7/10

W9-DAI-573

REQUIEM FOR A SLAVE

REQUIEM FOR A SLAVE

A Libertus Mystery of Roman Britain

Rosemary Rowe

This first world edition published 2010
in Great Britain and in the USA by
SEVERN HOUSE PUBLISHERS LTD of
9–15 High Street, Sutton, Surrey, England, SM1 1DF.
Trade paperback edition published
in Great Britain and the USA 2010 by
SEVERN HOUSE PUBLISHERS LTD

British Library Cataloguing in Publication Data

Rowe, Rosemary, 1942–
  Requiem for a Slave. – (A Libertus mystery of Roman
Britain)
  1. Libertus (Fictitious character: Rowe) – Fiction.
  2. Romans – Great Britain – Fiction. 3. Slaves – Fiction.
  4. Great Britain – History – Roman period, 55 B.C.–449
A.D. – Fiction. 5. Detective and mystery stories.
  I. Title II. Series
  823.9'2-dc22

ISBN-13: 978-0-7278-6877-0   (cased)
ISBN-13: 978-1-84751-217-8   (trade paper)

All Severn House titles are printed on acid-free paper.

Severn House Publishers support The Forest Stewardship Council [FSC],
the leading international forest certification organisation. All our titles that
are printed on Greenpeace-approved FSC-certified paper carry the FSC logo.

Mixed Sources
Product group from well-managed
forests and other controlled sources
www.fsc.org Cert no. SA-COC-1565
© 1996 Forest Stewardship Council
FSC

Typeset by Palimpsest Book Production Ltd.,
Grangemouth, Stirlingshire, Scotland.
Printed and bound in Great Britain by
MPG Books Ltd., Bodmin, Cornwall.

For Bryndis

Author's Foreword

The story is set in AD 190, at a time when a large part of Britain had been for almost two hundred years the most northerly outpost of the hugely successful Roman Empire: occupied by Roman legions, criss-crossed by Roman roads, subject to Roman laws and, in theory at least, administered by a provincial governor answerable directly to Rome.

However, the identity of the governor at this period is a matter of debate. Helvius Pertinax, the previous holder of the post (and the supposed friend and patron of the fictional Marcus Severus in the book) had recently been promoted, first to the African Provinces and later to the exceedingly important consular post of Prefect of Rome, making him one of the most powerful men in the Empire. The name of his immediate successor is not known. One theory is that several candidates were selected and then unselected by the Emperor, leaving power temporarily in the hands of important local magistrates and military commanders: several previous books in this series are based on this premise. However, it is possible that, by the time of this story, Clodius Albinus had been appointed, if not actually installed. (The date of his induction is not known, but he was certainly provincial governor by the end of 192 and had clearly been in post for some time by then.) This book, therefore, postulates the presence of a governor again, although the name of the new incumbent is not specified.

There is no such doubt about the identity of the Emperor. The increasingly unbalanced Commodus still wore the imperial purple, despite his lascivious lifestyle, capricious cruelties and erratic acts. (He had renamed all the months, for instance, with names derived from the honorific titles that he had given to himself, declared himself the reincarnation of the god Hercules – and therefore a living deity

– and announced that Rome itself was henceforth to be reti-
tled 'Commodiana'.) Stories about him barbecuing dwarves
and having a bald man pecked to death by sticking birdseed
to his head are probably exaggerated, but the existence of
such rumours gives some indication of the man. He was
widely loathed and dreaded, but he clung tenaciously to
power. Fearing (justifiably) that there were plots against his
life, he maintained a network of spies throughout the Empire,
including the notorious 'speculatores', who, although orig-
inally mere imperial scouts (as the name suggests) had
become effectively a private execution force, ready to strike
against suspected enemies.

Apart from personal enemies, there were historic foes.
In Britannia, most of the quarrelsome local tribes had long
since settled into peace (the Iceni revolt, for instance, had
been put down over a century ago), but there were still
sporadic clashes to the north and west. Among the red-
haired Silurians and the warlike Ordivices, in particular, the
spirit of their defeated leader, Caractacus, and his heroic
two-year resistance to Roman rule, lived on – if only, at
this date – among a few marauding bands. The army had
taken steps to suppress this discontent, creating special
'marching camps', where legionary and auxiliary forces
were kept in tented camps ready to move quickly against
insurgent groups, and, as the text suggests, most of the
inhabitants had bowed to Roman rule. But then, as now,
there were small groups of dissidents who refused to yield
and, from forest hideouts, mounted occasional assaults
(against military supply trains, in particular) though certainly
none as far east as Glevum. There is no evidence of actual
rebel activity at the time this tale is set, but records speak
of recent ambushes, and the western border remained a
byword for unrest until the end of the century.

This is the background of civil discontent against which
the action of the book takes place. Glevum (modern
Gloucester) was an important town: its historic status as a
'colonia' for retired legionaries gave it special privileges,
and all freemen born within its walls were citizens by right.
This was more than just a form of words. Citizenship at

this time was very highly prized. Celtic languages, traditions and settlements remained (as suggested in the story), but Latin was the language of the educated, people were adopting Roman dress and habits, and citizenship was the aspiration of all. Apart from its social and commercial status, it conferred upon its owner precious legal rights such as protection against the harshest punishments and the right to trial by a senior magistrate, with final appeal to the Emperor himself.

Most inhabitants of Glevum, of course, were not citizens at all. Many were freemen *not* born within the walls (and the interpretation of that law was very strict: birth within the 'sub-urbs' did not qualify). Such men did not enjoy the social and legal rights of town-born men, but were drawn by the commercial opportunity: the turnip-seller, stallholders and tanner in the book are examples of this stratum of society, each scratching a more or less precarious living from his trade. Even so, they were the lucky ones, as hundreds more were slaves – what Aristotle once described as 'vocal tools' – mere chattels of their masters, to be bought and sold, with no more rights or status than any other domestic animal.

Some slaves led pitiable lives, but others were highly regarded by their owners and might be treated well. Not all slaves were the possessions of the rich. Tradesmen (like the tanner) frequently kept slaves, sometimes in surprising numbers, to labour in their workshops. The work was often hard and dangerous (the description of the tannery is based on contemporary sources and is quite typical) but the owner had a vested interest in his labourers, who were generally certain of at least a modicum of food and clothes and some-where dry to sleep. A slave in a kindly household, in a comfortable home, might have a more enviable lot than many a poor freeman struggling to eke out an existence in a squalid hut.

Over this mixture, the town council ruled. As a colonia, Glevum had a high degree of responsibility for its own affairs (local tiles of the period describe it as a 'republic'), and local councillors were therefore men of considerable power. They were also, by definition, men of wealth, like

Quintus in this tale. Candidates for office were obliged by law to own a property of a certain value within the city walls, and, as the text suggests, they required a private fortune in support. Any councillor or magistrate (and many men were both) was also expected to contribute to the town by personally financing games, fountains, statues, and even drains – while at election time enormous sums were spent, though the donor might expect to gain a little in return, in service or in kind, from the contractors and tradesmen to whom they gave the work.

Power, of course, was vested almost entirely in men. Although individual women might inherit large estates and many wielded considerable influence within the house (like the tanner's wife and Gwellia in this narrative), daughters were not much valued, except as potential wives and mothers, although sons (as in the story) were the source of pride. Females were excluded from public office, and a woman of any age was deemed a child in law.

The Romano-British background to this book has been derived from a variety of (sometimes contradictory) pictorial and written sources, as well as artefacts. However, although I have done my best to create an accurate picture, this remains a work of fiction, and there is no claim to total academic authenticity. Commodus and Pertinax are historically attested, as is the existence and basic geography of Glevum. The rest is the product of my imagination.

Relata refero. Ne Iupiter quidem omnibus placet. I only tell you what I heard. Jove himself can't please everybody.

One

I was hurrying back to my mosaic workshop in the town, my mind on the important customer I had arranged to meet, when I stopped short on the street. I had caught sight of something which should not have been there. A street-vendor's tray! It was leaning against a pile of sorted stones outside my door. I heaved a heavy sigh. Not only was it likely to mark my precious stock – it was not so much a tray as a greasy piece of wood with an even greasier leather strap to hold it round the neck – but I was uncomfortably aware of what its presence meant. Lucius the pie-seller was at my shop again.

It was the fourth time in as many days, and no amount of hinting seemed to warn him off. My own fault, of course. I'd been too soft with him the first time he called, when I not only purchased one of his appalling pies but gave him a worn-out tunic out of pity for his plight.

I should have known better, especially about the pie. I had tasted Lucius's wares before, but I persuaded myself that they could not be as bad as I recalled. This 'example' was worse, if anything, clearly fashioned, as usual, from whatever ingredients he could rustle up for a few *quadrans* when the market stalls closed down: the questionable leavings from the butchers' blocks, a few squashed turnip leaves and the final sweepings from the miller's stones, more grit than flour – and those were only the things I could identify. The result was horrible. Even the dogs I fed it to when he had gone refused to finish it.

And here he was again, no doubt in the hope of tempting me to more. But this time even pity would not sway me, I resolved. I did not want him lurking around the shop like this; he was little better than a beggar and would horrify my wealthier class of customer, though one could not help feeling sorry for the man. He was so ugly, for one thing:

a dreadful scar had puckered half his face and he had only one good eye – the result of an accident years and years before, when his pie-maker father had been careless with the sparks and reduced himself to ashes together with the house. Lucius had been badly burned himself, but somehow the brick-built oven building had survived, and while his mother struggled to nurse him back to strength, she scratched a meagre living selling pies.

She still baked them for him nightly, in that same free-standing oven outside the dismal hovel which was all the home they had, but now it was he who hawked them around the streets. Amazingly, he often sold them all. They were warm and inexpensive and they didn't smell too bad, and in a big colonia like Glevum there was always someone passing through who hadn't tried one yet.

Besides, Lucius was so humble, and his one good eye had such a hangdog look, that even hard-headed locals like myself occasionally weakened and purchased another of his wretched wares. A few of the more sympathetic among his customers felt sorry enough for him sometimes to let him have broken and discarded things they didn't want them-selves – cracked bowls, chipped goblets, crusts of mouldy bread, or bits of cast-off clothing (as I'd done myself), odd broken sandals or a patched and faded cloak. Nothing of any value, as I assured my wife, but without them he would probably have perished in the cold.

My much-mended ancient tunic, fraying round the seams and with a stain from plaster halfway round the hem, was hardly the most remarkable of gifts, but the pie-seller had been embarrassingly tearful in his thanks and had pulled it on at once, over the filthy rags that he already wore. No doubt that garment too would soon reach the same sorry state, but in the meantime it looked quite well on him. It fitted him not badly when it came to length, though he was rather thinner than I have ever been, and the looseness of the front neck-line drew attention to the scar. However, he was clearly thrilled with the effect and capered off in it. He had shown his continued appreciation since by arriving at my workshop every afternoon to offer me the last pie on his tray.

'And it's no good my telling him I haven't any change,' I'd grumbled to Junio, my adopted son, the day before. 'He only insists that I take it as a gift.'

Junio gave me his cheeky sideways grin. He had been my slave for many years before I freed him and adopted him, and he still took liberties. 'It serves you right for being over-generous. He's only trying to repay a debt.'

'And whose fault is it if I was over-generous?' I muttered sheepishly. It was true that I had been in expansive mood. Lucius had turned up with his confounded pies a moment after we'd received the news that Junio's young wife had just been safely delivered of a son. 'Perhaps pride in being a grandfather did make me profligate. But you rushed off to make a sacrifice yourself. Isn't that impulse very much the same?'

'That was my obligation to the deities, to thank them for my son. Lucius's obligation is to you. He regards you as his patron now and he's bringing you his dues.'

I sighed. I hadn't thought of it, but it might well be true. If Lucius saw me in that light, no wonder he kept appearing at my workshop door: A 'client' is expected to attend his patron's home each day and offer any service in his power, and in return he is entitled to expect support. It was flattering, but I wasn't sure I wanted *clientes* to sustain.

'Well, we'll have to persuade him otherwise,' I answered crossly. 'I can't have Lucius taking up my time. My own patron will soon be coming back from Rome, and I have this new order for a pavement to fulfil by then.'

Junio knew when to let a matter drop. 'The pavement that Quintus Severus is commissioning, to go in the entrance of the basilica? It's to be in honour of your patron, isn't it? So he will want it finished by the time that Marcus comes.'

'Exactly. Quintus isn't satisfied with being chief *decurion*; he's hoping to be recommended for the Imperial Court.'

Junio grinned again. 'And Marcus is related to the Emperor, of course. Or so the rumours say.'

I frowned at him. It was not wise to be irreverent where Marcus was concerned. My patron had long been the most important magistrate in this whole area of Britannia, but he was one of the most influential men in the whole Empire these days, now that his friend and patron Pertinax held the Prefecture of Rome. And the Emperor has ears and eyes in the most unlikely spots, even in a far-flung colonia like Glevum. 'Marcus has never denied the claim,' I said reprovingly. (He'd never confirmed it either, but I didn't mention that.) 'So treat him with respect. And Quintus Severus also, when he comes. After all, as senior town councillor he's virtually in charge while Marcus is away – apart from the commander of the garrison, of course.'

'The decurion's coming here? I thought you would have taken the patterns to his house?'

I was not surprised he asked. I had a range of patterns, ready laid on cloth, and we often took them to a client's home in my little handcart so that wealthy customers could make a choice in comfort.

But I shook my head. 'Quintus wants something special. Marcus attending Neptune: Marcus in a wreath, and the god atop a dolphin with a trident in his hand, and a border of agapanthus and birds around the side. In honour of my patron's successful sea voyage, he says. I volunteered to sketch it, but he opted to come here. I'm expecting him tomorrow, around the seventh hour.'

Junio looked doubtful. 'Then I shall not be here, Father, to show respect or otherwise. Tomorrow I have to go and make arrangements with the priest and order a *bulla* for Amato's naming day.'

Of course, I had forgotten the necessity for that. Junio had been raised as a slave in a Roman family, and he took for granted all the ritual of the naming of a child. I was born a Celtic nobleman, seized by pirates and taken as a slave, and only formally received my Roman name at thirty years of age, when my high-ranking master died and bequeathed me freedom and the coveted rank of citizen in his will. There had been no bulla and naming day for me (or for Junio either, since he was born in servitude), but my grandson was a Roman citizen by birth and was entitled to all the proper rites. 'Of course you do,' I said.

'Let's just hope that Lucius does not come and interrupt

you,' Junio went on. 'It won't impress Quintus if the pie-seller is here, imploring you to take the greasy remnants from his tray. And I won't be here to help you get rid of him. Get Minimus to guard the door and send the man away.'

I nodded. Minimus was my private slave, one of a so-called 'matching pair' on loan from Marcus while he was away, and though he showed no aptitude for pavement work at all – more hindrance than help when I tried him out at it – he was good at turning people politely but firmly from the door. He would not be swayed by sentiment for one-eyed pie-sellers. I smiled grimly. 'That's just what I intend.'

But now the time was here, and so was Lucius, it seemed. It looked as though even Minimus had not been firm enough, and I would have to go and shoo him off myself. Suppose that Quintus Severus arrived and found him in my shop!

I confess I was annoyed. I was already flustered. I had been busy in the workshop until well past noon, fixing the remaining tiles on a mosaic plaque which Junio and I had been working on for days. It was a tricky commission, a half-circle piece with the Greek name 'Apollos' worked across the top. It was intended for a garden shrine in a country villa several miles away, but I had elected to assemble it at home, gluing the *tesserae* to a linen back, on which I'd sketched the pattern in reverse, so that I could instal it in a piece and soak the cloth off when the mortar set. (Inscriptions are always tricky and round letters most of all, and I didn't want my rather capricious client watching me and deciding that he wanted something different after all.)

So when I received a sudden summons from the customer – via a rather flustered little garden slave of his – I did not have much option but to go. Normally, I might have sent Junio to deal with this, but he was not available and it was no good sending anybody else. It was inconvenient: I'd hoped to have the piece finished and the workshop cleared and swept in time for Quintus's visit, but I hastened off – to find, when I got there, that the man was not at home.

(No doubt he thought my arrival was unduly slow, although I'd downed tools instantly and hurried all the way.) Such things were not unusual, but today it was especially tiresome. From the angle of the sun above the rooftops now, I calculated that the errand had taken me two hours. I was lucky that Quintus was not already here.

But there was no one waiting in the front part of the shop, where the chair was kept for important visitors. In fact, the place looked unattended. I frowned impatiently. I'd left Minimus in charge. He was supposed to stay at the counter in case of customers. But there was no sign of him. Inside, sampling the greasy pies, no doubt! And then there was the tray! Leaning on my most fragile and expensive pile of stock as well – the *lapis viridis*, a rare imported green.

So I was not in the best of tempers as I reached the outer shop, skirted the counter and pushed open the door into the dusty gloom of the partitioned area at the back which was my working space.

'Minimus! Where are you? What do you mean by this?'

No answer. In fact, no sound of any kind. No sign of anyone. It was more than usually dark in there. I had put the shutters quickly in the window space myself – lest cats or sudden gusts of wind should get into the room and disturb my careful work – but there was no taper lit and I realized that Minimus had let the fire go out. That was worse than careless – it was unforgivable. He knew we were out of the dried fungus tinder for the making of a fire. I would have strong words with that young scoundrel when I got hold of him. We would have to go out and buy or beg embers from the tanning shop next door before we had the means of any heat and light.

I tutted audibly. The darkness made it difficult to move about. I could distinguish the outline of the workbench well enough, but the floor was littered with little heaps of stone that I'd been working with – the painstakingly shaped and sorted tesserae – visible only as darker shadows in the gloom. One careless foot and they'd be scattered everywhere.

'Minimus!'

Where was he anyway? Obviously off with Lucius somewhere, eating pies, I thought. But where? There was no
back entrance to the workshop space. I had fully expected
to find them both in here, since it appeared that Lucius had
talked his way inside. Offered a bribe to Minimus, perhaps?
One of his wares, no doubt, since he had little else. So
where had they got to? It was a mystery.

Had Minimus been taken ill from sampling a pie? If that
was the case, I thought, it served him right. I would make
him finish it as a punishment. Then I glimpsed the trap-
door to the sleeping space above. That gave me an idea.
They could have climbed up to the attic room – it had been
damaged by fire a long time ago and was now used only
as a store, but Minimus had been up there many times and
it would make a good hiding place for illicit feasts.

I groped towards the ladder, calling, 'Minim—'

I broke off in dismay, for the first time feeling seriously
alarmed. My foot had nudged against something on the
floor. Something strangely heavy and horribly inert. I knew
at once that it was not a heap of tiles. I bent over, peering.
There was a suspicion of a sour, familiar smell, and I could
just make out a shape I thought I recognized.

I no longer cared about where I put my feet or keeping
my heaps of sorted tiles apart. I rushed to the window space
and took the shutter down, letting the light in, hoping I was
wrong.

But there was no mistake. I had found Lucius, and he
was very dead.

TWO

He was lying face downward on a heap of tiles, and I turned him over gently. In the dusty daylight, it was clear how he had died.

He had not simply fallen, as I had first supposed – tripped on the stone piles and hit his head against the bench – or perished from eating his own disgusting wares. There was a savage dark-red line of bruise around his throat. Around the burn-scars his face was swollen purple now, his tongue bulged from his lips and his one eye protruded horribly. His dead hands were still clawing at his throat, where they had dug bloody channels as he fought for breath. Someone had pulled a cord around his neck and throttled him. I could see the dark smudge behind the ear where the cruel knot had been. This looked like murder.

And it hadn't happened very long ago, I realized, when my shocked mind recovered sufficiently to think, because although the corpse was cooling, it was not yet actually stiff. As I had turned the body gently on its back, one arm had slid limply down on to the floor. Just to be certain, I raised the limb once more: it was unresisting, but heavy – like a roll of sodden wool – and in a sudden horror I let it go again. It fell grotesquely, like a stuffed thing, and hit the bench leg with a hollow thud. I rather wished that I had not made the grim experiment, but it confirmed the obvious: that Lucius had been killed quite recently, while I had been out of the shop this afternoon.

Not necessarily in this room, of course. He was not likely to have come into the back workshop without an invitation, especially when I wasn't here. Unless for some extraordinary reason Minimus had lured him inside? I thrust that theory instantly away. Minimus would never have murdered anyone. I was quite ashamed for having thought of it.

Besides, when I looked more closely, I could see two

faint grooves running in the stone dust from the doorway to the pile, and Lucius's toes and sandals were abraded at the front as if he'd been hauled ignominiously along with them dragging on the floor. It suggested that he had been murdered outside of the shop, then half lifted up, dragged in by the armpits and flung face down on the tiles.

That observation gave me some relief. It would have needed a stronger man than Minimus to accomplish that. My slave was scarcely more than a child, and Lucius, though there was little flesh upon his bones, was quite a solid corpse. He was at least as tall as I am, and – as I was now uncomfortably aware – was very heavy, dead. Only a full-grown adult could have dumped him here. Or more than one, of course.

But who would want to murder a man like Lucius? I gazed down at his face. Lucius had been an ugly man in life and he was uglier in death, but he was a harmless soul. True, his wares were terrible, but he was surely not a person to have serious enemies? Then I saw his belt. The loops that held his money-purse had been cut through and the leather ends now dangled uselessly. The purse itself was gone. Not that there was ever very much in it. Was that why he had died, for the sake of the few *asses* that he'd earned from his pies? It was more than usually possible, in fact.

There had been rumours of rebel bandits in the forests again: a band of straggling Silurians and Ordovices from the wild lands to the west, who, unlike the vast majority of those now-peaceful tribes, had never accepted Caractacus's defeat. Their targets were mainly military, of course, though anything Roman – such as a toga – might find itself attacked, and they sometimes ambushed travellers to steal money and supplies. At one time Marcus had nearly stamped the problem out, but in his absence it was getting worse, and once or twice the brigands had made forays into town.

Was that, I wondered, what had happened here? Had Lucius been loitering for me outside the door when he had been ambushed by robbers from the woods? They always killed their victims, so that they could not testify (the punishment for banditry was crucifixion still), and realizing that there was no one in the shop, they could well have dragged the body in and left it out of sight. Perhaps – supposing that the workshop was his own – they also doused the fire and snuffed the tapers out, to make the place look closed, so that discovery of the corpse would take as long as possible and thus delay pursuit. It seemed the likeliest explanation of implausible events.

It also suggested a disturbing thought. In his new tunic – grimed with stone dust now – Lucius did not look the pauper that he generally did. It was darned and mended, but that suggested care, and casual marauders would not have known his twisted face and recognized him as simply a wretched pie-seller. They might easily suppose that the coin-purse at his belt held gold and silver rather than a handful of the smallest of brass coins.

Poor Lucius! It seemed my well-intentioned gift had brought him only grief. Besides, I was certain that he'd come to the workshop to see me – and if he had not come here, he would not have died. If only Minimus had been here to send him home again!

Which raised another question. What had happened to my slave? Finding the body had driven that problem from my mind. For one mad moment I gazed around the room, half fearing that I'd find another corpse among the stones, but there was nothing. I even looked in the attic space upstairs, but there were no signs of footprints in the dust, and everything looked just as usual. I came quickly down again. I was really anxious now. When I came to think about things soberly, it was not like Minimus to have left his post. He was young and over-eager, but he was obedient to a fault.

So had he been taken away against his will? By the same bandits, perhaps? It was not a pleasant possibility. The best I could hope, in that case, was that he'd been seized to sell: there was always a market at the docks for young, good-looking slaves – overseas traders took them, and no questions asked – though what their ultimate fate might be was quite another thing. But there was a much more likely reason for abducting him. He had belonged to Marcus, one of the most important Romans in the world, and no doubt had useful information he could be forced to give, in ways too unpleasant to think about.

I went outside and looked rather wildly around. Minimus's knuckle-bones were spread out on the counter top – I had left him sitting on the stool ready to deal with any customers, and it was clear he'd been playing with them while I was away. He would not have dared to do so if I'd been about. This proof of childish mischief brought a constriction to my throat.

And there was the pie-tray, leaning on the stones.

I sighed, thinking of the owners of those two simple things: Lucius, with his one eye and his awful pies, who had sought my protection and was lying dead, and my little red-haired scatterbrain of a slave, for whom I was, naturally, entirely responsible. A fine protector I had proved to be!

I turned away and thumped my fist against the wall next door, then buried my head against my arm. I was aware of a shameful prickling behind my eyes.

'Hyperius, you can go ahead and let them know I'm here.' A voice behind me cut across my thoughts. I recognized the imperious tones of Quintus Severus. Dear Jupiter, I had forgotten about him and I was not prepared – I hadn't changed into a toga, my hands were dark with grime, and my face was smudged with most unroman tears. He would doubtless see all this as dreadful disrespect. And I could not even ask him to come inside my shop. What was the chief town councillor going to say to that?

I composed myself with an effort and turned to see the man himself. He was descending from a private litter in the centre of the street, assisted by a supercilious-looking slave. Quintus was always an imposing figure, tall and gaunt in his magisterial robes, and he looked every inch the civil dignitary now: completely out of place in this area of the town. Over his toga he wore a dark-red cloak, edged with expensive gold embroidery – causing a passing turnip-seller to turn and stare at him – and he carried a leather switch in one ringed hand. He wore his brown hair fashionably cropped, accentuating his huge brows and long, patrician nose, and his deep-set eyes were gazing around with evident dismay.

The source of his concern was evident. He was wearing an expensive pair of soft red-leather shoes, and there is no fancy paving in this suburb of the town (which has grown up, haphazardly, just outside the northern walls), merely a muddy road with a stone causeway either side.

I hastened forward, making the deepest obeisance my ageing knees could bear. 'Honoured citizen!' I stammered in dismay. 'I must apologize . . .'

He looked at me, and I saw the dawning consternation and horror on his face. I realized what a spectacle I must currently present, and devoutly wished that I had not agreed to meet him at the shop.

'Libertus? Pavement-maker? Is that really you? What are you doing there?' He seemed to recollect that I was a citizen, and he made a visible effort to control himself. 'I'm sorry, citizen, I did not expect to find you on the street. Hyperius, you dolt!' he added to the slave, who had obediently walked towards the shop and was now standing hesitating, goggling at me. 'Come back here at once. Can't you see I need you to help me cross all this?' He flicked his switch in the direction of the mire.

The attendant, a stolid man of middle years, whose scarlet tunic was almost as gorgeous as his owner's, turned a sullen red and hurried back to proffer a supporting hand. Quintus Severus took it and picked his way fastidiously across the mud and grime.

'Decurion,' I burbled, dropping another bow. 'A thousand pardons, distinguished citizen. I regret that I am not dressed to welcome you. Furthermore, I fear that I'm unable to invite you to my shop. But—'

He gestured me to silence and gazed at me, rather as a slave-master might assess substandard wares. 'Unable to invite me? What exactly is going on?' He took a deep, exasperated breath. 'I understood I was expected here?'

'Of course you were, distinguished citizen,' I said, still gabbling with dismay. 'But, you see, there's been an accident.'

'An accident?' That clearly shocked him, and you could see a kind of light dawn in the cold blue eyes. 'What sort of accident?' He frowned, contriving to convey that accidents were unacceptable, and that this one was evidence of my bad management. He looked me up and down. 'An accident to you?'

'Not to me, decurion. To Lucius,' I explained.

'Lucius?' The intonation suggested that this was even more absurd than permitting accidents. 'And who is Lucius?'

'A street-vendor,' I murmured. 'A pie-seller, in fact. I found him in my workshop just before you came.' I took a deep breath and made a plunge for it. 'I am afraid he's dead – murdered. Someone's throttled him.'

'A pie-seller?' Quintus echoed again, disbelievingly. He made it sound as if he thought that this was somehow all my fault and had been deliberately arranged to inconvenience him. 'Murdered in your workshop? What was he doing there?' *When I was expected,* his tone of voice implied.

'I don't believe that he was killed there, citizen. More likely set on in the street and robbed, and dumped there afterwards. I fear it may be bandits . . .' I outlined my reasoning.

'I see.' Quintus abruptly seemed to have lost interest in this. 'Spare me all the explanation, citizen. I know that you are skilled at solving mysteries – Marcus was always boasting of your skill – but the death of a pie-seller is hardly my concern.'

'But you understand that I can hardly ask you in the shop and show you patterns with him lying there.'

He cut me off with a dismissive gesture of his hand. 'Naturally not. It seems I've had a wasted journey here this afternoon. Unfortunate, but I concede that it is unavoidable. One cannot conduct business in the presence of a corpse. It would be inauspicious to a remarkable degree. What will you do with the body, anyway? I don't imagine that the pie-seller belonged to any guild?'

This was a problem that I hadn't thought about – I had been too shocked at finding Lucius dead. But, of course, he would require some sort of burial. There were special societies, even among slaves, to which people paid a small sum every month to ensure they received a proper funeral and were not condemned to walk the earth as ghosts, but, as Quintus had remarked, it was unlikely that Lucius had ever joined such a guild. Seriously poor freemen very rarely did – money was needed for more pressing purposes. I said, 'He has a mother – no doubt she would know.'

Quintus made a disapproving face. 'Better to inform the garrison authorities, and they will come round with a cart and put the corpse in a communal grave. It is not a council matter, since we're outside the gates. You will want to have the workshop ritually cleansed to get rid of evil omens as soon as possible, I suppose – and you can't do that until the body has been moved. Though it may cost you a little to have them bury it – he is not strictly a vagrant or a criminal.'

I winced. I had seen them put bodies in the common pit before – tipped in without ceremony and covered up with lime. It was not what I would have chosen for Lucius at all, but it's where he would have ended if he'd dropped dead in the street, and a proper funeral was an expensive thing and would mean a full two days of mourning closure for the shop. Besides, Quintus was right about the cleansing rites. No customer would come to a workshop where a murdered corpse had lain, for fear that it was cursed – only a proper ritual would dispel the fears. That would involve an expensive sacrifice at least, and probably a priest with incense, scattering water on the floor. This business was already likely to cost more than I could easily afford.

Quintus was looking questioningly at me. 'I could alert the gatehouse as I go home, perhaps. Then they can send a party later on.'

'Someone had better go and tell his mother, just in case,' I said aloud. 'Though I suppose that I will have to see to that myself. It's not a task that I look forward to.'

He looked at me, astonished. 'Get a slave to do it – you

do *have* a slave, I suppose. Don't I remember that Marcus lent you some?'

I nodded glumly. 'Two little matching boys. And that's another thing. One of them, who was attending me today, seems to have disappeared. I fear the killers may have kidnapped him.'

Quintus stared at me. His attendant made a stifled noise. 'What is it, Hyperius?' the decurion said.

'If I might be permitted, citizen . . .?' The slave had a peculiarly unctuous tone of voice. 'If the pavement-maker's slave has disappeared, why should we suppose that bandits are involved? Surely it is likely that it was the slave who killed the pie-seller? Stole his purse and made a run for it?'

Quintus looked absurdly pleased at this remark. 'Of course. Well done, Hyperius. Marcus is not the only one to have a clever man to help.' He turned to me. 'With your reputation, citizen, I am surprised you didn't think of that explanation for yourself.'

'I did, decurion, but I dismissed it instantly – and so would you, if you had known my slave.' It sounded impertinent and I hurried on, 'Anyway, there is evidence that there was a much stronger hand at work.' I explained about the tracks. 'You – or your slave – can come and see it for yourself—'

He cut me off with one impatient hand. 'Of course, we shall do nothing so absurd. To come into your workshop is to invite a curse. We have already lingered here too long. I shall get in touch with the garrison and have them move the corpse, but I shall also tell them to look out for your page and hold him on suspicion of involvement in all this. Hyperius is right. It wouldn't be the first time that a slave has stolen a purse and made a run for it.'

I shuddered. To be apprehended as a fugitive slave is a serious affair, unless the slave can prove that his master was unnaturally cruel and he had gone to seek protection from a kinder one. And it did not require the master himself to bring the charge. Quintus would doubtless do exactly what he said, and that would make three capital offences of which Minimus was accused – running from his master, theft and homicide.

'I'm sure that Minimus has done nothing of the kind,' I protested, ready to give my reasons, but Quintus was already bridling and he cut me off.

'That is only your opinion, which you can state in court if we do happen to apprehend the boy.' He gave an unpleasant little smile. 'Of course, the magistrates may wish to talk to you as well. We have only your word for it that you did not kill the man yourself.'

I confess that stunned me. I realized that it would be difficult to prove that I had not – there was no one else to witness where I'd been and when.

But Quintus did not pursue that train of thought. 'Hyperius! The litter!' he said imperiously. He turned to me again. 'I fear that we shall have to forget that pavement after all.'

Even in my state of shock I could not let that pass. 'But we have a contract. A binding one, I think. You told me what you wanted, and we shook hands on it, in front of witnesses. Two senior members of the *ordo* in fact.'

I was worried now. This commission had promised to be an especially lucrative one, and I had turned down other work on that account. That was not as imprudent as it seemed: I had a proper contract, and all decurions financed elaborate public works – it was expected of them (not surprisingly perhaps, since one of their chief duties was overseeing tax), and support for them among the populace was often commensurate with how much they spent. The new pavement for the basilica was a flamboyant one, and I had relied on earning quite a lot for it.

The litter-slaves had brought the litter up, and Quintus paused in the act of getting into it. 'I will speak to the *aediles*. Under the circumstances I think they will agree that the omens are too dreadful to proceed with this.'

'And if I have the workshop ritually cleansed? And prove that no one working here had any part in this?'

He shrugged. 'By that time I fear that there would be insufficient time to get the pavement done. It would be difficult to do it now, in any case. A message arrived at the *curia* today, nominating a candidate for the vacant ordo seat – you will remember there was a councillor who died, and we are due to vote in a replacement in a day or so – and saying that Marcus hopes to be here very soon himself.'

'Really?' I attempted to look unconcerned, but secretly I was a little stung by this. I had told my patron of the vacant seat myself, in the monthly bulletin about the town which I had sent to him (at his express request but at my own expense), though I'd never had an answer or acknowledgement. He was naturally concerned about the ordo seat, and any candidate he gave his blessing to was sure to be elected, so I could understand that he had written to the curia, but, I thought, he could have let me know as well.

Quintus was anxious to show how well informed he was. 'I understand he has found a ship in Gaul and is already on his way, so there is hardly time to have a pavement laid. I shall have to content myself with giving a grand banquet at my home to welcome him, as that fool Pedronius has already announced that he will do.' He saw my face and gave his sneering laugh. 'You hadn't heard that news? I had supposed you such a favourite that he'd have written to you first!'

I shook my head. 'If there was a message at my home today – as there might well have been – it had not arrived before my son and I set off for town,' I said. There was some truth in this. My roundhouse was not far from my patron's country house – indeed, he had given me the land to build it on – but in his absence the villa was closed up and only a few staff remained to keep it clean and aired.

I was thinking fast by now. Perhaps it was as well that the contract would be void. If Marcus was already on a ship from Gaul, then he would be here in less than half a moon. That made it near impossible to lay the floor in time – this was no stock sample pattern that I held prepared – and failure would have cost me a considerable fine. Besides, Pedronius would want his plaque completed by then too, and there was well-known rivalry between the two officials. Perhaps Quintus was doing me a favour after all.

But he had already climbed aboard the carrying-chair and pulled the litter curtains round him as a screen. So there was little that I could do except watch it move away, the bearers loping at a rapid pace while Quintus shouted 'Faster!' from the interior. My only consolation was to see Hyperius, already hot and breathless, trotting after them.

Three

I was still staring after them when I heard a noise behind me, and I turned round just in time to see the candle-maker from the tallow factory next door. He had opened his street-gate a crack to watch the litter leave and was about to slam it shut again, but I was too quick for him. He was a surly fellow, but he might have seen something which would throw light on events, though if he had information I would have to pay for it. I shouted out to him, 'Candle-maker, have you seen my slave at all? Or anybody calling at my shop this afternoon?'

He was always unneighbourly, and I would not have been surprised if he had ignored me and gone away inside. However, he simply scowled and shrugged. 'Your slave was here an hour or two ago; I haven't seen him since. As for customers, I have no idea. I'm far too busy with my own affairs. Why ask me anyway? It isn't my business to look out for yours.' He went in and slammed the door, leaving me standing in the middle of the road.

I stayed there a moment wondering what to do. Quintus intended to notify the authorities and have them move the corpse, but I wanted to speak to Lucius's mother first, if possible. And I wanted urgently to try to find my slave. However, I still had a dead man lying on my floor and I did not feel able simply to leave the place.

I could not even reasonably use the time to work, although I had a commission to accomplish fast. I hadn't quite finished the Apollo plaque, and it was urgent that I did, since it was more than possible that the superstitious Pedronius would decline to pay if he learned that it had been in the company of a corpse. What's more, I would be particularly dependent on the money from this job if the contract for Quintus's pavement was to be annulled.

If only we had taken the mosaic yesterday, when Junio

and I had laid the mortar base on which it was to sit! There
was only half an hour's work, at most, to finish off the
piece – all that was missing was a border at one end. It
would be possible to fix the mosaic into place today –
before any rumour of the murder got about and awkward
questions started to be asked – if I could only get it there,
but I did not have a handcart that I could move it on. Junio
had borrowed ours to fetch the numerous supplies that
would be wanted for tomorrow's naming feast.

It was doubly frustrating since I knew from my abortive
visit to the villa earlier that the tax-inspector was now likely
to be absent several days and could not possibly have heard
about the death. But although the plaque was very near
complete, glued upside down on to its linen back, and I
had a terracotta tray prepared that I could move it on, I
could not take it anywhere without a cart – not even from
the shop into the street, where at least I could argue there
was no question of a curse. Besides, I could hardly go inside
my shop and do what was required with Lucius's body still
on my heap of edging tiles. Neither could I leave him till
the army came.

If only I had Junio at my side just now!

'Important-looking customer you had this afternoon!' The
speaker made me jump.

I turned to see the turnip-seller I had noticed earlier. He
was a regular visitor to the area; a round, rough cheerful
fellow with a stubbly beard and a brownish tunic smeared
with earth and clay, which, together with his wide body
and oddly skinny legs, gave him a marked resemblance to
the wares he sold. People called him Radixrapum – 'turnip
root' – though never to his face: a man who regularly
wielded a spade and pushed a heavy barrow round the streets
for hours was likely to be fit and handy in a fight.

Radixrapum flashed his snaggled smile hopefully – I had
occasionally bought a turnip from him in the past. 'That
fancy cloak and private carrying-chair! Must be someone
wealthy. Hope he paid you well.' It was clear what he was
hinting: that I could spare an as or two.

I shook my head. 'I lost my contract with him, I'm afraid.

There's been an accident.' I was about to turn away when a thought occurred to me. 'You usually come here earlier than this. Have you been up and down this street previously today?'

'As a matter of fact, I came by twice before,' he muttered with an embarrassed grin as if I'd accused him of something untoward. 'I was hoping to find you.'

'You haven't seen anybody else outside my shop this afternoon?'

He thought a moment and then said doubtfully, 'No one that I can think of, except that red-haired slave of yours. He was here the first time I came – that would have been an hour or two ago.'

'You are quite sure of that?'

He nodded. 'Fairly certain. Of course, I wasn't taking any special notice at the time, and there are always lots of people moving to and fro – street-vendors and messengers and clients for the various businesses – but nobody near your workshop in particular. I would have noticed that, I think, because I was looking out for you. But you weren't here, of course.' He did the grin again. 'I decided to go on into town and come back later on. And when I did come back, I saw the litter and realized there was no point in calling while your customer was here, so I went off round the corner and waited until now. I'm trying to sell these last few turnips so I can go back home.' He gestured towards the barrow. 'Very good for soup.'

I shook my head again. 'I shan't be buying turnips to take home today,' I said. 'There's been a tragedy. Lucius the pie-seller – do you know the man?'

His round face puckered into a thoughtful frown. 'I think I know the one. Fellow with an awful burn-mark who only has one eye? Grey-haired chap who sells the dreadful pies?'

'Used to sell them,' I corrected. 'I'm afraid he's dead. I found him in my workshop. Someone's murdered him.'

The turnip-seller whistled. 'Murdered? Well, I'll go to Dis! Poor old Lucius! He was harmless. Who'd want to murder him?'

'That is what exactly I am trying to find out.'

He looked at me. 'Of course, you're supposed to be clever at this sort of thing. Will you be able to catch whoever did it, do you think?' He tapped his forefinger against his stubby nose. 'Oh, now I understand. That's why you were asking if I'd seen anyone. Well, I will think about it a bit more carefully, and if I remember anything, I'll be sure to let you know. And, of course, if there's anything else that I can do to help . . .' He was already turning as if to move away.

I prevented him by saying thoughtfully, 'Well, in fact, there might be something you can do.' I saw his startled face. 'It's nothing difficult. I want to find his mother and break the news to her. Would you be prepared to stand watch here for me? It doesn't feel decent to leave the poor man lying there alone, and in any case the military might come to take the corpse. That decurion who was here said he'd ask them to do that. Someone will have to be here to meet them when they come.' He was looking doubtful, and I added instantly, 'I'll give you half a *sestertius* if you'll stay here while I go.'

'Well, I don't know. I'm not sure that I'm very keen on keeping vigil for a corpse. Particularly a murder victim whom I scarcely knew.' But he was clearly weakening. Turnip-selling was not a very profitable trade, and a half-sestertius is a handsome bribe. The promise of a silver coin was far too good to miss.

I pressed my advantage. 'And perhaps I'll even buy a turnip too. But you must make up your mind. Will you stay here while I go and tell his mother what's occurred, in case there are arrangements for a funeral? She's only at the bake-oven, not very far away. But I'll have to get there quickly, because if I don't find her very soon, the army will be here and the body will be gone.'

'And she'll never have the chance to say goodbye or close the eyes. I know how much my wife would grieve if our son was lying dead and she could not perform those simple services for him. Very well, I'll do it – to oblige you, citizen. Half a sestertius, I believe you said?'

'Half a sestertius, when I get back again.' I didn't want him running off while I was gone. 'But, on second thoughts,

I don't think I'll ask his mother to come and close his eyes. They're bulging from his head. Someone has pulled a cord around his neck. He doesn't present a very pleasant spectacle.'

· The turnip-seller had that doubtful look again. 'Well, perhaps you'd better close them yourself before you go. They say that's where the soul gets in and out – and we don't want it coming back. I suppose you've called his name, and lit a candle at his head and feet?'

Of course, I had done nothing of the kind. 'I scarcely had the time,' I said, with more asperity than I really meant. 'In any case, as far as candles go, I didn't have the means – someone has blown the lamps and tapers out and let the fire go cold, and I don't have any tinder in the shop just now. I was going to get some embers from the neighbour's premises.'

'Well, I tell you what, citizen,' the turnip-seller said. 'You go and get them, and get the candles lit – I'll stay here while you do it – and then I will stand watch. I wouldn't want to do it otherwise: you hear how ghosts get restless if the earthly body isn't treated right, and come back to haunt the place and people where they died. But if you've done everything that you could do for him, it would be different. Even if the army put him in a pit, some of the rites will have been properly observed, and there's less chance of his spirit coming back to haunt.'

I nodded. It was not a nonsensical idea, even if I was not afraid of meeting Lucius's ghost! I could tell his mother that something had been done, and it might make the ritual cleansing afterwards a less expensive task. Besides, it would give the poor pie-seller a bit of dignity.

'Very well,' I conceded. 'I'll go inside and get something to put the embers in. While I am about it, I can close the eyes.'

He gave an enthusiastic nod. 'And call his name three times, the way you're supposed to do.' Any minute now he would recommend that I put a coin for the ferryman underneath the tongue, but he did not do that. Instead, he said, to my immense surprise, 'In fact, while you're about it, why don't I come in too? Then you have a witness that you did it properly. And I'll know exactly where to show the soldiers when they come. Or is the body too horrible to contemplate?'

I realized suddenly what I should have seen before: that he was consumed with curiosity but far too superstitious to go in on his own. Perhaps he was also worried by my description of the corpse. I said, to reassure him, 'It isn't pleasant, but imagination often paints things more dreadful than they are.'

He didn't answer, just nodded brusquely and followed me inside.

I wondered for a moment if he would turn tail. The body looked more gruesome than I'd remembered it, and the smell of greasy pies, mingled with stale sweat and body wastes, seemed to be even more pungent than before. But the turnip-seller seemed less affected than I thought that he would be.

'You are quite right, citizen,' he said cheerfully. 'You see worse sights beside the roads – executed criminals and that sort of thing. This is much less horrible than what they do to highway thieves.'

I nodded. Crucifixion is an awful death, though it didn't seem to deter the rebels in the forest very much. The Romans did their best. Those few bandits who were rounded up and convicted of their crimes were strung up in prominent positions by the road, so that their tortured bodies would be a grim warning to the rest. Lucius, by comparison, had died a speedy death.

I went over to the body, and Radixrapum followed me.

'Obviously strangled, as you say, citizen,' he said, examining the bloody neck with curiosity. 'But no sign of the cord. You don't suppose he might have hanged himself? Someone might have cut him down and brought him here, perhaps? Your young servant could have done it and then gone to seek for help.'

It was an attractive theory, but I shook my head. 'Look at where the cord was tightened.' I pointed to the place. 'You can see that the force was clearly back and down.

If he had been hanging – or had hanged himself – obviously the greatest force would be from overhead. Besides, if someone had simply cut the body down, why would they remove the rope from round its neck?'

He nodded thoughtfully. 'I expect you're right. Will you be able to force the eyelids shut?'

In fact, I was not at all convinced I could, and I was squeamish about touching that one protruding eye. I compromised by seizing a piece of linen cloth nearby – intended as backing for a piece of work – and binding it around the head to form a bandage, as embalming women sometimes do. The body was getting noticeably stiffer now, and I was glad to lay the purple face down on the tiles again. With the blindfold on, it did not look so bad. I got up, breathing heavily. 'No question of the soul finding a route back that way now.'

'Aren't you going to call his name?' the turnip-seller asked. 'In case his spirit is still somewhere nearby?'

I was quite sure that the soul had fled some little time ago and I was not anxious to encourage it to come back again. 'Don't you think I ought to go and find his mother first? Suppose that Lucius did not hold with Roman rites? He looks more like a humble Celt to me – or he might have been a follower of that Jewish carpenter, or Mithras or Isis, or some other modern cult. They all have their own customs when dealing with a death.' As I spoke, I made a point of washing my own hands, very carefully, in my water bowl.

The turnip-seller looked reproachfully at me. 'Anything is better than being picked up in a cart and flung into a pit with no rites performed at all. Call his name, pavement-maker. It falls to you, if anyone. It should be done by the senior person in the house. Well, you're the senior here. I am just a freeman, and you're a citizen. Besides, this is your workshop, and it will be you he haunts if you don't do it right.'

Perhaps it was this last thought that made up my mind for me. I am not an adherent of Roman rites myself – I make the required sacrifices on holy days, of course, to Jupiter and the pantheon, and the Emperor as well (it is never wise to alienate a deity, just in case), but I am more inclined to venerate the older gods of tree and stone. However, I have witnessed the ritual enough to know what I should do.

The window space was already open – as the rite demands – so I took a deep breath and stood beside the corpse and cried in a loud voice, 'Lucius!' It occurred to me that I didn't know if he had another name, so I added 'The pie-seller' to be doubly sure. There was – mercifully – no answer, so I repeated it twice more.

'There now, citizen. We have done all we could,' the turnip-vendor said in a prosaic tone, though I noticed that he'd flattened himself against the wall as I called on Lucius's name – presumably lest he should impede the spirit's path. Now, though, he was smiling cheerfully. 'You go and get the embers and I'll stand watch outside.'

I picked up an oil lamp and a copper bowl. 'I will go to the tanner's and see if they will let me light the lamp, as well as have some embers to start the fire again. Then we can set some tapers round the corpse. Besides, I can ask the tanner some questions while I'm there, in case he noticed anything unusual this afternoon. I've already asked the candle-maker on the other side.' The tanner might be less churlish with his answer too, I thought.

Radixrapum nodded. 'It would be a good idea. When I was here before, I saw someone with a donkey at the tanner's gate, unloading hides. They might have noticed if anyone else was in the street.'

'I'll ask them,' I agreed, though I would scarcely have much time for questioning if I wanted to reach the pie-house before the soldiers came. I turned to Radixrapum to say as much to him, but he was already on his way outside and there was nothing for me to do but follow him.

Four

The tanner was a small, squat, swarthy man, with bandy legs and eyes that were noticeably crossed. His face was lined and so raddled with the fumes that it had become the colour of his hides, and he rejoiced in the possession of a single tooth. It was impossible to guess what sort of age he was – he looked fully fifty or sixty years of age, but he had looked much the same when I first moved into the shop and that was now some fifteen years ago. Perhaps his tanning had preserved him too.

I could see him through the open gate as I pulled the rope to ring the bell. He was arranging finished skins into a pile and selecting the best ones to hang up on display in a dingy little area which served as a front court. He came towards me, grinning – if, with one tooth, it could be called a grin.

We knew each other slightly. In the days when, like him, I had lived above the shop, he had called round several times seeking an arrangement to collect my urine pots, so he could mix the contents with various leaves and herbs for a concoction which helped loosen the hair from stubborn hides. However, I already had a contract with the fullers-shop nearby, and nothing came of it. This was the first time that I had called on him.

He was still baring his gums at me, in what was obviously intended to be a friendly smile. 'Citizen Libertus.' His voice was mumbling and cracked, though I have heard him raise it in anger many times when one of his workers' efforts failed to please. 'To what do we owe the honour of a visit? Do you wish to purchase hides? Or a piece of goatskin – I've got some nice ones here. For a blanket, or a pair of shoes for your good wife, perhaps?' He gestured to the hides that he'd been stacking earlier.

I was tempted to tell him the whole story but rejected the

idea. Unlike the turnip-seller, my neighbour loved to talk, and I knew he had dealings with the wealthy in the town, including the customer for the Apollo piece. I thought of asking if I could borrow a handcart for an hour but rejected that as well – he would be bound to ask questions as to why I wanted it. So I simply shook my head and jerked my chin towards the oil lamp and the bowl. 'I am not bringing business, neighbour, I'm afraid. I come requesting coals. A flame for the oil lamp and some glowing embers to get the fire alight. There's nothing in the workshop that I can light them with.'

He focused both eyes vaguely on my face. 'Not even your Vestal flame alight? And you a Roman citizen?' he said.

It was true that there was a little altar-niche on my premises, dedicated to the goddess of the hearth – no doubt he had seen it when he came to call – but it dated from the time the little shop was built, in the previous owner's time. Even when the upper storey had been a sleeping space, I never lit a sacrificial flame on it except on occasions like public holy days or the feast day of the Emperor, when such observances were generally required.

I had made no answer, and he took that as assent. 'That was careless, neighbour.' He raised his thinning eyebrows in a knowing arch. 'Too busy talking to that fine customer of yours? I saw the expensive-looking litter at your door. And wasn't it the chief decurion getting out of it? I sold him an ox-skin once. I hope he gave you a nice contract and made it all worthwhile?'

'I lost the work, in fact.'

He made a little grimace of sympathy. 'I'm sorry to hear that, citizen. Someone came in with a lower estimate, I suppose. They're all the same, these very wealthy men. Quibble about a quadrans with the likes of us, then spend a fortune on public works and games to woo the populace, especially when they want to win a vote. Like that Gaius Greybeard or whatever he is called, who's been trying unsuccessfully to get an ordo seat for years, putting up that fountain at the crossroads recently. And your decurion's the same – promised new hangings for the ordo room, they say, simply to impress the other councillors. Put extra on the taxes, I shouldn't be surprised, so we shall pay for it.'

I muttered something indeterminate. The tanner loved to gossip and was enjoying this, but I did not wish to be lured into something indiscreet, which might reach the ears of Quintus Severus later on. I tried to change the subject, hoping that I might learn something about Minimus's fate. 'You didn't see anyone else outside my shop, I suppose, talking to my slave this afternoon?'

He shook his head at me. 'Too busy looking after my own affairs. But if it was a time-waster, I more than sympathize. I had just the same thing happen earlier today. Fellow came in here and asked to look at hides, and when I'd spent half an hour showing off my wares, he suddenly decided it was all too dear. Though judging by the jewelled cloak-clasp that he wore, he could have afforded anything I had.'

I listened with appropriate noises of concern, but inwardly I was impatient to get my embers and be off. I was about to offer money, but all at once he said, 'Well, we humble tradesmen had better stick together, hadn't we? You come this way and we'll see what we can do. You'll have to come right through to the workshop, I'm afraid.'

He led the way along the narrow path beside the house, to the large rear courtyard where hides which had been preliminarily soaked were hung out on racks to dry. 'Come in to the tannage room and get the coals. You've timed it very well. I'm boiling up a batch of tanning agent now – alder bark and acorn cups with alum in the blend – the fire's very hot. Mind that horse hide, it's still full of stripping mix.'

I stepped back in time to miss the skin that he had gestured to, which was hanging dripping on a rack. It still looked disturbingly and recognizably like a horse, and as I looked about I could identify several sheep- and ox-skins drying off, and there was a group of smaller pelts as well, which I could not identify. The smell was terrible.

He had noticed the direction of my glance. 'Weasel, otter, stoat and seal,' he said proudly, pointing each one out. 'And that one there's a wolf. The army like them for their *signifers* and pay a hefty price. This way, then, citizen.'

I ducked around a deer hide and followed him inside.

The tannery room occupied the whole front half of his house, which had been specially adapted to accommodate the trade. The entry door was situated oddly halfway down, and the front part of the space – which we had just walked past outside – was partitioned off from the rest by a low internal wall, and the area thus created was busier than a hive. A series of round vat-pits had been dug into the floor, and a large number of men were hard at work. Some were pushing the hides into the tanning mix with long wooden poles; others were actually standing in the pits with their tunics tucked up above their knees and – supporting their weight on ropes set in the walls – treading the hides into the evil-smelling brew with brown-stained legs and feet. I wondered for a moment how they got in and out, until I realized that the steep sides of the vats were lined with plaster and that there was a series of toe-holes in every one of them.

Between the pits, an army of small children scuttled to and fro with jugs of tanning mix, filling the clay vessels which were set into the floor and which seemed to feed the liquid to the adjoining vats along a deep channel with a glazed pipe in it. The smell, if anything, was even worse in here.

'You certainly demand good concentration from your slaves,' I said, surprised to notice that most of the workers didn't raise their eyes at our approach.

He laughed. 'It isn't anything that I do, citizen. It's simple common sense. One false step and you fall into the vat. It isn't so much drowning – though that's always possible – but the mixture doesn't do you any good, especially if it goes into your mouth and eyes. I lose a couple of people that way every year. You get off lightly if it only stains you brown and makes you smell disgusting for a week or two.'

I nodded. I could see that the whole floor was a series of traps for careless feet. I had to pay attention to where I put my own.

'Anyway,' he went on, 'these are not all slaves. I couldn't afford the workforce to do all of this. The treaders are mostly my property, of course, but most of the other hands are freemen who are glad to have the work – there've been some dreadful harvests and winters recently – or lads whose parents have bound them to the shop. I get a fee for having them while they learn the trade. Some of the work requires a lot of skill and it takes time to train them properly. Through here, then!' He gestured to the other side of the partition wall, towards the other, smaller section at the back, where he clearly intended we should go.

There was a solid floor there, to my relief, though it was fully occupied by two lines of trestle tables flanked by high three-legged stools on which the workers perched. There must have been a dozen older lads and men: each had a partly treated hide pegged, stretched out, on a rack in front of him, and was either painstakingly scraping it with strangely shaped bronze tools, or, once that was completed, plucking any recalcitrant last hairs out by hand. This time the men did glance up to look at us, overtly curious, as my guide led me down the narrow zigzag space between the rows.

'The tannage room is through here,' he said, gesturing to a doorway to the rear. 'Come in and we will see what we can do about your coals.'

He led the way into a second room, which clearly gave access to the private living area beyond. This area had the benefit of a stone hearth and a window space, and thus served for the preparation of the tannage mix.

It was clearly brewing now. A copper vat was slung on chains above the fire, and something most unpleasant was bubbling inside, filling the area with clouds of acrid steam which the window space did very little to dispel. The boiling was being supervised by an ancient slave, dressed only in a loincloth, a pair of tattered boots and a heavy metal slaving-ring of linked chain around his throat, reaching from his skinny shoulders almost to his ears – the sort of thing one sometimes sees on female Nubian slaves and which it requires a skilled blacksmith to remove. As we came into

the room, he was being chivvied by a stout woman in a
stained tunic and torn shawl, whose grey hair and skin had
been dyed brown by smoke. She held a long wooden
cooking-paddle in her hand – I suspected that the slave had
felt the blade of it.

'Get a shovel, wife, and fetch us some embers from the
fire,' the tanner said. 'The citizen pavement-maker has a
need of them. And fetch a taper while you're at it, and light
his oil lamp too.'

The woman looked resentfully at him. 'Fetch a shovel,
is it? Just like that? You know it's kept outside. And who's
to look after my tannage while I'm gone? Neither you nor
your smart visitor could do that, I suppose. And don't tell
me that old Glypto will keep an eye on it – the old fool's
so stupid that he'd fall into it. He takes more looking after
than the brew itself. Don't you, eh, Glypto?' She poked at
the old man with the paddle as she spoke. He smiled, a
patient foolish little smile.

The tanner turned to me. 'Glypto came to me many
years ago, as part of my wife's wedding portion,' he
explained. 'I'm not sure that he was not the better part of
the bargain, too.'

His wife flashed him a look that would have tanned skins
on its own, then turned to me. 'Glypto has got old and deaf
and foolish with the fumes, but I can't get rid of him. My
husband keeps him just to taunt me, I believe. Says nobody
would buy him, but that we cannot simply turn him out on
to the street – though he's good for nothing these days
except stoking up the fire and taking rubbish to the midden
now and again.'

Poor fellow! I knew the midden-pile she meant. There
was a narrow gap between the tanner's shop and mine –
hardly wide enough to be called an alleyway – which had
once led through to a coal store behind the tanner's house
and to the lane beyond, but the tanner had moved the coal
heap and the path was now disused and blocked by stinking
refuse from the houses round about. From time to time,
some enterprising fellow with a handcart came to sort it
through and sell the rotting contents to the farmers for their

fields, but otherwise the rubbish simply lay there mouldering until the river flooded and washed it all away. It was not a place where people chose to go.

Glypto gave another of his feeble smiles. 'You want me to take the rubbish to the midden now? But, mistress, I took some just an hour ago?'

She made an infuriated sound and tossed her head. 'You see what I have to suffer, citizen?' She rounded on Glypto and raised her voice at him. She said very loudly and distinctly, 'Listen, you old fool, I want you to stay here while I go and fetch a shovel. My husband wants me to supply some coals to this stranger, though I don't know who he is or what he wants them for. But like you, Glypto, I must do as I am told.' Then, with a last long hostile look at me, she disappeared into the living quarters at the back, leaving the old slave to glare at me suspiciously.

'This is the pavement-maker from the shop next door,' his master told him with a patient sigh. 'He needs some hot embers because his fire's gone out.'

Glypto looked appraisingly at me, and then a look of illumination crossed his face. 'That's right, master. All gone out next door. I heard the green man say so when I took the rubbish to the pile.'

I stared at him. I have seen men whom one might describe as 'blue', when they were painted from head to foot in woad, but . . . 'The green man?' I echoed.

The tanner raised his eyebrow at me to signal what he thought. 'Ignore him, citizen. He's apt to give these fanciful reports. I think he gets strange visions from the fumes.'

It would not have surprised me – the pungency of them was already getting into my eyes and nose and throat – but, in the light of what was currently lying in my shop, I was interested in anyone – green or otherwise – who might have been paying especial attention to my premises. However, I did not want to raise suspicions in the tanner's mind and make him curious.

I was debating what I could say to Glypto that would elicit more, but at that moment the woman came back in with a lighted taper and a piece of shaped metal on a stick – obviously the home-made 'shovel' she had gone to find – and thrust them unceremoniously into her spouse's hands.

'There you are, then, husband,' she said belligerently.

The tanner turned to me. 'I apologize for my wife's bad manners, citizen.' He was lighting my taper even as he spoke and motioning to Glypto that he should shovel some hot coals from the fire into my pot. He nodded towards the woman who was still glowering. 'I'll chastise her by and by.'

It was clear that he had never chastised her in his life, or she would not have dared to turn on him and snort derisively, 'You lift a hand to me and I will walk out of that door. Who would concoct your wretched tannage then? And I'd take my dowry with me – then see how you cope.'

'I've a good mind to send you packing anyway. I would have a legal cause, since you never managed to provide me with a child,' the tanner said mildly, and that silenced her.

It was clearly an argument that they'd had before, and I was glad when the tanner handed me the pot. The embers in it were still red with heat and it was hot to hold – a good deal hotter than I had bargained for – so I almost dropped it. The tanner said at once, in a loud and careful voice, 'Get a proper carrying-brazier, Glypto, and take these coals next door. Help the citizen to light his fire. When you have finished, you can bring the brazier back.'

I was about to make excuses and refuse the help – I didn't want the old slave seeing Lucius's corpse and returning here to tell the tale – but it occurred to me that if Glypto accompanied me alone, I would have a chance to ask him more about the mysterious green man. I could always keep him standing at the workshop door while I discreetly took the brazier in. In any case, by this time he had scuttled from the room, his booted feet ringing on the stone-tiled floor.

The woman looked resentfully at me. 'So, Husband, now I'm expected to stoke the fire as well, while you lend this man my slave – as if giving him the coals and light he wants was not enough. I hope you are going to charge him for the privilege?'

I am fairly certain that the tanner would have done – it was no more than I had expected, after all – but probably because his wife was urging it, he shook his head. 'We local tradesmen must help each other, wife. Come, then, citizen,' he added cheerfully to me, as Glypto reappeared, wearing a tattered blanket as a cloak and carrying the embers in a proper brazier now. 'I'll see you to the street and then get back to work. Glypto will accompany you and get your fire alight.'

'Or at least he can carry the brazier to my door,' I corrected hastily, before the slave could take his master's words as a command. 'Tanner, all this is very kind of you.' I nodded at the woman. 'Good-day, then, goodwife, and accept my thanks. Perhaps one day I can return the compliment and find some service I can do for you.'

She mumbled something in reply – to the general effect that she would rather find herself in Dis – then picked up the wooden paddle and turned back to stirring the tannage savagely. I took my lighted oil lamp and followed the tanner through the door, across the workshop and so out to the gate, with Glypto's heavy footsteps clattering at my heels.

Five

The turnip-seller was still standing outside my workshop, of course, his barrow parked beside my pile of stones, but as I came on to the street, his back was turned to me. He seemed to be giving furtive glances at the door, as if he feared the corpse were likely to do something untoward if no one was keeping a careful watch on it.

But I didn't hurry back to him. Glypto claimed to have seen someone in the alleyway, and that was information which might help me find my slave. I still clung stubbornly to the belief that Minimus was alive. If he'd been killed with Lucius, his body would be here. Captured, he would have some value in the slave market or someone would demand a ransom for his safe return. I hoped the latter, but I could not be sure, and it was vital I had any information I could find. The living must take precedence over the dead, I told myself.

So I turned to the old slave and gave him what I hoped was an encouraging smile.

'You saw the green man in the alleyway, Glypto? The one that runs between the shops?'

'You want Glypto to run between the shops?' The slave looked mystified.

For a moment I was bemused at this, until I thought about it and realized he'd misheard. I should have remembered that he was a little deaf. There was nothing for it but to repeat what I had said, though this time in a louder voice, carefully articulating every word just as I had heard the tanner do. I saw the turnip-seller glance around at us. So much for trying to be discreet, I thought.

This time it was clear that Glypto had understood, though he was clearly suspicious of my motives for addressing him at all. I guessed that, as a general rule, no one said a word to him except to give orders. 'I was putting rubbish on the midden-pile,' he said in a reluctant mumble.

'Of course you were,' I reassured him, still in ringing tones. 'Your mistress sent you there. I heard her say as much. And then you saw the man.' I dropped my voice a notch. 'Why was he a green man, Glypto? Was it the clothes he wore? A green tunic, maybe? Or even hair, perhaps?' That was not a wholly preposterous idea. There are some Celtic elders, especially among the rebellious western tribes, who still maintain the ancient customs of our ancestors and bleach their hair and long moustaches with the traditional lime. That sometimes gives a faintly greenish hue.

Glypto shook his head decisively. 'Green man,' he said again. 'I heard them talking,' he added, as though that settled it.

I abandoned my attempts at making sense of what the green man was, and seized on the implication of what he had just said. 'You heard them talking?' I repeated. 'So he was not alone. How many of them, Glypto? The green man and who else?'

The thin shoulders underneath the tattered blanket shrugged. 'I don't know. I only saw the green man. And I heard another voice.' He stole a look at me. I must have been looking doubtful, because he suddenly burst out, 'But pay no attention to Glypto, citizen. Perhaps there was nobody in the lane at all. My mistress says that I imagine things. Glypto is too old and deaf and foolish to know anything. She told you, didn't she? She tells my master, and he believes it too.' He said it with such bitterness and force that he made me reconsider my own approach to him. A man who could express himself like that was not an idiot.

'I think Glypto notices a lot of things,' I said. 'More than his master and mistress ever dream he does.' I realized I had adopted the form he'd used himself, talking about 'Glypto' as if he wasn't there. It sounded belittling and I corrected it at once. 'So you know there was someone with the green man, Glypto?' I said patiently. 'Because although you didn't see him, you did hear the voice?'

My only answer was a reluctant nod.

I was finding this questioning very difficult, for more reasons than one. Not only was it hard to coax answers

from the slave, but a breeze was threatening to blow my
oil lamp out, so that I had to concentrate on shielding the
flame with my free hand. To say nothing of the fact that I
was obliged to raise my voice and I was afraid the tanner
would overhear and come out to reclaim his slave. But, for
the sake of Lucius and my own missing servant, I had to
persevere, in case there was something Glypto knew and
hadn't told me yet.

So I persisted. 'Did you recognize him, Glypto? The
owner of the voice? A man who had dealings with your
master, possibly?'

'No one Glypto knew.' He shot me a knowing glance.
'And not a man at all. It might have been a woman, but I
think it was a boy.'

'A boy.' I felt a surge of hope, wondering if it could have
been a small red-headed slave. 'You guessed that from his
speech? But you didn't even glimpse him? Not his hair or
clothes?'

Glypto shook his head. The smile he gave was not so
foolish now. 'Not any part of him. He was hidden from me
on the far side of the pile. I couldn't see him for the rubbish
heap. Anyway, the green man's back was in the way.'

'So the other person obviously wasn't very tall? Another
reason why it was probably a boy?'

'Exactly, citizen. Glypto is not as stupid as he looks.'
The old slave's manner was quite triumphant now. He gave
me a crafty look. 'Why are you so interested in all this,
citizen?'

It was a reasonable question, even from a slave, but it
took me aback. I debated inwardly as to how much I should
tell and decided on a partial version of the truth. 'There is
a problem, Glypto. My slave has disappeared. And – before
you suggest it – I don't believe he's run away. He was very
happy here. I think someone has seized him – perhaps to
sell him on. But he was very young – only a pageboy that
my patron Marcus Septimus Aurelius lent to me. That's
why I'm so interested in what you have to say. I thought
it might have been his voice that you heard, that's all.'

He gave a sly laugh. 'A slave belonging to your patron,

citizen? And you've lost him, have you? No wonder you are worried and want to get him back. Even Glypto has heard of Marcus Septimus – he's the most important man for miles around.' He was almost gleeful at my predicament. 'But I'm afraid that I can't help you. The boy I heard was not a private slave, or not an indoor one. Certainly not the kind of page His Excellence would have. Might have been some sort of land slave, I suppose, but what would a land slave be doing around here?' He shook his head. 'Most likely a street urchin, from the sound of him. No education – you could tell that at once. He had rough manners and his speech was coarse, and his Latin was even worse than mine.'

In fact, Glypto's Latin was not bad at all and he had just used it to surprisingly intelligent effect. I should have noticed that and encouraged him to talk. But I was too busy following my own train of thought. 'Yet this urchin person said that everything in my workshop had gone out?' I mused. 'How would he know that?' A thought occurred to me. 'Or was it every*one*? Are you sure you heard correctly?'

The foolish, vacant look came down across his face, as suddenly as an actor might hold up a mask to depict an idiot in the theatre. 'Pay no attention to Glypto, citizen. I told you that before.'

Dear Mars! I had offended him again. I tried another smile. 'On the contrary, Glypto. You're an excellent observer and you've helped me quite a lot. And there's more that you can do. What did this green man look like? Was he tall or short? I know that you only saw him from the back, but what was green about him? Did he have a cloak, perhaps?'

It was a mistake to press him on that point again. His voice reverted to a senile whine. 'Glypto didn't notice. He didn't stop to look. His mistress flogs him if he stays out too long.' He gave a long, exaggerated sigh. 'As she will do now, when he gets back to her, if you don't release him quickly and allow him to go home. So he begs you will be quick. Glypto has already told you what he knows, and you can see that it is nothing related to your slave.'

I felt a little guilty, as he clearly meant I should. It was

true that I had kept him from his work, and I feared that
the flogging was a possibility. Besides, it was clear that he
wasn't going to tell me any more, and the turnip-seller was
awaiting us impatiently by now.

I turned away, and almost managed to let the lamp go
out. I shielded it hurriedly and it flared up again. 'Of course,
I shouldn't keep you any longer than I must. I'm sorry,
Glypto,' I said, and led the way towards my workshop door.

Radixrapum was watching us as we approached, and he
was looking decidedly displeased. 'You've been a long time
coming, citizen,' he said. 'I thought you were in a hurry,
to sort things out in there . . .' He gestured vaguely in the
direction of the corpse. 'You've been so long about it that
the cart will soon be here and you won't have time—'

I interrupted him, aware that Glypto was alert to every
word. 'The tanner has been good enough to light my lamp
for me, and to give me embers so that I can start the fire,'
I said, trying to signal with my eyes for him to be discreet.
'You and I will go inside and quickly get it going. Glypto
here' – I nodded at the slave – 'will stay outside and keep
watch on your barrow while we've gone. But his mistress
needs him; we must not keep him long. We'll bring the
brazier back to him as swiftly as we can.'

The turnip-seller raised a pair of bewildered eyes to mine.
'But . . .' he began, and then I saw illumination dawn. 'Ah!
I see. Of course.' He mouthed the words as if the slave was
blind. 'You haven't told him . . .?'

But Glypto had seen it and was obviously aggrieved. He
had put on his feeble, stupid face again. I gave the turnip-
seller another warning frown. 'Of course I have told him
that I have lost my slave,' I said, with careful emphasis.
'That's what we were discussing in the street just now. And
he's been a lot of help. He overheard some people talking
in the alleyway – it may turn out to be quite relevant.' I
didn't know how sharp the turnip-seller was, but I hoped
that he would realize that I had not mentioned Lucius.

I need not have worried. Radixrapum thought a moment,
then flashed a knowing grin, clearly delighted to be in my
confidence, though his reaction was so careful and extreme

that he might have been an actor in the theatre representing a conspirator in a comedy. 'So, of course, you want me to help you with the fire, seeing that you no longer have a slave.'

That was clearly nonsense. Glypto was obviously skilled with building fires himself and was looking mystified, but Radixrapum had already taken the brazier from him and was on his way around the counter and through the inner door. I followed with my lamp, and we closed the door on Glypto, shutting him outside. The smell in here was noticeably worse, although, compared to the tannery, not so bad at all.

'You don't want to tell him that there's been a murder here?' the turnip-seller murmured.

'There has been a murder, but I'm not sure it was here. I think that Lucius was killed elsewhere and brought here afterwards.' I went over to Lucius's body as I spoke and started to move it very gently from the pile. The army would do that very soon in any case, I thought.

The turnip-seller took the legs and helped me with my task. 'I see. But you are still afraid that news will get about?'

'The tanner is a dreadful gossip and he loves to talk,' I said, when we had done. I went over to the wall, took down a bunch of home-made tapers that I kept hanging on a nail and selected two of the most perfect ones. 'At the first opportunity he'll spread the news abroad, and I will have customers refusing to come near. Especially the one that ordered that piece there.' I indicated the almost-completed Apollo piece still laid out on the floor. 'Pedronius is inclined to change his mind in any case.'

He nodded. 'Pedronius the tax-collector? Even I have heard of him. Didn't he buy that fancy villa just a little while ago, from the councillor who died so suddenly?'

'Or from his heirs, at least,' I said, and made him smile. 'In fact, the man in question left no living family, so everything went to the "residuary legatees" – most of the important men in town got some of it.' I knew that for a fact. Marcus had been a beneficiary himself.

This was not unusual. Any man who wished to rise in life would make a will like that, nominating a series of

influential men to inherit his estate if no other heirs were
found: it prevented confiscation by the imperial purse, which
would otherwise have been inevitable, and had the additional advantage of ensuring patronage from the people who
were named, although in practice they rarely profited from
the will. However, it did sometimes happen, as in the present
case. 'In fact, the villa was left to the chief town councillor,
the very customer that you saw outside my shop, but he
didn't want it – he had a bigger one – so he put it on the
market before it cost him tax. I believe that's how Pedronius
came to hear of it.'

The turnip-seller handed me the taper-spikes to stick the
candles on. 'I gather the tax-gatherer paid an enormous
price for it – and then discovered that the deal did not
include the slaves.'

'So my patron told me at the time,' I assented. 'It was
not entirely the decurion's fault – the slaves had been
bequeathed to someone else – but Pedronius threatened to
take him before the aediles, and in the end Quintus agreed
to provide him with a chief slave to run the place, though
Pedronius had to provide the other servants for himself,
and, of course, there were lots of them needed in an establishment like that. There's been bad feeling between the
households ever since.'

'Not a good beginning,' Radixrapum said.

'Exactly! And Pedronius is a superstitious man,' I said.
'And that is just the trouble. The other owner died there
suddenly, you know. Pedronius fears that the house attracts
bad luck. He wants this Apollo piece in his garden to ward
it off and to appease the gods. Now he's likely to suppose
that the plaque is cursed as well. I only wish that I could
get it into place before the story of the murder gets around.
Unfortunately, I haven't got a cart to move it on.'

'But surely your decurion noticed it was here? It sounds
as if he'd take delight in crowing over the tax-gatherer's ill
luck.'

I shook my head. 'He didn't come inside. So you and I
are the only ones who know the plaque has been here with
a corpse.'

'I see.' He looked delighted. 'Except for the murderer, I suppose. But he's not going to tell.'

'Exactly!' I said dryly. 'And we must work quickly now before Glypto's curiosity gets too much for him and he comes in to look. If he tells his master, it will be all over town.' I placed the lighted candle by Lucius's bandaged head. 'Though I expect it's hopeless anyway. I can't pretend there hasn't been a death. Quintus will doubtless tell his dinner guests in exaggerated terms, and the tanner will see the army when it comes to get the corpse. But, all the same, I may yet find a way – if I can find my son and have a cart again. So another half-sestertius if you get the fire alight and keep your own counsel about what you have seen.'

'Another half-sestertius, citizen? You have a bargain there.'

He said it so eagerly that I rephrased the offer. 'I will give the money next time that you call – after I have got that plaque in place and I'm sure that your gossip hasn't reached the customer.'

He grinned. 'You can trust me, citizen. I'll help you keep the secret in any way I can. For the money you are offering, I would do more than that. First, though, I will get the fire alight. Flame is known to purify a room and keep evil ghosts away.' He knelt at once beside the hearth and began raking out the ash and dust. He tipped the embers from the brazier in and covered them with the dry leaves and kindling that I kept nearby, blowing gently on them until a flame appeared.

The promise of money had worked its charm again. Perhaps I should have tried bribery with Glypto too, but I hadn't thought of it. Anyway, I was not carrying much money in my purse and I was counting on bribing the watchmen at the gate – in case there was news of Minimus being taken out that way. I placed a second lighted taper at the corpse's feet and turned to see how the fire was getting on.

The turnip-seller had my leather bellows in his hand and had coaxed the flame to brighter life, and as I turned, he leaned back on his heels and tossed a log of wood into the

hearth. He grunted and clambered slowly to his feet. 'There
you are, citizen. I think that's well alight. But it won't burn
properly until you clean the hearth. You'll have to get your
slave to sweep it thoroughly some time.'

'That is supposing that I ever find my slave again.'

'Of course. But you said the tanner's man had information that might help? Something that will help you to find
the murderer as well?'

'I don't know,' I said. 'Glypto says so, but he has strange
ideas. He talks about a green man in the alleyway. The
tanner thinks he's foolish and imagines things, but I am not
being half-deaf so sure. It's not the clothes or hair, apparently. In what way could a man be green apart from that?'

The street-vendor scratched his turnip head. 'I don't know,
citizen. You're the clever one.' His face brightened. 'Unless
you're right about the bandits, and the man had come from
hiding in the woods. There's rumoured to be someone in
the town supporting them, and I hear they do sew leaves
and branches to their clothes, so that they blend in better
with the trees.'

I nodded. I had heard that rumour too. 'Though in that
case you would think that when they came to town—'

'Of course!' Radixrapum used a dusty palm to strike his
brow. 'They would have to take them off, or they'd look
conspicuous. I should have thought of that. I'm sorry,
citizen.'

'Don't apologize,' I said. It always helped to talk things
through with someone else and I was coming to respect the
turnip-seller's intellect. He had raised more than one idea
I hadn't thought of for myself. It was nice to have an ally
in whom I could confide, since there was no Junio or
Minimus to help.

The turnip-seller was clearly flattered by my praise. He
said, in an obvious attempt to help again, 'Did you ask that
slave if there were any customers next door this afternoon?'

In fact, I hadn't. The story of the green man had driven
it from my mind. 'Not yet,' I answered. 'I'll do it as soon
as we get outside again. If you're ready, we'll take the
brazier back.'

He nodded. 'At least poor old Lucius has got his candles now, and his ghost won't be offended that he was not shown respect.'

It crossed my mind that being throttled from behind, dragged along and thrown face-down on a pile of jagged tiles was hardly a demonstration of decent reverence, but I did not say so. Instead, I picked up the empty brazier and went outside with it.

Glypto was standing close beside to the door, but as soon as he saw me he stepped guiltily away, although I am certain that being half-deaf he could not have overheard. I gave him the empty brazier with a smile. 'Take that to your master and thank him for his help.'

'Is that all, citizen? Can poor Glypto go back to work again?'

'Just one thing more, since you have sharp eyes. Tell me, did anyone come to your shop this afternoon? Anyone besides me, of course, I mean. Anyone who might have seen what happened to my slave?'

The old man did his simpering face again. 'How would old Glypto know a thing like that? Glypto is kept busy in the tannage room.'

That was true, of course, but I knew the man by now. He was resentful and holding something back – I could tell that from the way that he would not meet my eyes. 'But you went out with the rubbish and you fetched the fuel to stoke the fire. And – whatever your mistress supposes to the contrary – you keep your eyes about you. Was there anyone?'

He was torn between stubbornness and a desire to show what he could do. You could almost see the battle on his face. At last he said, 'Only the usual delivery of hides. And the quartermaster from the barracks wanting a wolf-skin for the army signifer.'

I nodded. The standard-bearers of the legions often wore such hides draped across their head and shoulders when they were on parade, leading the troops on ceremonial marches through the streets. They wear them into battle too, apparently – presumably to make the standard easy to

Rosemary Rowe

pick out – and I have even seen wolf-skins worn on the daily route march, although I always thought that they must be insufferably hot. 'I saw one at the tannery.'

'That's the one he's bought. He was lucky to get it,' Glypto said. 'You can't get the wolves these days, with all those rebels in the wood.'

'But that was not the only customer?' I said. 'There was another fellow who came in looking round – a man with a fancy cloak-clasp, I believe. I remember your master mentioned him to me.'

The mask had come down on Glypto's face again. 'Glypto can't tell you, citizen. He wasn't in the shop. He has already told you about everyone he saw, and his mistress will be furious with him for being late.'

There was no point in pressing him, and I let him go, though I did call after him as he scampered off, 'There will be a quadrans for you the next time that we meet – more if you happen to remember something else.'

He paused and turned around. 'But how can I be sure to see you, citizen? They don't let Glypto out. Only to put on the rubbish on the pile.'

'Then I will meet you at the midden-heap,' I said. 'If you can contrive to be there tomorrow' – I was about to say 'when the sun is at its height' but I remembered that I had a naming ceremony to attend, and I amended it – 'in the late afternoon. I will keep a watch for you.'

He nodded. 'Till tomorrow then,' and he went back through the gate into the tannery. Almost at once I heard the shrill voice of the tanner's wife. It raised in hectoring reproof, followed shortly after by the sound of blows. I cringed a little. I felt responsible.

Six

Radixrapum caught my eye as I turned back. He raised an eyebrow. 'Funny sort of fellow, that old slave. I wonder what he did see in the alleyway – or whether he really saw anything at all.'

'I hope I'll discover that tomorrow, when we meet,' I said, but even as I spoke the words they sent a chill through me. If Minimus was in danger, that seemed too long to wait. Surely I had to find him before that! Yet my best hope of finding him was to trace the murderer, and I had little idea of where to start with that. Besides, there were other urgent things that needed to be done, and – what with questioning Glypto and lighting candles by the corpse – I'd already delayed too long. 'I had planned to tell Lucius's mother what had happened to her son,' I told the turnip-seller, 'but now there's scarcely time to reach her before the cart arrives.'

'There's no chance at all of reaching her, I shouldn't think, and certainly no time for you to get back again.' He gave a little grin, tilting his turnip head at me. 'Don't look so stricken, citizen. You never did have time – and if you stop to think, you'll realize that as well. When we were in the workshop just now, you mentioned that your recent customer was chief decurion, didn't you? I could see he was wealthy, but I hadn't realized he was as important as all that. If the senior town councillor tells the garrison to send the cart round here, obviously they're going to do it straight away.'

I nodded thoughtfully. 'I suppose that's true.'

'Then perhaps you don't need me to stay and keep a watch? Or do you still intend to go to the pie-bakery and find her anyway? You said it would be better if she didn't see the corpse.'

I suppose that had been vaguely in my thoughts, but I

answered stubbornly, 'I think she ought to know. And she may know something that will help me trace the murderer – for instance, whether Lucius had personal enemies.'

He looked at me quizzically. 'You wouldn't like to put that piece of work up on a plank and rest it on my barrow before you go? I'll give you a hand, of course, and you can wheel it out into the street. Then it will be out here when the army comes, and nobody need ever know that it was in there with the corpse. The decurion did not see inside the shop, you say – and I want that half-sestertius, so I won't be gossiping – but you can't prevent the soldiers from telling everyone. And they will have to go inside to pick the body up.'

He was quite right, of course, and it was a concern. Quintus's reaction to a dead man in my shop had been enough to tell me what my customers would think if rumour got around. I was beginning to look at Radixrapum with more and more respect. His suggestion was not a foolish one. In fact, I rather wished I'd thought of it myself.

Although his barrow was much smaller than my hand-cart was, and currently full of earth and bits of turnip-top, it would be the work of moments to clear that away, and, with care, the Apollo plaque was not too large to carry in that way. The piece was already mounted on its linen backing cloth, ready to be reversed and cemented into place, and I had that terracotta tray on which to carry it. That could be managed on the barrow, though it would take a lot of care. The mosaic was not quite finished at one edge, of course, but that was, if anything, a help. It made it slightly easier to move, since I could protect the edges in transit with a rolled strip of cloth, and a border can always be filled with larger tiles, or even with painted mortar if required.

I had border tesserae already cut and quite a lot to spare; the extra pieces could be taken with it as they were, and I could put in the final touches when it was in place. I had already left the necessary tools and mortar at the site, when I put down the preliminary layer yesterday. So it was tempting to do as the turnip-seller said. But there was Lucius's mother to consider too.

Radixrapum saw that I was havering. 'It won't make any difference to his mother, citizen. She cannot help him now. If you go off and tell her, what are you going to do? Stop the army carting him away and ask her if she wants to take the corpse herself? That will just be an impossible expense, because she'll have to provide the funeral – you and I are both aware that he would never have contributed to any guild. So you'll end up paying for it all yourself. And you couldn't decently just put him on a public pyre. If you're going to stand as patron, you would have to do it right – with at least a funeral director and bier, and very probably a priest and some sort of sacrifice. It would cost a huge amount. To say nothing of all the cleansing rituals you'll have to get performed before you can reopen your shop in any case. And you weren't officially his patron, were you, citizen?'

He was voicing the very thoughts that I'd had earlier. I made a groaning sound. With the loss of Quintus's order, things were hard enough, without additional expense – especially if the Apollo piece fell through. 'Not officially his patron,' I said reluctantly. 'Though he'd half-adopted me as one, this last half-moon or so. I simply feel an obligation to do something, that is all.'

He cocked a brow at me. 'If the corpse had turned up anywhere but here, it's likely that nobody would have told the mother anything, and she would only have deduced that Lucius was dead when he did not come home. You will have saved her that, at least. This has been thrust on you, and you have done your best – you've lit candles for him and called three times on his soul. No reason why you should lose your customers as well. You can go and see the mother afterwards, if you feel you must, and offer her such consolation as you can. But if we are going to move this piece of work of yours, we ought to do it fast, or the army cart will turn up and catch us in the act.'

It was no good arguing. The man was not such a turnip as he looked. He was obviously right. I nodded doubtfully. 'We'll do as you suggest.'

He gave me another conspiratorial grin. 'Of course, you'll

have to buy those last few turnips first, to clear the space. Shall we say another half-sestertius for the lot, and for the temporary hire of the barrow too?'

Dear Mars! He almost seemed to be enjoying this. 'Oh, very well,' I said. 'If you look behind the counter, you will find a leather bag I sometimes use to carry bread and cheese. Put the turnips in it, and we will make a start.'

It did take a few moments to clean the barrow out, but, despite his protests, I insisted it was done – the mosaic would be balancing dangerously enough, without there being lumps of earth beneath the tray preventing it from lying properly. When we had finished, we went into the shop.

It was my turn to feel disconcerted by the corpse. The tapers were still burning at Lucius's head and feet (though the most pervading smell was not of smoke and tallow grease), and despite the blindfold round the head, I was uncomfortably aware of the memory of those bulging eyes – as if the dead man was somehow staring through the cloth.

I was glad that we had moved the body earlier; it made it easier to turn our backs on it, though I had an eerie feeling that it was watching me – reproachful because I hadn't gone to find his mother first. But the turnip-seller seemed to be free of such uncomfortable fantasies and he was already kneeling by the plaque and laying hold of the linen backing piece. So I suppressed my fancies and, with his help, I shuffled the whole plaque on to the tray, stuffed strips of cloth around it and lashed it into place. Then between us we carried it out on to the barrow. It fitted, in a fashion, though it was precarious. Then we went back and gathered up the extra tiles into another length of cloth, knotted it securely into a roll and wedged the bottom of the load with it, so it could not slip forwards if the barrow lurched. The whole thing looked incongruous, but all the same it was a great relief to have it safely out.

And just in time, it seemed. There was an unfamiliar sound of wheels and jangling chains, and the military cart came lurching into view, moving slowly in the narrow, muddy confines of the road. It was not forbidden to bring horse-drawn transport here during the hours of daylight, as it was within the walls (and anyway this was an army vehicle and would have been exempt) but the area was not designed for wagons of this size. There was barely room for it to inch along. I leaned against the wall and tried to look insouciant, as though I had been waiting there since Quintus left.

The turnip-seller, however, was not content with this. He glanced towards the barrow. 'This looks out of place with a mosaic on – they'll notice it for sure. I'll take it round and put it in the alley while they're here.' He seized the wooden handles and made as if to trundle the whole thing out of sight.

I shook my head. 'That would only take you past them. Go the other way. Push it a little further down the road,' I urged. 'That will arouse much less suspicion than you going skulking by the midden-heap. These soldiers have no idea that you have been with me – to them you are just another vendor with a barrow in the street. They won't know what's on it, if you take it far enough.' I saw him hesitate, and added urgently, 'When they've taken Lucius, we can decide what we do next. But move quickly if you're going to. They are almost here.'

They were indeed: one obviously senior soldier with a swagger stick, and two reluctant younger ones behind him with the horse. The older one, whom I had nicknamed 'Scowler' in my mind, was already striding purposefully towards us.

The turnip-seller must have seen him coming too. He did not even glance in my direction as he said, 'I could always take it to the site for you. I know where it is – the villa is even on my own route home. When you've been to see the woman, I will meet you there and take the barrow back.' He gave a fleeting grin. 'That's worth another half-sestertius, don't you think, citizen?' And, without waiting for an answer, he set off down the street. I swear I heard a distant cry of 'Turnips!' as he went.

'Are you this pavement-maker we've been sent to find?' Scowler was barking the question in my ear.

I turned to face him. He was standing close beside me:

deliberately close, in a posture designed to be threatening. His feet, in their hobnailed sandals, were planted wide apart and he carried a helmet tucked beneath one arm, while the other hand rested lightly on his hip, the fingers caressing the handle of the baton at his belt. His head was tilted arrogantly back.

'Well?' he said.

I looked him up and down. The man was swarthy, crop-haired and stocky, with a self-important air, though the chain-mail tunic and the sweat-stained leather underskirt marked him as an auxiliary officer at best – one of the many from the southern provinces, perhaps, lured by the promise of citizenship when he retired. In that case, I outranked him – in one respect at least.

'I am the citizen Longinus Flavius Libertus, certainly, and this is my workshop,' I said evenly, stressing my title and my full three Roman names – a signal that I was already a citizen myself.

He must have got the point, although he showed no outward sign. His voice, however, became less peremptory. 'I was sent here on the orders of the chief decurion. Said there was a body of a pauper to collect.' He leaned a little closer as he spoke. He smelt of sweat and horses and cheap watered wine. 'Seems to think your slave has robbed and murdered him.'

I looked at him coldly. 'Decurions can be wrong.'

That seemed to strike a chord. He used a sharp elbow to dig me in the ribs. 'I don't think he can believe it much himself – about the murdering at least. If he wanted to bring a charge against the slave, he'd want to produce the dead body, wouldn't he – not have it disposed of quickly in the pit?'

I looked at him sharply. I had not thought of that, although perhaps I should have done. I'm not entirely familiar with the details of the law.

He gave me another nudge. 'Though we've been told to hold the boy if he turns up. Says that he will haul him to the courts and have him charged with robbery and with attempting to run away. He claims the boy belongs to Marcus

Septimus – not to you at all – and in the owner's absence he will act for him and make the formal accusation that the law requires.'

I tried to keep my voice completely unconcerned. 'The boy was lent to me, however, and I make no such charge. Quintus Severus is wrong about the theft as well. Whoever killed the pauper stole his purse and took my servant too – which I hope to prove by producing both of them. But the decurion is right about the corpse. You'll find it in my workshop, lying on the floor.'

Scowler furrowed his low brow a little more. 'What's it doing there? And why, in that case, have they called on us?'

'As to what he's doing in my workshop, I don't know. Someone dragged him there when he was dead – and if you are going to ask me why, I don't know the answer to that either, I'm afraid. And I did not call you; the decurion did.'

He gave me an understanding look which said that one could not argue with officialdom. His frown relaxed a little, but he shook his head. 'Shouldn't touch it really, when it isn't in the street. Criminals and vagrants, and dead travellers whose bodies cannot be identified, that's what me and my fatigue party are supposed to gather up.' He scratched his cropped head with his baton-end and seemed to be thinking. Then he looked triumphantly at me. 'Suppose I told you to dispose of him yourself? He was murdered in your workshop after all.'

'I doubt that the chief decurion would approve,' I countered. 'Anyway, I've told you: the body didn't die here – it was dragged here afterwards. I have proof of that. You would have had to take it if it had been left out in the street.'

He looked perplexed again. The mention of Quintus had clearly worried him. 'Well, since you put it that way . . .' He turned back to his men who were still waiting with the cart. 'Come on, you idle scum. Do what you were sent for. Take a look in there!'

They were ruthlessly efficient; I'll say that for them. It seemed no time at all before they brought Lucius out, suspended between them by his arms and legs. They swung him up and tossed him on the cart, on top of another body already lying there – it might have been a leper or a beggar with one leg. The soldiers didn't even pull a blanket over them. I was glad that Lucius had the bandage on his face, and that his mother wasn't there to see.

Scowler was supervising all this with disdain. He hadn't moved an inch. When they had finished, he turned to me again. 'Well, that's it, citizen. We'll leave you to it now. There's a couple more corpses that we have to fetch. A pair of brigands who have been put to death – we've got to pick their bodies up before we put these in the pit.' He jammed his helmet on and turned back to his men. 'Don't just stand there lounging, you useless sons of whores! We've got more work to do. Get that horse down to a place where you can turn the cart around.' And he went swaggering off.

I watched them inching down the street, then went back to the shop, blew out the tapers – which had been thrust aside, though fortunately not where they would start a fire – and put the outside shutter for the doorway up. I was going to go to the bake-house to find Lucius's mother now. Everything else would simply have to wait.

With a chill feeling, I picked up the greasy tray, which was still lying on the stones outside my shop. What would happen to the poor woman without her son? Who would bring her remnants from the market now? I considered for a moment, then went back and picked up the turnips too.

Seven

I t did not take me very long to reach the place where Lucius had lived. I even half-recalled the route, although it was a long time since I'd visited this ramshackle area of the town, which was constantly flooded when the Sabrina rose.

The dwelling was every bit as squalid as I had remembered it, a broken-down hovel amongst the ruins of what had once been a house, now with only a piece of tattered cloth across the front to form a door, and – in place of what had been handsome tiles – woven reeds as a rough sort of thatch. Behind this stood a fire-blackened conical stone building which was the oven, or so-called baking-house. A well-worn path ran in between the two, among a mass of tangled weeds and fallen masonry, interspersed with the usual litter of a public street: bits and pieces of broken pot, rusty nails, and fish and chicken bones.

I saw the old woman as soon as I approached. She was small and wizened, and even thinner than her son had been in life, but she was impressively energetic for her age. When I arrived, she was by the baking-house, hacking ferociously at a piece of tree, apparently in order to make it fit the oven fire. She had obviously been out earlier collecting fuel for it, because there was a carefully created pile lying close nearby – dried grasses, fir cones, branches, birds' nests, even bits of rag. She clearly made the most of anything that would burn.

She lowered the hatchet as she saw me arrive (I wondered if it was the same one that she used to chop ingredients) and stood up to greet me, pressing one hand into her crooked back as if to ease the ache. She looked at me with shrewd, glittering green-grey eyes. 'If you are wanting pies at this hour, mister, then you're unlucky, I'm afraid. There's none of last night's left. My good-for-nothing son has taken them to sell, and I shan't be starting baking any more till he comes home with the supplies – and even then it will be hours before they're cooked enough to eat.' She gave me a brief, well-practised smile, showing a surprisingly handsome set of teeth – large but not discoloured and remarkably complete. 'Come back tomorrow and I'll set one aside for you.' She turned back to her work.

I shook my head. This was going to be even more diffi-cult than I had supposed: she was so unsuspecting of what lay in store! I went up, removed the hatchet gently from her grasp and made to take her arm, ready to lead her in the direction of the hut. 'I think that you should come and sit down in the house. What I have to tell you is distressing news. It concerns your son.'

She snatched her arm away and stood confronting me. 'He hasn't gone and got us into debt a second time? I suppose he's been gambling on the chariot races again? Well, as I told the other man your masters sent around, Lucius cannot pay you with what he hasn't got.' She wiped a bedraggled sleeve across her face. 'And it is no good coming here and threatening me for it. I haven't got a quad-rans, as you can clearly see. I didn't know he'd got caught up again. I thought he'd given up betting after what you did to him. But my son is single-minded when he decides to be.'

Rather like his mother, I thought inwardly, but all I said was, 'So he'd been in debt before?' It was not at all what I had planned to say, but this was a very unexpected piece of news. I hadn't envisaged Lucius as a chariot devotee.

There was no reason why he shouldn't be – apart from poverty. There is no permanent chariot circus in the neigh-bourhood – the arena in the amphitheatre, where gladiato-rial games take place and where criminals were sometimes thrown to the beasts, is too confined to stage a proper race – but there is a site where a temporary structure can be set up for the day, complete with turning posts, dolphin-shaped devices to indicate the laps, and viewing stands where all but the more exclusive seats are free. The lack of facilities ensures there are no full-time local teams, but there are chariot-racing festivals from time to time, sometimes with famous visiting drivers on display, funded by some local dignitary as a part of a campaign to win favour with the populace. All the same, poor working freemen like Lucius did not usually attend, still less did they ever bet money on a race. They simply did not have the time and cash to spare, and anyway, since they did not have the vote, the entertainment was not aimed at them. But Lucius, it seemed, had placed a bet or two – no doubt on borrowed money, as he had none of his own.

So I wondered if I'd stumbled on a motive for his death. The men who run the betting syndicates are famous (or infamous) for their ruthlessness. It would not have been the first time they'd made a cash advance on the promise of repayment if the team came home and then exacted a terrible revenge on someone who had failed to pay them what was owed.

In that case, the killer would be hard to catch, I thought. Victims are reluctant to identify the men behind these gambling rings. Assaults and murders are not reported to the authorities, partly because people fear reprisals if they do, and also because betting on the chariots is, itself, a technical offence. (There has been too much corruption and race-fixing in the past, my patron told me once, sometimes resulting in riots in the street.) Yet it remains absurdly easy to find someone who will take your stake – agents approach you as you wait outside – and even the law which forbids gambling booths at the course is, very often, effectively ignored.

So, 'Lucius was gambling on the chariots?' I said again.

She looked suspiciously at me. 'You didn't know that? So you didn't come from them? And you don't want a pie?' Her voice was sharper now. 'Then, what have you come for? You said it was bad news.'

I took a deep breath. 'I'm afraid it's Lucius.'

She made a tutting sound. 'It almost always is. What is it this time? Accosting travellers to buy his pies and having them complain? If you are an aedile from the market police—' She broke off and stared at me. 'But, of course, you aren't. You wouldn't be wearing that tunic if you were.

But this must be serious. I see you've brought his tray. Have they arrested him?'

I nodded and laid it carefully against the oven wall. 'It's serious, but not for the reasons that you think. And there's no kind way to tell you. Lucius is dead. Got himself murdered somewhere in the street.'

'Murdered?' I had expected her to cry or shriek or groan, or give some other indication of her grief, but she said the word quite softly. 'Well, that's the end of that. Not much of a life he ever led, poor lad.' Her face was calm but all the light had gone out of her eyes. 'Did you see him dead? Do you think he suffered? Tell me it was quick!'

I found a way to answer that at least. 'He was set on from behind. He could scarcely have realized what was happening.' It was almost true. There was no point in telling her about the clawing hands and bulging eyes. But there was one thing I had to be quite certain of. 'They've taken him for a pauper's burial. He wasn't a member of a funeral guild?'

She shook her head – to my infinite relief – then turned away and fiddled with the branch she had been cutting up. 'You don't know who killed him?'

I shook my head. 'I only wish I did. Do you know if he had enemies?' It struck me that she had seemed somehow unsurprised, and a name might lead me to Minimus, of course.

She made a little uninterested face. 'Not that I know of, mister. He was a gentle man – unless it was a matter of a gambling debt: they gave him a dreadful beating once before. And there was another day he was attacked – that time was because he'd given somebody false coin. He didn't mean to; he'd been given fake silver and simply passed it on – never bothered to test it with his teeth, though I have shown him how to do it at least a dozen times. Of course, the man he passed it on to didn't wait to hear all that, simply sent his slaves around to "teach the ugly cheat a lesson", as they said.' She broke off again. 'But what gives you an interest in my unhappy son?'

I said, very simply, 'He was murdered near my workshop, and whoever killed him has also made off with my slave, it seems – and, I'm afraid, with Lucius's purse as well.'

She snapped a brittle twig between her hands. 'So the money is all gone? And you discovered this?' She did not meet my eyes.

It occurred to me that she might think I'd taken it. 'Your son was on his way to see me, I believe, hoping that I'd buy another of his pies. I'd given him a tunic not very long ago.'

She did look at me then. 'So you are the pavement-maker that he told me of? And that lovely tunic. What's happened to it now? I suppose the army will have taken him away?'

I nodded.

'It would have fetched something in the marketplace,' she said in a defeated tone. I was secretly a little bit appalled by this turn of things – as if a few asses were more important than what happened to her son – but I reflected that perhaps if one has nothing in the world, a few copper coins may be life or death. But she shamed me for my thoughts. 'I cannot even buy a taper to light before the gods.'

'I did light candles at his head and feet, and called his name three times,' I said, as though that made a difference.

It seemed it did. She gazed at me and said with obvious sincerity, 'You are a good man, mister. I could have done no more myself. Thank you for treating him with some respect in death, and for being so kind to him in life.' She reached out her wrinkled hands and grasped my own. 'And thank you also for coming all this way to tell me of his death.'

I was embarrassed by this display of gratitude. 'It was really nothing,' I muttered, recognizing with guilt that this was true.

She pressed my fingers. 'But you looked after Lucius. I will not forget. You come this way any time, pavement-maker, and you shall have a pie – gratis. That is, supposing that I ever bake again. Jove alone knows how I'll manage for ingredients.'

I gave her the turnips. It was the least that I could do. This time it did bring tears into her eyes.

'Bless you, mister . . . or should I say "citizen"? Didn't Lucius tell me that you held that rank?'

I nodded. Of course, I wasn't wearing my toga at the time.

'And to think that a proper citizen should have done all this for us! Jove bless you, citizen, a hundred times.' She hugged the bag of turnips to her chest. 'If there is ever anything that I can do for you – anything at all – I am at your service.' She shook her head sadly. 'Provided I survive. I don't think I care. Now Lucius has gone, I have lost the last thing that I had to live for in the world. I lost my husband and my business in the fire years ago. I think it was only worry about Lucius that kept me going.'

She was about to cry. I rather hoped she would – pent-up grief is worse than any tears – but I also hoped that she would wait till I had gone, or we should both be made embarrassed. 'There is one thing that you can do for me,' I said, in a weak attempt to deflect her from her tears. 'I'd like to have the bag I brought the turnips in.'

It didn't make her smile. 'Of course. One moment, citizen.' She rummaged behind her frowsty curtain and produced an iron pot – with one of its three legs missing, I noticed, and no handle on the top. 'Lucius brought this home for me the other day – one of his customers made him a gift of it. I'll put them in here, and you can have the bag. It is a good one and must be worth an *as* at least. I should have thought of it.' She emptied the three turnips into the damaged cauldron as she spoke. I wished I'd never mentioned getting back the bag.

'If you make turnip pies, I'll buy one of them,' I said. It didn't sound a very appetizing meal, but it would be a more wholesome filling than had often been the case. 'Or were you intending to make a meal of those yourself?'

She shook her head. 'I hadn't thought what I would do with them.'

Of course she hadn't. Poor woman, she hadn't thought of anything at all. But I had to press her. I said gently, 'I want to find his murderer on my own account, you know. I think he has my slave. If anything occurs to you which might shed light on this, please come and let me know, for both our sakes.'

'You asked if Lucius had any enemies – if I think of anything, I'll come and find you at the shop. But unless he was gambling on the chariots again, honestly I can't think of anyone at all.' She stared down at the turnips as if she might find inspiration in the pot. 'Yet I can't believe that he'd gone back to it, after last time and what they did to him.'

'And what was that? Took him to an alley and beat him to a pulp?'

She looked at me wryly. 'Exactly, citizen. I nursed him for a week. And even that was not enough: they threatened him with worse if he did not contrive to pay the money back within a moon.'

'And did he?' I saw her face. 'Or rather you did it for him, I suppose.'

She looked away. 'Of course, I was a great deal younger in those days. I had to go and let them shave my head and offer my hair to a fancy wigmaker, as well as sell my only pair of shoes – and do other things I'd rather not admit – so we could pay them back. They'd have killed him otherwise.' She shook her head. 'Lucius never forgave himself when he found out what I'd done. I can't believe he'd get involved with gambling again, however excited he was about his team.'

'His team?' I said startled. So he'd not just been a casual visitor, caught up in the excitement of the day. 'Lucius followed the chariots enough to have a team?'

'Not his own team, of course. He just supported them – or rather he dreamed of fame and fortune driving chariots. You do hear of people who manage to do that. I even had a brother who was sold into a team – my parents thought it would ensure his livelihood – and he showed some aptitude, before he broke his legs and turned into a cripple overnight. Then, of course, he was no use to the team and completely worthless in the marketplace. His slave price was so small that my husband bought his freedom with the profits from the pies.'

'So you took care of him? That was most generous.'

She gave a weary smile. 'We could afford it then. You would not believe we used to have a thriving business once. People even used to pay us to let them cook their food, in the heat left in the ash when we had finished for the day, not to mention the bread and pastries that we made to sell.'

I looked around at the ruins of her life and could make no answer.

She saw the direction of my glance and said, 'But that was long ago, when we had proper fuel, and I could afford good flour and fine ingredients. And then there was the fire – and everything was burned. My husband and my brother with the rest, of course. I was forced to survive in whatever way I could – thank Jupiter the oven itself was made of stone, and I can still heat the oven if I can get the fuel, though I can't keep it running the way we used to do.' She sighed. 'But Lucius was always passionate about his uncle's team. That is how he lost the money last time, I'm afraid. I suppose he might have been sucked into it again.'

'I see. Well, thank you for your help.' I turned away. All this had put a different slant on things. If Lucius had been killed because he'd failed to pay a gambling debt, and his money had been stolen as part payment – which was possible – then I was dealing with a different class of murderer, even more dangerous than brigands from the woods. I would have to be careful when I made enquiries. But why would such people seize young Minimus? Did they intend to try to ransom him and thus extort the missing sum from me? And where did Glypto's stranger in the alley fit into all this?

The green man! I whirled around again. Of course! The chariot teams were known by the names of the colours that they wore. 'Which team was it?' I almost held my breath. 'Let me guess. Was he by any chance a follower of the Greens?'

To my disappointment she shook her head again. 'The Greens? Great Mars! He hated them. He was a life-time supporter of the Reds.' Her voice was quavering but strong. 'The team comes over from *Corinium* now, I think. Is there anything else that I can tell you about that?'

I shook my head. There was nothing further I could think of asking her, so I took my leave again. At the corner I glanced back at her, expecting to find her hard at work, but she had simply sat down on the littered grass, buried her head in her tattered sacking overskirt and was sobbing helplessly.

I had meant to thank her for the offer of the pie, but I left her to her grief.

Eight

I quickened my pace and hurried back through town. I had done all that I could do for Lucius by now. I had no idea where Minimus had gone and I was powerless to look. Suppose rebels had him . . . but I would not think of that. If I didn't wish to have my family starve, I had to get that Apollo plaque in place before my customer had second thoughts. Besides, by this time Radixrapum would be waiting for me there, no doubt demanding the money that I'd promised him today.

I loosened the drawstring on the purse I carried at my belt and without slackening my pace, drew out the three coins that I found inside and looked at them hopefully. The result was not encouraging. I owed the turnip-seller a whole sestertius by this time: a half-sestertius for his help and another for the hire of his barrow, both to be paid when I got back to him. Thank heavens I said he'd have to wait until the plaque was safely laid before I paid him for his silence too. By the time I had paid Radixrapum what was due to him, I would only have a single quadrans left.

But even that I was going to have to spend. My household would begin to worry if I did not return by dusk. I had to let them know that I would be rather late, but there was no Minimus to act as messenger. That meant paying someone else to go. Of course, my wife would wonder why I hadn't sent the page, but I decided that the full distressing truth about his disappearance and the murdered pie-seller could wait till I got home. No need to cause her additional concern.

I found a skinny urchin lurking in a lane – one of the *egentes* that frequent the town, hoping to earn enough to eat by doing menial tasks like holding horses and selling the manure. He wore a ragged tunic and was anything but clean, but he had a pair of fairly serviceable sandals on his feet, which made it not impossible for him to walk so far, and I guessed that he'd be grateful for my paltry coin. I gave him a verbal message to deliver to my house, and he accepted the errand very readily.

It was not very satisfactory. I had no guarantee that he'd actually deliver it: it was several miles to my roundhouse, and I had no means of writing anything so I could not tell my wife to pay him extra when he came, which might have ensured that he actually arrived. But in the circumstances it was the best that I could do. I watched him out of sight and then I set off myself in the direction of Pedronius's country house and the garden where the plaque was to be laid.

I did pause at the gatehouse at the city wall to ask if the sentries had seen my missing slave but, as I feared, there was no news of him. I gave them a good description and a different account (they had been alerted to watch for runaways), then I set off again.

It was a long trek from my workshop, and longer still from the swampy river suburb where the pie-oven was, so by the time I neared the villa the day was well advanced. I began to wonder if they would let me in, and, even if they did, whether I could complete the task before I had to leave. (I would have to go before the sun was set – the walk home meant several miles of lonely forest road, I had no lantern and there were bandits in the woods, as Gwellia, my wife, was always telling me.) But if I could get the plaque inside the gates at least, and put it in the garden where it was to be installed, it would be difficult for the customer to refuse to pay. I hurried down the roadway that led up to the house.

It was a large and handsome dwelling, conspicuously constructed to impress, as befitted a very wealthy man. No doubt that's why the tax-collector had acquired it. A handsome high wall ran around the whole perimeter, with a gatehouse and a gravelled drive in front, leading through gardens to the handsome portico, while a smaller, rougher country track led round the side of it, winding off to farmsteads in the hills, and from that there was a rear entrance to Pedronius's estate for the stables, servants and deliveries.

That was where I was expecting to find Radixrapum with his load, but a glance along the lane there showed no sign of him. Surely he had not gone knocking at the front?

I was about to retrace my steps and look when a small boy in a turquoise tunic scuttled from the back gate out into the lane. He was not a lad I recognized from my previous visit, but that was not surprising. He was almost certainly a page, and – apart from the chief steward, who showed me where I was to put the plaque – I'd had no dealings with the indoor slaves.

I accosted him at once. 'Are you a servant of Pedronius the tax-gatherer?' I said.

The pageboy looked suspiciously at me. 'And what is it to you, tradesman, whose slave I am?' His voice was piping, but he spoke with an impudence far beyond his years. 'Who are you anyway?' He looked me up and down. I was still in my tunic and working clothes, of course. 'What is your business here?'

'I am Libertus the pavement-maker,' I replied with dignity. 'A tradesman, certainly, but a Roman citizen.'

I saw him blanch a little. 'I'm sorry, citizen, I—'

I cut him off. I wanted information, not apology. 'I have been working in the house. Your master has commissioned an Apollo plaque from me. He wants it put around the garden shrine. The site is all prepared and I have come to lay it now if that is still convenient. The work is delicate and I constructed it at home. Someone was to have delivered it for me.'

His young face cleared. 'Ah, the mosaic. I heard that it had come, though they are not best pleased with how it has arrived. Still, you're here now, citizen, and it will be all right, I'm sure. If you go through that gate' – he gestured with his hand, almost gabbling in his desire to help – 'you'll find the chief slave there. He's the one who told them where to put it when it came. I fear he'll have a thing or two to say to you as well. But now, if you'll excuse me, I have work to do. I have a message to deliver before the town gates shut – the steward is displeased enough with everyone as it is.' And without a backward glance, he ran off down the lane and disappeared in the direction of the town.

I was a bit nonplussed. I had hardly expected Radixrapum to take the barrow in, but perhaps he had been asked to do so by the gatekeeper.

I asked the man on duty in the niche beside the gate but he shook his head. 'I don't know anything about a visitor. I've been here on duty all the afternoon – in fact, I'm due to be relieved at any minute now – and the only one to pass me has been that little slave in the blue tunic. Which reminds me, I don't think I am familiar with your face. What did you say your name was, and what's your business here?'

I told my tale again, and in the end he let me in. I looked around a moment, wondering what to do. When I had been there previously that day, there hadn't been a gatekeeper – the chief steward himself had come to greet me at the gate. And tonight there was no one to meet me when inside or escort me to where I was to work, and no one accosted me as I walked through the stable yard. I went straight across into the outer kitchen court, avoiding the large *amphorae* let into the ground for the storage of the household's oil and grain supplies.

I knew from previous visits where the chief slave had his room – in the front entrance of the servants' quarters, a large shed-like building forming one side of the court. It was a stone-built, cheerless room, no bigger than a cell, but it was private and, being central, it gave him a useful vantage point, not only across the kitchen court and yard, but also over the separate sleeping areas which lay to either side: male slaves to the left and females to the right. The arrangement doubtless required vigilance, since slaves are the property of their owners, and any relationship between the sexes is not only frowned on but classified as theft.

The steward's door was open and I could see him sitting there, on the straw mattress in his sleeping space, poring over something spread out on his bed. I could not see what it was, because at my appearance he bundled it away, put it into a stout brass-bound wooden chest and turned a key on it.

'Well, citizen Libertus?' His voice was not friendly as he greeted me. 'You have come back, I see. We were not sure if we were expecting you or not. Your plaque is waiting for you in the stable block; I had them put it there where it was safe. Do I take it that you hope to do some work tonight? Another hour and it will be dusk.'

Something had disturbed him – the turquoise slave was right. The long thin face, which had been kind enough before, was cold and angry now. I wondered, from his welcome, if I was too late in more respects than one, and if the rumour about Lucius's death had, by some accident, already reached the house. It was just possible. Quintus could have sent a message here himself. After all, the steward had once worked for him, and the decurion would have taken a perverse delight in sending word that Pedronius's intended talisman was cursed.

But I dismissed the thought. The steward had not told me that the plaque was not required, or even complained that it would bring bad luck and demanded to renegotiate the price. Indeed, it seemed that he'd actually had it brought inside from the road. That much was promising.

I gave him a placatory smile. 'I hope that I can make a start tonight. I should get most of it in place, even if I cannot completely finish it. Tomorrow there is the naming ceremony of my grandson at my house, so obviously I cannot absent myself from that, but I will be back to put the final touches on as quickly as I can.' I had an inspiration and added, 'I hear that Marcus Septimus is already on his way from Rome, and I'm sure that Pedronius would like this done before he comes. I understand he hopes to hold one of the welcome banquets here, and I know he places some value on the plaque.'

He looked down his long, thin, bony nose at me. 'You are aware of how much store he sets by it? Then you have a most peculiar way of demonstrating that! It has been treated most disrespectfully.'

So that was the trouble! Perhaps I should have guessed, since I knew how superstitious Pedronius could be. I sent up a quick prayer to whatever gods there were that my apparent disregard for his favourite deity would not be enough to make the tax-collector change his mind.

'Of course,' I babbled, 'I can see he might consider it inappropriate for an image of Apollo to be transported in this way.' *Wheeled through the streets on a street-vendor's barrow by a ragged turnip-man*, I meant, but I did not draw additional attention to the facts. 'My own slave, I fear, was not available and it was the best expedient that I could devise.' I tried the smile again. 'Where is the fellow who delivered it? I promised him money when I got here myself.'

The disdainful eyebrows came down half an inch. 'Citizen, that is unfortunate, but hardly my concern. You have a contract, and the price was fixed. If you were obliged to use the services of someone else and were thereby put to some expense, that is your own affair. But was it necessary to have him leave it outside the villa wall and not even send a message to say that it was there? If the gatekeeper had been a little less alert, it could have been stolen or damaged in some way – no doubt those forest bandits that we hear so much about would find a ready use for a sturdy handbarrow, if only to sell it in the marketplace.'

It was my turn to frown. 'Left outside the wall?' I was surprised at this, and slightly irritated with the turnip-man, but, on reflection, perhaps I was unjust. Manoeuvring that barrow with its fragile load over a mile or so of stony road would be no easy task but, as he promised, he had done that for me. If I was longer at the pie-oven than he had bargained for, perhaps he'd been obliged to leave and hurry home himself, since, like me, he would not wish to travel in the dark. He had assured me this villa was on his own route home, though he hadn't mentioned how far out he lived. But, all the same . . . 'He left no message? Not of any kind?'

'The gatekeeper did think he heard a noise outside, which might have been a knock, but when he looked out through the grille he saw no one at all, only the barrow leaning up against the wall. Fortunately, he took a closer look and, knowing that a pavement was to be installed, he realized what it was. He had the wit to send and tell me it was there, so I ordered a pair of slaves to go and bring it in. They've put it in the stables, as I said before.'

'This all happened in the back lane, then?' I said, working out that this must certainly be true. 'And no one saw a turnip-seller? Not at either gate?'

He looked at me impatiently. 'Not that I am aware of. Were you expecting one?' He said it with such obvious disdain that I did not press the point. It was enough that the mosaic had arrived and was safely at the house. Doubtless I'd hear the truth from Radixrapum very soon; he'd want his money, and he'd earned it too, though I was surprised that he had simply left the barrow here and gone. Had he – my mind was racing now – seen something unexpected to lure him down the lane? A band of rebels in that stand of wood? Or someone who might have been described as a green man?

I shook my head. More likely that a waggoner he knew had passed and offered him a lift.

The chief slave had seen my movement and took it for dissent. 'You are deciding that it is too late to make a start?'

'On the contrary, steward, I will get to work at once, if I could have a slave to bring me water in a pail. What about the land slave who helped me last time I was here? If you could spare him, he could lend a hand. It requires someone lively, but there is nothing skilled – just passing things and keeping mortar mixed and wet – and then there is a good chance that I can finish this tonight.'

He looked disapproving. 'I'll see what I can do. But the land slave you mention is away on loan. My master often leases servants – just for a day or two – to help defray their price, and that one's helping a decurion today to move his kindling pile. And all the other servants have allotted tasks.'

Suddenly, I had another of my little inspirations. 'There is a rear doorkeeper who is due to come off duty, I believe. He will be fit and strong. Do you think he could be spared? No doubt he wants to eat. But tell him I will give him a substantial tip.' It is not uncommon for visitors to give gratuities to slaves, who try to save their slave price and buy their freedom back, but gatekeepers rarely get very much at all. I could afford a half-sestertius as Radixrapum wasn't here, and I might learn something to the purpose from the man – and earn an ally in the house as well.

'I'll see if he is available,' the chief steward said, meaning, of course, that such an arrangement was a favour on his part: the gatekeeper would come if he was told to come – a slave has little choice. 'In the meantime, I'll get your water sent and two of the garden slaves will wheel the barrow out to you. You go to the garden and they will meet you there.'

I made my way around the outside of the house to the area of walled garden where the altar was. It was a lovely place, a small secluded spot, with a terraced walk fringed by tiny hedges of sweet-smelling herbs and a collonade of pillars up which creeping flowers had been trained to grow. The Apollo statue stood at the farther end of it, in its own special niche, with a curved space in front of it where the plaque was to be placed, and a low stone bench on either side of it. Tucked under one of these was a stout hempen bag. I knelt and retrieved it, since it was my own. It contained the tools and mortar box that I had left behind the last time I was working at the site, ready for the task which now awaited me. I had prepared the area with a roughened mix to help the mortar grip, and given it the faintest tilt towards the back, so if my careful measurements had been accurate, I could hope that the linen-backed mosaic would slot into the space and I could quickly build the missing edge to fit.

I was still eyeing all this up when two large slaves appeared wheeling the barrow – with insufficient care. They were trundling it far too much upright and were in danger of unshipping the fragile load it bore. I realized what a task Radixrapum must have had in bringing it so far along the public road without mishap, although he was accustomed to handling it, of course. I spoke to them sharply and they laid it down, then shambled off again, just as my friend the gatekeeper appeared, carrying my water in a wooden pail.

He was looking anything but friendly now, in fact. He put the bucket down and stood a little bit apart. 'I'm told

I have to help you, though only Jove knows why. I won't be any use. It's not my job to carry water like a kitchen slave, and I don't know anything about laying plaques.'

'The job I want you for requires no special skill. But I wanted someone strong and only you could answer what I want to ask, so I requested you. You are supposed to be off duty, I'm aware. I wonder if a half-sestertius would help to compensate?'

A greedy little glint came into the brown eyes, and he said at once, 'A half-sestertius, citizen? What can I do to help?'

He was surprisingly helpful for a man who'd never dealt with tiles before. He fetched a board for me to mix the mortar on – I had prepared the right proportions of wet lime and ground brick dust in my box – and he kept it stirring while I drizzled water in until I felt the consistency was right. Then he helped me cover the back of the mosaic with the mix and slide it carefully into place, linen uppermost. It fitted very well – you could already see the pattern showing through the cloth – and a row or two of plain-coloured tesserae all round would fill the jagged edge. I inserted a layer of mortar in the gap and began the careful work of putting in the border to complete the plaque.

He squatted down beside me as I worked, handing me the colours as I asked for them. 'Never gave much thought to mosaic floors before. Wonderful when you see how it is done. What about the linen – will you scrape that off the top?'

'Not for a day or two, until the cement is set,' I answered. 'Then it will soak off fairly easily. It will look well, I think.' I glanced up from my work to steal a peek at him. 'I understand that I owe thanks to you, because you saw it in the lane and realized what it was. That was observant and intelligent of you.' I saw him preening slightly at my words, and I went on at once, 'I expected my messenger to bring it to the house. The chief steward told me that you thought you heard a knock.'

He scratched his tousled head. 'Well, not exactly that. Just a peculiar noise. I peered out through the grille but there was no one I could see, only an ox-cart going lurching down the lane.'

'But you went out yourself?' I set another border tile into the wet cement. Only a few more large ones and the job would be complete.

'I heard the wagon pause. Naturally, I went outside to see if it was someone coming here, but the man was simply stopping to rearrange his load. He grumbled that there was something cluttering the lane, so, of course, I went round to investigate and found the barrow there. I hadn't seen it come, and he had no idea. He hadn't seen anyone else along the road, he said, except a young man taking rolls of woven cloth to Glevum on his horse.'

'I see,' I said, although I didn't see at all. This seemed to disprove my theory about Radixrapum getting a lift home – unless the cart-driver wasn't telling us the truth.

But, it seemed, there was nothing more to learn, so I concentrated on placing the last few tesserae. When I had finished, I clambered to my feet. Tomorrow or the next day I would wash off the cloth and the god Apollo would have his naming plaque. It looked impressive even as it was. Pedronius should be more than satisfied, I thought.

I gathered my tools together in the bag and tied it to the barrow, together with the tray, using the rag I'd wrapped the pieces in. 'I'll leave this here,' I said, 'and take it back to town the next time that I come. But if a turnip-seller comes and wants the barrow back, then you should let him have it – it is his property. I only meant to hire it for an hour or two, but it looks as if he got a ride home after all – if not on the ox-cart that you noticed in the lane, then something similar – and doubtless that saved him a long walk in the hills. Speaking of which, it's time I left myself.' I fished into my purse and brought out a silver coin. 'Here is the half-sestertius which I promised you.'

The gatekeeper took it and tried it in his teeth, then tucked it underneath his tunic belt. 'I'll take good care of your possessions, citizen, you may be sure of that,' he murmured with a grin. 'That is what I call a very handsome tip. If you call again, I would be pleased to help: I'm saving to buy my freedom, if I ever get a chance – just as the steward is, though it will cost him a lot more. With this contribution, I am almost halfway there.' He picked up the handles of the barrow as he spoke. 'So may Janus, the god of gates and gatekeepers, smile on you and bring you safely to your own door this night – and your turnip-man as well.'

And with that he took the barrow and wheeled it swiftly through the court, leaving me to make my puzzled way towards the gate.

Nine

The failure of Radixrapum to meet me at the house and receive his payment had one unlooked-for benefit for me. I still had a half-sestertius in my purse, and that meant that I could afford the unusual luxury of hiring horse-drawn transport for my journey home – an unexpected bonus, for which I thanked the gods. The sun was already getting lower in the west, and if I had been on foot, I should have been overtaken by darkness long before I got back to my little roundhouse and my worried wife. I was anxious to tell the family about the loss of Minimus, and, to tell the truth, I was glad not to be walking on my own. I am generally sceptical about the tales of rebels in the woods, but, in the circumstances, I was not feeling sceptical tonight.

I hastened to a hiring stables that I'd had dealings with before, where I knew that they kept a *cisium* for hire – a swift and lightweight gig for single passengers. The gig was there all right; the problem was to find a driver willing to undertake the trip at such an hour, since there was little possibility of a finding another fare for the return. But the proprietor of the stables owed me a favour, and, after some bickering as to price, a deal was duly struck.

The hire establishment was just outside the western gates, and I live to the south, but, of course, we could not take a horse-drawn vehicle through the streets till dusk, so we went the other way, taking the minor, gravelled road that skirted round the outside of the walls and joined up with the major road again beyond the southern entry to the town.

I had been hoping to ask questions of the sentry there, in case he'd seen anyone with an unwilling red-haired slave, but it was not possible. The main road back to town was already crammed with carts and wagons, lining up to try to get in through the gates and make deliveries. I should have known, of course. This happened every evening in the half-hour before the gates were closed, and there was always a jostling competition to be first, with quarrelling drivers wielding curses, fists and whips. No one was going to let a mere workman in a hired gig get through.

But going the other way the road was clear – a military Roman road is deliberately built with enough width for a century of soldiers to march down it eight abreast, which means two loaded wagons can also pass, with care, if they each put a wheel on the margin path. So there was little hindrance for a narrow gig. I was slightly regretful as we drew away, but my hope of learning anything was, in any case, remote. If rebel brigands had captured Minimus, they were unlikely to have walked him boldly through the gate – he would have struggled and drawn attention to himself. They were far more likely to have tied him up and smuggled him out hidden in some donkey-load or, it occurred to me, a handcart full of hides. So I sat back as the gig-man drove past the throng, and we were soon clear of the confusion and in open countryside.

'There is a turning on the left-hand side three miles or so down here, and half as long a stretch of gravelled track before we reach my door,' I murmured to the driver at my side. 'A full half-sestertius if you get me there in half an hour.' (I had struck the deal for just a little less, with precisely this intention in mind.)

'Provided we don't meet any soldiers on the way, we should do that with ease,' he told me with a grin.

He was right to make no promises, of course. If we did meet a contingent of legionaries on the move, we should be obliged to pull over on to the muddy margins and wait until they passed, with all their supplies and followers as well – and that could take a considerable time. Even a training party from the local garrison engaged on their daily eight-mile exercise could cause us some delay.

We were lucky. We did not encounter any marching troops. In fact, once we had gone a little way from town, there was very little traffic of any kind at all. We did see one official messenger, riding hell for leather with the imperial post, and, of course, we ceded priority to him, but he was past us in an instant and we moved off again.

It was a comfortable journey, as such journeys go – the body of the gig was hung on leather straps to minimize the jolts – and normally I would have quite enjoyed the ride, but I was very anxious to be home. We were passing through darkening forests by this time, and my mind was full of Minimus. I wondered where he was – supposing that he was anywhere at all. I only hoped that he was unhurt and not too terrified. If he was being held captive in this very forest now, I wondered whether he could hear the clatter of the gig. Or was I foolish to suppose that he was still alive?

I wished again that there was something I could do to look for him, but I had no idea at all of where to start. None of my enquiries had told me anything. My only hope was that if the rebels had him, they planned to ransom him, in which case they would doubtless send me a demand. There had been nothing of that nature at the shop, but perhaps it would be waiting for me at my home, since Minimus could obviously tell them where I lived. Then, at least, there would be a place to start. I was increasingly impatient to get there and find out.

I clung to the leather strap beside my seat as we jolted from the major road on to the country lane which led past my roundhouse to my patron's large estate, and so on to the distant farms beyond. The roadway was much narrower and darker here, though it was kept in good repair, and the last half-mile seemed agonizingly slow.

The driver was anxious for his extra money too. 'I'm sorry, citizen, I'm doing what I can. At least it's better than the other route.'

I nodded. There was another way into the town which cut off several miles, but that was an ancient farm track, twisting and precipitous, full of rocks and roots and sudden gradients, and far too treacherous for horse-drawn vehicles to use.

At last we reached the junction with that other lane. My roundhouse had been built not very far away – we were already at the corner of my enclosure fence. I was leaning forward in my open seat, craning to see the welcome glow of firelight through the door and smell the cooking on the central hearth. But, to my amazement, there was no sign of life, not even a wisp of smoke curled from the chimney hole.

The driver drew up at the gate where I had told him to and turned to me. 'Doesn't seem as if they are expecting you,' he said. 'That's a pity – I was hoping you could light my torch for me.' He gestured to the bundle, ready dipped in pitch, which he carried in the torch-frame at the front corner of the gig. 'It will soon be really dark, and it will take a lot more than half an hour to get back again.'

He was clearly mentioning the 'half an hour' as a way of reminding me that he had earned his fee – as probably he had – but, of course, I had no accurate way of measuring the time. My promise had only been a way of ensuring he made haste, as we were both aware.

I gave him his coin and took the torch from him. 'Wait here a moment. I will see what I can do. I don't imagine that they've entirely put out the fire.' As soon as I had said that, I felt a shiver of alarm. I was reminded suddenly of my cold hearth at the workshop earlier. What was awaiting me in my roundhouse now?

My heart was thumping as I went in through the gate. I knew that Maximus, the other red-haired slave that Marcus had lent me, was in Glevum with my son, but the lad who tended the animals and the garden should be here. He helped in the kitchen when there was no other slave to spare. 'Kurso?' I shouted, but there was no answering sound of running feet. 'Gwellia?' I called more urgently. My wife did not reply.

I glanced into the dye-house and the servants' sleeping hut, but there was no one there. Apart from the contented clucking of the ducks and chickens in the coop, and the rustle of the sheep and goats within the barn, the whole enclosure was as devoid of life and as sinisterly silent as the inner room of my shop had been this afternoon.

So it was with trepidation that I pushed open the door

of the roundhouse that was my modest home. The circular room was empty, but a glance was enough to show me that it was not disturbed. Everything was just as usual. The bed of reeds and rushes was ready to one side, two three-legged stools stood by the central hearth, and a bench beside it held the cooking-pots and food. Even my wife's loom was standing up against the wall, the stones that weighted down the weft still neatly in a row.

I found that I was almost shaking with relief. There was no sign of a struggle, and – thank the gods! – no corpse awaiting me. The fire had not been strangled either. It had been carefully banked up for the night, though there was no clay cook-pot in the embers, or any sign of Gwellia's usual baking bread. That was doubly a surprise. There was a naming feast tomorrow and, though it would not be a grand affair as Marcus's had been, we had invited a good many people to attend. If ever there was time for baking, it was now.

I went across to look more closely at the fire. One or two of the larger half-charred logs were still giving off a glow. I set down the torch-bundle, put some tinder on the hottest portion of the hearth and began to coax the fire back into life with the leather bellows which my wife had made. After a minute, a feeble flame arose, so I thrust the pitch-torch in it until that caught alight, then bore it in triumph back out to the gig. The little victory had somehow cheered me up. 'I'm sorry that this took a little while,' I said. 'There's no one in. I had to coax the fire.'

The driver put the lighted torch into the rack. 'I thought the place looked empty. I wonder where they've gone? You don't want to go back into town again? I'd only have to charge you half the price, seeing that I'm going that way in any case,' he added hopefully.

I shook my head. 'I am sure there is some explanation of all this, and they will soon be back,' I said with more conviction than I felt. 'They'll expect to find me here.'

He nodded and, saluting with his whip, turned the gig around and trotted off into the gloom. I watched the bright flare of the pitch torch out of sight, then turned back to the house. I lighted a home-made taper at the fire and looked to see if there was a note or any demand to ransom Minimus, but there was nothing of the kind. Not even a communication from my wife to me as there would usually have been if she had been called out unexpectedly.

I found a crust of bread and a small piece of cheese, and prepared to eat them squatting by the hearth, washed down with half a beakerful of water from the jug. I felt suddenly and dreadfully alone.

Then a thought occurred to me. Junio's roundhouse was only a little further up the lane – his enclosure was right next to mine – and though Junio was out, his wife and child would certainly be there. And, of course, if my urchin had delivered the message that I'd sent, Gwellia would not be expecting me so soon, since she would suppose that I was walking home.

Perhaps she had gone to sit with Cilla and the child, and help with the preparations for the naming day, and taken Kurso with her. Of course that's what she'd do. Cilla and Junio did not keep a separate slave – indeed, at one time they had been our slaves themselves – and we combined our households for most purposes. Though no doubt we would soon have to think of buying extra help, I thought. Marcus was coming and would want his servants back – supposing I could produce little Minimus, that is – and, with the new child, Junio and Cilla would want attendants of their own.

I hurried to the door and thought I could detect the welcome whiff of woodsmoke drifting down the hill. Absurdly grateful for this evidence of normality, I seized my cloak – for it was getting very cold – lit another pitch-torch for myself and set off in the direction of Junio's home.

The wind was rising, whistling in the trees. I devoutly wished I hadn't left my winter cape – a warm woollen *birrus* with a useful hood – hanging in the workshop when I set off this afternoon, and I was glad of the torchlight on the rocky path.

I soon caught the glimmer of firelight through the thatch and the delicious smell of something cooking on the hearth.

Preparations for tomorrow's feast, no doubt, I thought. More than usually anxious to see my family, I speeded up my steps and was soon outside the door, half-expecting to find little Kurso there awaiting me as makeshift doorkeeper. (He was not by nature suited to the task, but he was more hindrance than help when it came to cooking and was renowned for dropping things: his previous owner had treated him so harshly that the lad still shook with nerves and could even now move faster backwards than forwards.)

But there was no sign of him or of my wife when I peered around the door. It had been left half-open to let the steam and smoke escape, and I stood for a moment taking in the scene. The baby was sleeping in a hammock on the wall, and my daughter-in-law was standing with her back to me, bending over something bubbling in a pot, from which the appetizing smells were rising even now.

So the first that Cilla knew of me was when I said aloud, 'Greetings, daughter. Where is everyone?'

Perhaps I should have given her more warning that I was standing there.

The effect of my words was truly startling. She whirled around and screamed, dropping the spoon that she was holding into the boiling pot. The infant, woken by the sound, screamed louder still.

She snatched up the swaddled baby and clutched it to her breast, crying as she did so in a sobbing voice, 'Creature of darkness, leave this house at once! I command you! Go back where you belong.'

Ten

'Cilla, what is it?' I thrust the torch into a holder by the door and strode across to her.

But, instead of being reassured, she gave another shriek. She put down my screaming grandson in his hammock-bed and stood in front of it, taking up a sharp knife from the kitchen bench. She brandished it at me. 'Keep away from us.' Her voice was low and strangled, scarcely like her own – even the child had sensed her fear and stilled to whimpering.

'Cilla!' I said reproachfully. 'You know you wouldn't kill me or stick that blade in me!' But I was not so sure. Her eyes were so wild that I feared she'd lost her wits and at any moment she would slash at me. My heart was thumping hard against my ribs. Slowly, very slowly, I reached out and gently took the hand that held the knife. I was intending to prise the weapon from her grasp but there was no need for that. She dropped it as though my touch had scalded her.

'Cilla, whatever is the matter?' I exclaimed, feeling more confident now she was disarmed.

She didn't answer, only shook her head and moaned, turning her face away and shutting her eyes tight as if she could not bear to look at me. She tried to snatch her hand back, but I recaptured it. I could feel that it was trembling. I squeezed her fingers gently in my own.

'What's been happening? Something's frightened you.' I reached down with my free hand and picked the knife up from the floor and laid it on the table safely out of reach. To my surprise, I was trembling myself – I felt I had barely escaped without her stabbing me. This day of surprises was getting ever more bizarre.

However, it was clear that she was truly terrified, and the only way that I could think of soothing her was to ask, in as normal a voice as I could muster, 'Where is Gwellia?

With Kurso, I presume? I thought she would be here. I sent a message that I would be late, but I was hoping for a bite of hot supper all the same. All I could find was a bit of bread and cheese, and it has been a very tiring day. I was bending over for at least an hour laying that Apollo piece in place.' Perhaps these mundane details would bring her to herself.

It seemed to work. She opened one eyelid and said uncertainly, 'Libertus, father, is it really you?' She squeezed my fingers briefly, then reached out an exploratory hand and touched my face.

It was my turn to be startled. 'But of course it is. Who did you think that it was going to be?' A sudden dreadful thought occurred to me. You sometimes hear of people blinded by the gods. I held her fingers close against my cheek and added quickly, 'Nothing terrible has happened to your sight?'

She shook her head and disengaged herself. 'I saw that it was you.' She sat down very heavily on a wooden stool. 'That was the trouble. I thought that you were dead . . . and the torchlight made your eyes look glittering . . .'

'Dead?' For a moment I was incredulous. Then I understood. 'You took me for a ghost?'

She looked at me and laughed – a little sheepishly – then gave a wobbly smile. 'I can see that I was wrong. You are quite warm and solid and obviously real. And I doubt a spirit would complain of eating bread and cheese.' There were tears of relief in her eyes, though she wiped them briskly on the corner of her robe and said in something more like her normal voice, 'I'm sorry, Father. I would offer you some stew, but you gave me such a fright I've dropped the serving spoon into the cooking-pot.'

I had to laugh at this. 'I would love to taste the stew,' I said, and meant it too. My mouth was positively watering. 'I am no phantom, I assure you. But whatever led you to suppose I was?'

Cilla had turned an embarrassed shade of red. 'I suppose it does seem foolish, when you are sitting there. But what were we to think? There was a messenger.'

That startled me. 'What kind of messenger? An urchin from the street?' I asked, thinking about the boy that I had sent myself.

She nodded. She was already on her feet, trying to fish the ladle from the pot, but the spoon that she was using wasn't long enough. I did not try to help. I knew that this was woman's work and it would be insulting to offer to assist.

'I would say so, from the look and sound of him,' she said over her shoulder as she struggled with the spoon. 'Not a proper courier, certainly. A ragged sort of boy. He must have run here all the way – he was completely out of breath. But he managed to blurt his message and tell us you were hurt.'

'So naturally you thought there'd been an accident,' I said. 'And it was a short step from there to think that I might be a ghost?'

I meant to tease her, but her plump cheeks did not dimple into a smile. Her voice was serious. 'He didn't say anything about an accident. He said that you had been set on from behind and robbed, in your workshop or very near to it, and it was doubtful whether you would live. He'd been sent to tell us and to summon us to come. Gwellia gave him money and let him catch his breath, then she found Kurso and they all set off for town at once.'

'To look for me?' I said.

'To bring you home if that was possible, or to find a *medicus* if there was time for that. I stayed here with the baby to wait for Junio in case the others didn't pass him on the way.' Her eye had lighted on an iron hook hung on a nail nearby, from which a large plucked chicken was dangling upside down. and in a moment she had it taken down and cleaned, and was using it to reach the ladle. She turned to frown at me. 'How did you guess it was a street urchin who came?'

'I sent a message with such a boy myself,' I said, and added unnecessarily, 'but that wasn't it.' I hazarded a smile. 'Though I think I understand what might have given rise to this. There really was a tragic incident at my shop today

– someone was set upon, exactly as described, and he died in fact. Only, of course, the victim wasn't me.'

She stared at me. 'Who was it, then?'

'It was that one-eyed pie-seller you've heard me talk about.'

'The one that you were kind to, who has plagued you ever since? Junio was telling me about his awful pies.' I was relieved to see the suggestion of a smile. As if on cue, like an actor at the theatre, little Amato began to cry again.

Over his wails, I raised my voice to answer her. 'I am afraid my generosity was the death of him, in fact. In his new tunic he looked quite prosperous. He was outside my workshop, by the look of it, and whoever killed and robbed him dragged the body in.'

She shook her head. 'You can't feel responsible for that! You meant to be a help.'

I gave a rueful smile. 'That decision may be the ruination of us both – Lucius lost his life and every penny that he owned, and I lost that important contract I was hoping for. Quintus refused to buy a pavement from me, since the corpse was in the shop. The omens were too bad to contemplate, he said.'

She had retrieved the serving ladle while I talked and was now spooning steaming stew on to a wooden platter. 'Oh, Father, what a disappointment. And what a dreadful shock, finding the poor pie-seller in your shop like that. No wonder you are tired and hungry after such a day. Sit on the stool and eat, while I see to the infant and try to settle him.' She poured a little stew on to the stone-carved altar by the wall. (It still seemed incongruous to me – an altar to the Roman household gods in a Celtic roundhouse of this kind. I never made private sacrifices to the Lars myself, but Junio and Cilla were brought up in Roman households in their early youth – child-slaves, both of them – and the altar was almost the first thing they had bought to furnish their new home. It was the same altar that would be used tomorrow for the bulla ritual.)

I watched in silence as she made the token sacrifice, then she handed me a spoon and turned to rock the baby in its hanging crib. 'When you came in, I'd just got him to sleep and I'm afraid I woke him when you startled me.'

The yelling was already fading into gulping sobs. I took up a tiny sample of the stew and blew on it. It tasted even better than it smelt.

'Hush, little one,' Cilla crooned to Amato. 'You go to sleep again. You may have a big day tomorrow after all.' She turned to me. 'And I'd better set to work and get some baking done, and there's that chicken and a fat goose waiting to be cooked – Gwellia and Kurso plucked and gutted them this afternoon – but nothing will be ready if I don't make a start myself.'

I was tucking with enthusiasm into hot lamb stew, but I managed to reply, 'Ready in time for the bulla feast, you mean?'

'If you are alive, I suppose it will be held – I wasn't sure if it was going to be. It's hardly fitting to hold a naming day when there has been a family death – as Quintus would have said, the omens are too bad – although tomorrow is the ninth day after Amato's birth. I was waiting for Junio and Gwellia to come home, to find out whether you were still alive before we finally decided what to do. When I first heard footsteps, I thought you might be them – they would have had time to come and go to Glevum by this time. Mother-in-law and Kurso left here hours ago. There's a good boy, Amato.'

The whimpers had stopped as if by magic now, and my little grandson was gurgling up at her. She gave him a finger and he sucked at it, then slowly closed his eyes. Only then did she withdraw her hand and tiptoe back to me.

'What happened to the corpse? It has been disposed of properly, I hope? Otherwise the auguries will still be terrible.' She spoke in a low voice, as if the fates might overhear.

I nodded through another mouthful of delight. 'It has been taken care of, don't worry about that. Quintus got the military cart to come and take it to the pit. And I did what I could to respect the dead man first: lit a candle at the head and feet, closed the eyes – as nearly as I could – and called his name three times. And washed my hands three times with water afterwards, as ritual demands. I told his mother what I'd done and she was much relieved – she could not have afforded a proper funeral.'

Cilla smiled. 'Poor father. I suppose you had to go and break the news to her?' She moved to the table and took up the knife again, though this time it was only to chop a bunch of herbs. 'You've had a busy day. The pie-seller was killed when you were out laying the Apollo piece, I suppose?'

I was about to tell her otherwise when a thought occurred to me. 'I wonder how your urchin came to know about the death? I was there when the army came to take the corpse away, and there was no one in the street who could have spread the news – I remember being grateful about that at the time. But obviously somebody learned of it, and very early on if the message got here long enough ago for Gwellia to have time since to get to town and back. At what sort of hour did the boy arrive?'

She shrugged. 'I can't tell precisely. But the sun was past its height – I noticed it was just behind that tall tree over there.'

I looked in the direction of the oak she pointed to and did a little calculation in my head. The Romans divide daylight into twelve equal hours, and the dark into the same, though obviously the length will differ with the time of year. But taking the season into consideration and looking at the tree, I could make an estimate.

'So it was around the eighth hour, more or less, which means he left the town an hour or so before. Certainly, Lucius was dead by then. But even if the urchin ran here all the way,' I fretted, 'I can't see how he knew in time to manage that. Unless one of the soldiers gossiped straight away when they got back to base. The commander at the garrison knows me, after all? And he's one of Marcus's friends. He might have sent the message, possibly.'

I saw that Cilla was making a gesture of dissent.

'You're right,' I said. 'That makes no sense at all.

The commander would have sent a soldier, if he'd sent anyone, and anyway the army knew that I was still alive – they'd seen me when they came to take away the corpse. Yet someone must have sent the boy and given him directions as to where I lived. And no doubt paid him too. But who in Glevum was likely to do that?'

Cilla had picked up the dead chicken by its feet and now held it by its claws, so that the head drooped downward as she made little knife-slits in the dimpled skin. 'Nobody paid him; he was promised money when he got here,' she replied, stuffing the chopped herbs into the slits she'd made. 'That's why Gwellia gave him a coin before she left. As to who sent him, that's not a mystery. It was Minimus – at least that's what he said.'

'Minimus!' I almost dropped my own spoon into the stew. 'It cannot possibly have been.'

She looked surprised. 'A red-haired slave had sent him, that's what the urchin said – or, rather, panted out. That is why we never doubted that the message was the truth.' She stopped with a handful of chopped parsley in mid-air. 'He might have been talking about Maximus, I suppose, but Minimus was attending you, so we naturally supposed that it was him.' Her plump face creased into a puzzled frown. 'Where is he, anyway? Isn't he with you?'

I gave a despairing groan and shook my head. 'That is another of the mysteries of today. Minimus is missing – he has disappeared. It seems whoever murdered Lucius has kidnapped him as well. I feared the rebels might have been responsible and I was hoping to find a demand for ransom waiting for me here. But there has been nothing?' I enquired, knowing with a sinking heart that this was true.

'Nothing,' she confirmed. She had turned very pale. 'Oh, poor Father, what a day you've had. That will have upset you, more even than the death. Let me heat some water and prepare hot mead for you. I'm sure that you must need it, and, for once, I might have some myself. The midwife recommends it as a restorative.'

I was instantly flooded with remorse. It was only eight days since the poor girl had given birth, and it was no wonder that she was looking white and strained. In a wealthy Roman household, she might still be lying in, though in humbler houses women rise as soon as they have strength. All the same, I understood why she'd not cooked the fowl or tried to bake the bread and oatcakes on her own – not only was she tired, but some sects will not permit their followers to eat the food prepared by a new mother after a birth until she has undergone a cleansing ritual. Some of the guests invited for tomorrow's bulla feast might well hold such superstitious views.

I said, 'Hot mead is a very good idea. You've had a shock as well – although a needless one. I will prepare it. I have done it many times.' Without a murmur, she sat down on the stool. I took the half-stuffed chicken and placed it on the bench, and went to find the jar of mead that the household kept in store for me. Junio has more Roman tastes and likes a jug of wine; there was a full amphora of it leaning by the wall.

She watched me put water on the fire to heat. 'Poor Minimus, I can't bear to think of it,' she said. She had worked beside him at my patron's for a time and was quite fond of him. 'I hope that he's unharmed and you get him safely back – for your sake, father, just as much as his. Otherwise, what will Marcus say when he returns?'

It was almost the first thing that everyone had said, and something which I did not want to contemplate. I knew exactly how my patron would react. He would be furious and then demand the slave price, which would be very high. Both of those pages were very highly trained and worth a great deal more than I could possibly afford. And he might demand the right to restitution too – four times the value was the usual amount. My hand was trembling as I poured the mead into a jug and added a scoop of honey to the mix.

'I wish I knew where I could start to look for him,' I said.

'You don't suppose that Minimus really sent that messenger? He didn't see the pie-seller attacked and thought that it was you? It might have looked quite like you from a distance, I suppose. The pie-seller was wearing your old tunic, after all. If Minimus had been absent – on an errand, let us say – and from a distance witnessed the assault, wouldn't he have tried to send a message home and set off somewhere to find help himself? He might be at your work-shop with a medicus right now!'

This was an attractive theory, and for a moment I was tempted to agree, but an instant's contemplation made me shake my head. 'Minimus would have known me from the pie-seller, however far away he might have been. Besides, if he thought he'd seen me set upon and hurt, he would have come running to look after me and he would soon have realized that it was Lucius.'

She was obliged to recognize the truth of this and nodded dismally. 'And if he thought it fatal, he would have brought the news himself.' But she did not give up. She was deter-mined to help me think this through. 'Perhaps it was someone else who looked into the shop? Some customer who didn't know you very well, but saw the corpse and thought that it was you? Though the pie-seller is very distinc-tive isn't he – with a scarred face and only one good eye?'

I considered her suggestion. It was a hopeful one. Perhaps something of the kind was possible. Lucius had been lying face down on the floor, and anyone who glimpsed him would not have seen his face. But then I saw the truth and shook my head again. 'That is an interesting idea, but there's a flaw in it, I fear. The murderer had doused the fire and lights and put the shutters up. The whole shop was in dark-ness. I nearly fell over Lucius myself. No mere passing customer could have seen that he was there.' I mixed the water with the honeyed mead and poured some out for her.

She sipped it thoughtfully. 'Yet someone red-haired sent that messenger. Who was it, if it wasn't Minimus? It must have been someone who wanted to assist – that is hardly likely to be a rebel, you would think.'

'Dear Jupiter!' I jumped upright, almost oversetting the mead jug in my haste. 'Glypto's green man was talking to a boy – an urchin-boy at that. I thought at first the green man was the murderer, but perhaps I was mistaken, after all, and he's the one that sent the messenger.'

'Green man?' Cilla was looking at me with alarm, as
though it was my turn to have lost my wits.

'I'll explain it later,' I assured her. 'Though I'm not sure
exactly what it means myself. In the meantime, this might
be important in finding Minimus. What was he like – this
urchin who brought the message here? What about his
speech?' I was still remembering the bandits in the woods
– pockets of rebels from the western areas who had never
really given up the fight – their accents would be quite
distinct.

Cilla looked surprised. 'He was so out of breath that it
was hard to tell. Let me remember what he sounded like.'
She had a natural aptitude for mimicry and she used it now
to imitate the voice – bad Latin with a coarse, uneducated
twang – very much as Glypto had described. '"I had a . . .
dreadful business . . . finding where to come. I . . . wouldn't
have agreed if I . . . had known how far it was . . ." A little
bit like that.'

I grinned. She loved the opportunity to tell a tale like
this, and the hot mead was clearly loosening her tongue. I
crouched down beside her and refilled her beaker again.
'And what did he look like?'

She scarcely needed the encouragement. 'He was ragged,
as I told you, very small and thin and rather in want of a
visit to the baths. Wore a brownish tunic and a sacking
cloak, though I noticed he had a pair of stout boots on his
feet. His hair was short and curly, and I think that it was
brown, though it might have just been muddy, like the rest
of him.'

I swallowed my hot mead in a gulp. 'That would fit with
Glypto's estimate of the boy whose voice he heard. So
perhaps the green man is our red-head after all. He might
be Silurian, I suppose, like Minimus himself: lots of
Silurians have that red-haired look – just as the Ordovices
are tall and fair, like Quintus Severus. And there is nothing
to say that the messenger was not a slave. That would
explain that part of it – but I wonder how he came to know
exactly where I lived?'

She had emptied her own beaker for a second time. 'Who

is this Glypto anyway?' she said. But before I could reply, we were interrupted by the sound of running footsteps crunching up the path, and, as we looked at each other in surprise, a hooded apparition burst in through the door.

Eleven

I am not by nature a superstitious man, but the creature looked so like one of the evil dwarves our poems speak about that for a moment I was truly shocked, just as my daughter-in-law had been when I arrived. So when the apparition pushed back the heavy hood and revealed himself as Kurso, the little garden slave, swamped in my *birrus britannicus* from the shop, my first reaction was of sharp relief.

'Kurso, what are you doing in my cape?' I said. Alarm had made me sound severe and I regretted it at once. Any reprimand was apt to make him shake so much with fright that he was generally incapable of speech.

But tonight was an exception, it appeared.

'Master, thank all the gods that you are safe!' Stripping off the cape, he ran towards me and fell prostrate at my feet, kissing my sandals in an embarrassing display.

'Now then, Kurso,' I muttered awkwardly, 'I'm glad you're so delighted, but please get up at once.' I took him by the arm and assisted him to rise.

He was still grinning at me in disbelief, though he was trembling. 'We went to Glevum – we heard you'd been attacked and might be in danger of your life. There was a message . . .' He looked ready to kneel down and embrace my feet again.

I prevented him by saying, 'So I understand. I don't know who sent it, but, as you can see, it was a mistake. I am sorry to have occasioned everyone alarm. I am touched that the household was so concerned for me, but I'm sorry that you and your mistress had a long walk in the dark for nothing, and no doubt in anxiety as well. It must be disappointing to find me boringly at home, safe and well and drinking honeyed mead.'

I meant to tease him, but he did not smile. 'Not disappointed, master, only glad. Though we already knew that it was a false alarm. We heard in Glevum that you were unhurt. The mistress was so relieved she sent me out for wine and poured it on the workshop altar as a sacrifice.'

Gwellia is no more an adherent of the Roman gods than I am, and I recognized how distressed she must have been to have thought of engaging in this little ritual. 'I've never been the subject of thank-offering before. I must thank her for her care,' I told him with a smile. 'She is not far behind you, I assume?'

'She and the young master' – he meant Junio, of course – 'are coming down the old lane this moment with the cart. But it's difficult and dark.' He shuffled a little closer to the fire, and I realized that the trembling was partly due to cold. 'They sent me on to get the fire alight and take them back a torch.'

I nodded. 'Then I can save you time and trouble. I have already banked the fire, and when I came up here I brought a torch with me.' I nodded to where it was still burning on the spike. 'You can take that one. But have a little sip of something warming first.' I stirred some more hot water into the last few drops of honeyed mead and handed it to Kurso. We rarely gave him alcoholic drink, of course, but he was shivering.

He drank it from the jug with a grimace and you could almost see the warmth come seeping into him.

'So,' I said, when he had finished it, 'they sent you for a torch. What brought you up to Junio's roundhouse, then? Surely the mistress told you to go home?'

He saw another reprimand in this and backed a step or two but the mead had given him the courage to reply, 'Master, I was to come and see the young mistress anyway, when I'd got the torch.'

'Of course – to tell her that I was safe and well, and that the bulla feast could therefore go ahead. I should have thought of that.'

'To tell her we believed that you were safe, although we were not absolutely sure, because we couldn't find you in the town. But I thought I heard voices in here, so I came here first – and realized it was you. The mistress will be very glad to learn that you are home.' Kurso relinquished the jug reluctantly. 'I ought to go back at once and let her know.'

I nodded. 'I will come with you and set her mind at rest,' I said, thinking of his safety as much as anything. Gwellia at least had two young men with her, but timid Kurso would be travelling the woodland lane alone. I had not forgotten the rebel bandits in the wood. 'And I see you are wearing a thin tunic with no sleeves,' I added. 'You're no use to anyone if you have caught a chill. Put that birrus on again before you go out in the wind.'

My patron would have thought I was a fool, of course, but I felt responsible. It was clear that the poor boy had set off for the town in such a rush that he had not thought to provide himself with a cloak. He threw me an uncertain glance. 'You won't want it yourself? That other one you have is only half as thick.'

I shook my head. 'I'd left it in the workshop, so I could not have used it if you hadn't brought it here. It was the mistress who told you to wear it, I suppose?' I saw him nod, and I smiled. 'So who am I to contradict her words?'

He was still looking doubtful but he put on the cape, and pulled the heavy hood around his ears again. The garment was much too long for him and almost reached the ground, and with his face completely hidden in the hood, he looked again as he had looked when he first came through the door – like some mysterious creature from the underworld. He took down the torch and stood at the doorway, ready to depart.

I turned to Cilla who had been sitting silently, cradling her mead cup and listening to all this. 'We shan't be very long.'

Kurso nodded, anxious to be gone. 'If we don't hurry, they'll be almost here. And I was to tell you, mistress, that the young master could not find a calf, but he has managed to buy a whole lamb for tomorrow's feast.'

I was astounded at this news. 'But surely there's not time to cook it now?' I gestured at the fire.

Cilla nodded. 'The slaves dug a cooking-pit earlier today and set a fire in it, so that we could buy a butchered beast and cook it overnight – the way that Gwellia says you used to do when you were young. She meant it to be a nice surprise for you. In fact, she promised that you could show us how. There should be time to do it – the pit will still be hot – provided that Junio gets here with it fairly soon.'

I was delighted at the prospect of a Celtic roast. I grinned at her. 'Then we will go and light him on his way. Come, Kurso,' I said, and we set out into the night.

I was glad I had my cloak on. It was very cold indeed, and the south wind had blown in heavy clouds which covered up the moon. In the darkness, the forest made alarming sounds: every rustle of a creature and every snapping twig made me think of rebel footsteps in the wood, and the breeze sighed in the treetops like bandits whispering. Even the torchlight did not seem to help: the light sent monstrous shadows skittering everywhere. For Kurso's sake – as well as for my own – I began to chatter in a cheerful tone.

'There are a lot of questions that I've not had time to ask,' I said, as we picked our way along, stumbling over tree roots and boulders on the track. 'Who was it told you that I wasn't hurt – or dead?'

'It was the tanner in the shop next door.' He peered at me from under the darkness of the hood. The torchlight was oddly reflected in his eyes, giving them an unearthly glitter in the shadow of his face.

'You went to talk to him?'

He nodded. 'We got to the workshop as quickly as we could, but there was no one there – and no sign of any struggle or blood or anything. The fire was still alight, and there were some snuffed-out tapers on the floor. The mistress was terribly upset to find no sign of life and sent me to the tannery to enquire if anyone there had any news of you.'

I grinned, thinking of my neighbour's love of gossiping. 'Which no doubt they did?'

The dark hood nodded up and down again. 'The tanner was very anxious, master, when he heard you might be hurt, and very keen to help us when he realized that you weren't.

He even left his shop and came round to reassure the mistress personally. I'm glad he did. She would have doubted the message unless she heard it from his lips: that he'd seen you only an hour or so before and you seemed in perfect health. He saw you set off into town with some turnips in a bag.'

My turn to nod. So the tanner had been watching my departure from the shop. I was glad that Radixrapum had escaped by then and taken Pedronius's pavement safely out of sight. 'Did he say anything about an army cart?'

There was a short pause as Kurso skirted a little patch of mud, and then he said slowly, 'That was true, then? We wondered about that. He assumed there'd been some kind of accident – he'd seen the army cart drive up and take something away. He thought it was a body, but he couldn't tell us more – except that it wasn't you. He seemed to hope that we'd enlighten him, but, of course, we couldn't – we did not know ourselves.' He gazed enquiringly at me, but he said no more.

I answered the question that he had not dared to ask. 'There was a corpse,' I told him, 'but it was just a street-vendor who used to sell me pies.' I sent up a mental apology to poor Lucius for that 'just', but I wanted Kurso to be reassured. I did not tell him either that it was no accident. Here in the dark there was enough to worry him. 'He died outside the shop. I imagine that's what made someone send that messenger to you – though I don't know who did that. I'm fairly sure it wasn't Minimus.'

'From his description, we assumed it was. A red-headed slave. Who else could it have been? It wasn't Maximus. He turned up later on, with the young master, and they were just as mystified as we were by it all—' He broke off as the silence of the night was broken by the distant howling of a wolf. Kurso huddled a little closer to my side and slowed to crawling pace.

'Keep walking,' I told him. 'And keep your voice up too. They are said to be just as nervous of us as we are of them. Besides, they're afraid of fire and we have a torch.' I tried to pretend that I believed that, but I doubted every word, and when the torchlight shone upon a pile of broken branches near the path, tied into little bundles with a cord – somebody's pile of kindling, by the look of it – I selected two stout ones that were longer than the rest and handed one to him. 'And now we're armed as well,' I said.

He didn't answer. He was rooted to the spot. The courage from the mead had quite deserted him. But it was dangerous to linger. I took the torch and strode away from him, knowing that he would have to follow me or find himself benighted on the path. It was unkind – Kurso was such a nervous creature anyway – but it was the only way that I could think of to keep him on the move.

After a moment, he trotted after me, and I observed in a deliberately loud and ordinary tone, as if there'd been no interruption in our talk, 'Junio turned up at my workshop after you?'

He nodded. 'We felt a bit foolish when the tanner left, not knowing what to do. But then the young master came along, trying to find you to walk home with you.'

'Why was that?' I wondered. 'I was not expecting him.'

'He and Maximus were struggling with the handcart,' Kurso said. 'They had a huge heap of purchases to manage – lots of food and metal trinkets, to say nothing of the lamb – and it was obviously going to be much harder when they got out of town. They were hoping you would come along and help to steady it.' It came out in a rush, but it had done the trick. He was thinking about the story, not the dangers of the night. 'Of course, they were surprised to find us there, but we told them what had happened, and then they understood. We waited a bit longer, but you didn't come, and it was getting dark . . .' He tailed off unhappily.

I said, to change the subject to happier things, 'And you thought you'd better give me up and set off home again?'

He gave me a sideways, apologetic look, as if I had accused him of deserting me. 'We did try to find you before we left the town – we even asked the sentry on the gate if he had seen you recently. But no one had seen you on the road at all.'

'I didn't come that way – and I hired a gig,' I said. 'I can see why you were worried.'

'The mistress was beginning to wonder if the messenger was right, and someone had indeed attacked you after the tanner had seen you leave the shop! But Junio persuaded us that this could not be true – the messenger would never have got to us in time, not even if he'd come here on a horse.'

'Which he clearly hadn't, from what you say of him.' I frowned. The more I thought about that messenger, the more of a mystery he seemed to be. 'And he didn't give you any clue as to who might have sent him, or where he heard the story that I'd been set upon? Even though you went all the way to Glevum in his company?'

Kurso shook his head. 'Oh, we did not do that. He left us almost as soon as we set off – he could move much faster than the mistress could and he was wanted back, he said. We hadn't got as far as this when he ran off again, and we did not see him after that. I'm sorry, master, I can't tell you more.'

So there might have been a horse or an accomplice in the woods, I thought, but then I shook my head. Why should I suppose that there was something sinister? I had never been set upon at all – it had been Lucius. Yet why should someone have supposed that it was me? And why, by all the gods, should a green man – or anybody else – care enough to alert my family?

Kurso saw the shaken head. 'What is it, master? Something startled you?' He stiffened and then added in a frightened whisper. 'I can hear a noise myself.'

I was about to assure him that there was nothing of the kind when I realized he was right. There was a faint sound of voices and a rumbling sound – and it was getting nearer all the time. I tightened my grasp upon my makeshift staff, and said, with more conviction than I felt, 'Only a farmer looking for his sheep . . .' I trailed off as I heard a distant thump, and the sound of cursing drifted through the night.

'What is it, master?' Kurso's voice was shrill. 'Do you think it could be the rebels after all?'

'I don't believe so.' I found that I was grinning out of pure relief. 'Listen!'

In the distant darkness a familiar voice was saying very loudly, 'To Dis with this handcart! It's impossible. Where has Kurso got to with the light?'

Twelve

I t took us a little time to reach them even then, and what a reception I received when we arrived! I might have been a hero returning from the wars, the way that Junio and Maximus behaved. They dropped the handcart as quickly as they could, grinning like a pair of idiots, and hastened over – my son to clap my shoulder heartily and the slave to fall on one knee and kiss my hand. But my wife seemed less delighted to find me safe and well. She shouldered past the pair of them, and – far from giving me a fond embrace – pummelled against my chest with both her fists.

'Libertus! Husband! How could you worry me so much! First I thought that you were dead, and then you were missing—' She broke off, and I recognized that she was in tears and this was the anger of extreme relief.

I captured both her hands and held her tight. 'It's all right, Gwellia,' I murmured in her ear and felt her sobbing cease. Then, in a complete reversal of her mood, she collapsed upon my neck and – in full view of the servants – hugged and kissed me tenderly.

In the end, I had to extricate myself and say with what dignity I could muster, 'I am glad to see you too. It has been a worrying day.' I was on the point of telling her that we'd lost Minimus, but decided that this unhappy news could wait. For one thing, I was not certain that I wasn't being overheard by unseen listeners behind me in the wood, and I did not want my wife's distress to give any satisfaction to the kidnappers. So, instead, I went on in a normal tone, 'But we should not linger out here on the lane. I've come to lend a hand. Give me that lamb you've got there on the handcart, Maximus: that will lighten the load for you and balance it as well.' I gestured towards the unattended cart which showed an increasing tendency to topple to the right.

Maximus obeyed, though he struggled under the dead weight of the animal. It was a big lamb and bulky, though the fleece had been removed – there was always a separate market for sheepskin in the town – and he is small and slight, despite his name. But he contrived to help me drape it round my neck, so that I was carrying it on my shoulders as the shepherds do. The sheep was surprisingly heavy – I have felt a new respect for shepherds ever since, though the creature was stiff and perhaps more difficult to manage than a living animal. When I had it balanced, I gestured to the slave to hand me back my makeshift staff, which I had dropped on to the ground when Gwellia ran at me.

Meanwhile, the others had begun to rearrange the cart, which was still piled high with purchases for Amato's naming day. It was an awkward load: metal trinkets from the silversmiths, the whole family's garments from the fuller's shop where they'd been newly cleaned (everyone is expected to wear white at a Roman naming day) and incense for the shrine. There were leather bags and wooden boxes full of foodstuffs too: special sweet cakes from the baker's shop as well as dates and figs and every kind of fruit. There was also a small amphora full of wine, another one of oil, and even a cage of white doves for the cleansing sacrifice, which had been balanced precariously on the top of all of this – no wonder Junio had wanted an extra steadying hand.

However, with the heavy carcass now removed, the rest was soon arranged and roped securely into place. Junio and Maximus between them pushed the cart and, with Kurso carrying the doves, and Gwellia the torch, our little procession set off in the direction I had come – back towards the roundhouses again.

Only then did I outline the happenings of the day. I kept it very brief and did not mention Minimus at all. The corpse that they'd heard about was the pie-seller, I explained. When the tanner saw me, I was on my way to Lucius's mother to tell her the news, and then I'd hurried over to put Pedronius's pavement down. 'I didn't want to lose the Apollo contract too,' I finished. 'And then I found a gig to drive me home from there, so we didn't pass through the gates.'

'So that's why we didn't find you in the shop,' Junio exclaimed. 'And why no one had seen you at the gates. I did think to enquire.' He looked at me for approval. I had trained him in my methods while he was my slave. 'I was expecting that you would catch up with us. I wondered why you hadn't, even if you left Glevum a long time after us. This is the way you usually come and, as you can see, we were not moving fast.'

They would have been slower still without a light, I thought, using my staff to help me as I picked my way among the muddy potholes and roots along the lane. But all I said was, 'You must have been alarmed, especially after that peculiar message saying I was hurt.' Then, suddenly conscious of the distant wolves again, I added, 'Gwellia, tell me about this mysterious messenger.'

She had nothing to add that I'd not already heard from Kurso, in fact, but I heard her out, knowing that she would be comforted by simply voicing it and also distracted from the terrors of the night.

Junio looked across at me and caught my eye. As usual, he had understood my ploy and he took up the tale as soon as she had stopped – though he had very little to report. He had spent the day exactly as he'd planned, making his purchases, collecting the clean clothes and paying a visit to the local priest of Mars, who was to perform tomorrow's ritual. 'The *pontifex* made it very clear to me,' he added wryly, 'that he was not coming out of duty – he would not normally come out all this way – but simply because he was "a friend of Marcus's". No doubt he hopes to be rewarded when your patron returns.'

'Then I hope he isn't disappointed,' I remarked. 'Marcus is famously careful with his wealth.'

'He's promised to officiate in any case,' my son replied, 'and to make the preliminary sacrifice for cleansing Cilla and the roundhouse from the impurities of birth. He doesn't even want a fee, he says – though he does want you to make a point of telling His Excellence all this. By the way, he says there's been a messenger and Marcus is already on his way. The letter came to the curia today, apparently.'

I was about to say that I had heard as much from Quintus earlier when Gwellia put in unexpectedly, 'And to the villa too. One of the servants came to the roundhouse shortly after noon, in great excitement, to tell us the news. The travellers are expected back here in a day or so – though not in time for the bulla feast, of course. But Marcus has sent a gift ahead of him in honour of the day – a beautiful silver trinket for little Amato.'

'That was very generous of my patron,' I said, privately suspecting that his wife had organized that piece of thought-fulness. Marcus is not given to expensive gifts and I had not expected him to send a present for the naming day, even if he knew that it was happening.

He might well not have known. I had written every moon, as he had requested, to keep him informed of what was happening in the town, and obviously in my last I had told him of the birth. However, such letters took a long time to arrive, and since, as Cilla had remarked, the bulla day is traditionally held only nine days after a boy is safely born, I could not be certain that Marcus had received the message yet. I had sent an invitation for him to the villa, naturally – since he was my patron it would have been an insult to do otherwise, even if he was not in residence – but I had hardly expected such a generous response.

So I was more than a little startled when Gwellia said, 'They are going to send someone to attend on his behalf, though the servant that I spoke to did not know who it was. Marcus suggested it himself apparently, since he cannot be here in person.'

I was surprised and said so.

Gwellia shook her head. 'It is the sort of thing that Marcus sometimes does – he's sent you to represent him at a social function before now.'

'But I am a citizen, and that is different,' I protested. 'Marcus has had the villa closed up while he is away and there are only servants there – no one of any proper status as a representative.' Not that I had any objection to welcoming a slave – after all, I had once been captured into slavery myself – but Marcus would have felt the impropriety of a low-born substitute.

Gwella smiled. 'So he'll send the most senior person in the household, I suppose – the chief slave himself, I shouldn't be surprised. That would be quite fitting really, since Cilla was a maidservant at the villa once. It would be awkward for Marcus to be here as her guest. I know that you and Junio are the official hosts – you as the head of the family, and Junio as the child's father – but Cilla will be present and the roundhouse is her home. And a very humble one he thinks it, I've no doubt. So he'd feel that a high-ranking servant is a perfectly appropriate emissary.'

She was right, of course, but I said stubbornly, 'Marcus was the magistrate who invited her to dine, and thus enabled me to set her free. And she is a Roman citizen by marriage now, so there can no impropriety in her inviting him. As to it being a humble roundhouse, why should he object? Ours is very similar and he has been there several times.'

Gwellia tucked a hand into the arm that held the lamb in place over my shoulder and said gently, 'Only when you were ill and could not go to him. Besides, you have invited local farmers to come and join the feast – they may be freemen, but they are not the class of people that Marcus mixes with. And there's another thing. If your patron were to come in person, he would naturally take precedence in everything, instead of you. So this is quite a clever solution on his part, isn't it? He attends by proxy and there is no offence – and no embarrassment on either side. And Amato will have a lovely gift to show for it.'

She was right again. I could think of no intelligent reply, so I changed the subject to arrangements for tomorrow's little feast, and we talked of other matters for a while. It was still dark and chilly, but the wind had died and the forest seemed less threatening now there were more of us – even the wolves had ceased their howling now. After a little we passed the pile of branches by the track, and, as the faint smell of woodsmoke and burnt charcoal reached us on the breeze, I realized that we were getting close to home.

Before I could say so, Maximus piped up, as though he read my thoughts, 'That must be the roundhouse. I can see a glow. And there's someone standing by the door. I can see the dark outline. I'll bet it's Minimus.' His face was radiant with a sudden joy, and I remembered how close the two of them had been – so close, in fact, that when I knew them first, they used to finish each other's sentences.

That recollection clenched cold hands round my heart. I said, as gently as I could, 'I don't believe so. I'm afraid I have disturbing news for you – something I haven't told you which occurred today. I will tell you all about it when we get back to the house.' I was still reluctant to discuss this where we might be heard.

But Maximus seemed to sense that something was amiss. He dropped the handle of the cart and came around to face me in the middle of the path. I thought for a minute that he was confronting me, but he was too well-trained a slave to do anything like that. He only bowed his head and murmured brokenly, 'Something has happened to Minimus, master? Is that what you mean? Has there been an accident? Is he hurt?' He searched my face with anxious eyes, before he said, 'Or dead?'

I shook my head. 'I really do not know. I hope not, but I don't want to talk about this out here in the lane. We'll get back to the roundhouse and unload these things, and then I'll tell you everything I can.' But he didn't move, and I had to speak severely before he reluctantly obeyed and went back to his position helping with the cart.

The others had been listening to all this, of course, and a strange unhappy silence settled on the group as we struggled on along the lane towards the house. Those last hundred paces seemed to take a year, but at last our small procession reached the roundhouse door. The smell of smoke was much stronger now, and I could see that in our absence Cilla had got the fire-pit ready for the lamb.

The cooking-pit had been sited a little to the back, which is why I had not noticed it when I arrived before, and my first action now was to go and look at it. The fiery embers had been raked aside and the stones which lined the pit were glowing red, bathing the scene in an unearthly light. I signalled to Kurso to toss in a layer of damp straw, which had been left ready in a nearby pile, then – with a grunt of relief – I dropped the heavy lamb into the hole. In the torch-light, we gathered aromatic leaves to sprinkle over it, added another layer of the straw and finally enough fresh earth to seal the pit. The animal would cook quite slowly in the heat, but by the feast next morning it should be ready to consume. Already it reminded me of feast days in my youth.

I brushed the loose dust from the fire-pit from my hands and went indoors with little Kurso still trotting at my heels. The others had unpacked the handcart by this time – the contents were stacked around the roundhouse on all sides and Junio and Gwellia were consuming stew beside the fire, while Maximus was waiting with the water jug to serve them as they ate. Two smaller bowls, clearly for himself and Kurso, were standing on the bench.

Cilla was presiding at the cooking-pot, where there was still a pleasing quantity of hot and fragrant stew. She saw us enter and waved the ladle cheerfully at me. 'You have set the lamb to cook, then?'

I nodded. 'With Kurso's help. He has deserved his meal. And Maximus too, I think.'

But the red-haired pageboy did not rush to eat. He stood like a statue with the water jug. 'Master, you promised . . . the news of Minimus? I see he is not here.'

I took a deep breath. 'Minimus has gone – I don't know where or when. He simply disappeared when I had left the shop this afternoon – about the same time as Lucius was killed. I fear he has been kidnapped by the murderers and, worse, they may be taking him somewhere to be sold.' I didn't mention rebels – that was too terrible a possibility to share. 'I had been hoping to receive a ransom note for him, but I haven't had one.'

Maximus had turned a deathly shade of white. 'So he may be dead! If he saw the murder, perhaps he was killed too – just to make sure he couldn't tell.'

It was Junio who answered. 'But your master doesn't think so, and I think I can see why: because, in that case,

surely we would have found the corpse. There would be
no sense in hiding it, when Lucius's body was left for us
to see. Is that not so, Father?'

'Exactly,' I replied. Junio had put it bluntly – for
Maximus's sake I might have avoided talking about
Minimus's 'corpse' – but, in fact, that was precisely how I
had reasoned things. 'So there is every chance that he is
still alive.' Though if the rebels had him, I thought, he might
wish that he were not.

Minimus, however, looked a little comforted. 'But surely
someone must have seen him taken from the shop. If we
knew at least which way they went, we could try to get
him back.'

I shook my head. 'I can't find anyone who witnessed
where he went, not even the tanner – although I've asked,
of course. But I can't believe that he went willingly – I left
him in charge of the workshop while I was away – so I am
still inclined to think that he's been carried off, most likely
by the murderer himself.' I didn't add the obvious: that he
might have been knocked unconscious and stuffed into a
sack, to make it easier and less conspicuous to drag him
away.

Gwellia had obviously worked this out herself. 'But he
would have no value if he's damaged very much,' she said
softly. 'I suppose that is some comfort. Poor little Minimus.
But there is nothing else that we can do tonight?'

I shook my head. 'I don't believe so. After the bulla ritual,
I will go straight back to town and make as many enquiries
as I can. I'll go to all the gates. Someone, somewhere, must
have noticed him – or something which will put us on the
track.'

'And I will come with you,' Junio put in. 'Two people
asking questions will save a lot of time, and the sooner we
have news, the sooner we can act. But, in the meantime,
there is a feast day to prepare.'

Gwellia nodded briskly. 'There is a lot to do. Maximus,
eat your supper and then come back with me and help to
set the bread and cakes to rise before you go to bed. Then,
first thing in the morning, you can go and cut some reeds,

and Kurso can gather some sweet-smelling herbs that you can put with them. Then both report to me. We'll come up here and strew them on this roundhouse floor, as soon as Cilla's swept it for the day, so that it smells delightful by the time the high priest comes. He'll be fairly early because he'll want to make sure that everything is properly prepared. Libertus, husband, you will mix the wine while Junio and Kurso get the lamb out of the pit and carve it ready for serving to the guests. Don't put on your nice clean toga till you've finished that – you don't want it dirty when the people come. Just make sure that there is time to change.' She turned to Maximus. 'Well, don't just stand there staring, come and eat your stew. It's early bed for you. We'll have to be up before the dawn to get all this done in time.'

She had not mentioned the missing slave again. I nodded to Junio, who had caught my eye. Gwellia was dealing with worry in her usual way, by keeping so busy that there was no time to think, but I needed someone to discuss things with.

I talked to Junio well into the night, mostly about Glypto and my fears for Minimus. 'Don't say this to the others,' I said in a low voice, 'but if the green man has red hair and is Silurian, it looks more likely than ever that the rebels are involved.'

He shook his head. 'Not necessarily. Most Silurians are loyal citizens these days – those two slave-boys of Marcus's are the proof of that. It's only a few fanatics that keep mounting these attacks. And why should a rebel be concerned enough to send a message here, even if you really had been hurt?'

We argued in circles for an hour or more, but we made no progress with the mystery. Finally, I crept away and went to bed myself, reluctant to keep the little family awake. I did not want to spoil Amato's naming day.

But I slept only fitfully – and when I did, I dreamt of Minimus.

Thirteen

T he bulla ceremony was a great success. Despite the women's fears that there was far too much to do, everything was ready by the time the high priest came next morning to perform the cleansing ritual for Cilla and the house, though it was early and the sun was not yet high.

I was secretly delighted that we had arranged to hold the sacrifice on the same day as the naming ceremony, instead of the usual day or two before, because it meant that the purification (which included everybody and everything in the house) would release me from any evil influence which might have clung to me as a result of being in the company of a corpse. The doves that Junio had purchased for the sacrifice turned out to be genuinely spotless too – with no dark blemishes daubed over in white lime – and their entrails were clean, which was, of course, a splendid augury.

The doves were duly offered, the whole roundhouse ritually swept, and we all washed our hands in water the pontifex had blessed. Then the altar was swiftly cleaned with purifying salt and dressed with snow-white blooms – white as the freshly laundered garments we all wore in honour of the day – fresh herbs were scattered on the floor, and by the time the other well-wishers arrived, the little roundhouse was as well-adorned as any Roman villa could have been.

However, this was clearly not a Roman house, so, at the suggestion of the priest, a little piece of symbolic play-acting took place in which Cilla placed the swaddled baby on the floor, and Junio literally 'lifted up' his son. (I call it 'play-acting' because in fact this had all been done in private days and days before – almost as soon as the child was safely born. Junio was sufficiently versed in Roman ways to have made a point of 'lifting up' Amato there and then, and thus pronouncing him legitimate – indeed, he was so proud of fatherhood that he had gone to Glevum later the same day and registered the birth with the authorities, even though he was not required to do that for another moon.)

Nonetheless, the little raising ritual was performed again in front of witnesses – some of whom were Roman citizens – so there could be no future suggestion that it had not occurred. This was far more than a simple symbolic act, of course. Until a child was 'lifted up', it did not formally exist and therefore could be disposed of at the father's whim: given away or sold into slavery, exposed and left to die, or even, in the cruellest cases, chopped up for the dogs. But now that Amato was formally recognized as Junio's son, he was legally a citizen himself – albeit a very junior one – with all attendant rights and privileges, and he was additionally identified as his father's chief presumptive heir.

Once that was over, and the guests' applause died down, Kurso and Maximus fetched the ceremonial offerings for the gods (not birds or animals this time, since there was nothing here to expiate, just the so-called 'bloodless sacrifice' which was traditional, exactly as the annual anniversary of this day would be marked by similar oblations till Amato came of age). Wine and oil and incense were poured out on the shrine and burned as sacrifice, together with a piece of specially marked sweet cake (bought for the purpose from the baker's shop), while baskets of white petals were scattered for the gods. Little Amato was very well-behaved throughout, even when the high priest passed him three times through the smoke.

'Another good omen,' Junio said to me, almost bursting with paternal pride.

There were the usual prayers and speeches, mostly by the priest, and then the bulla, placed in its special leather pouch together with a number of lucky amulets, was duly hung around the baby's neck, and citizen Junius Libertinus Flavius Amato was officially a person under law. He would not take that bulla off until he came of age and put on the white toga of an adult male. Until then, if he wore anything toga-shaped at all, it would be a purple-striper like the patricians wore, which was the badge of boyhood throughout the Empire. All that, of course, would be in years to come: for now he was close-swaddled, as Roman infants are.

Suddenly, I felt an unexpected lump rise in my throat. It was partly pride, of course – I had never hoped to be the head of a family of my own, even an adopted one like this – but there was something else as well. Junio and Cilla had both been raised as slaves in Roman homes, and today was essentially a Roman naming day: so different from the customs in my own Celtic youth that I felt for a moment completely out of place. I was a Roman citizen, of course – and very proud to be – but I had rarely even seen a bulla ritual. Even in this Celtic roundhouse which I'd helped to build, I felt like a stranger in a foreign land.

But I brushed aside such sentimental thoughts. It was time for the presentation of the gifts.

All the guests had brought presents for the child and they lined up to bestow them – important callers first, which meant that my patron's representative led the way, carrying the lovely little silver bell. The question of status had been very neatly solved. Marcus had asked his messenger to come and act on his behalf: a young man called Virilis, who was not a slave at all, but a very smart and handsome military courier, who, my patron's note assured me, was a freeborn citizen and destined for high office in the cavalry one day, or even in the Emperor's private entourage.

Virilis was full of youthful vigour, as the name implies, and he strode up to play his part. He struck a pose and turned to face the company, and it was immediately clear why Marcus had selected him. He was a most impressive sight. His horseman's leggings were of scarlet cloth, and his loose over-tunic bore two purple stripes which ran from neck to hem and was held at the waist by a narrow sash of plaited purple silk – and silk was literally worth its weight in gold: the traders who sold it put it on the scales! He wore a splendid pair of red leather knee-length boots, and he carried a dagger on a baldric at his breast, though he bore no other arms and had no breastplate on. (Naturally – in normal times at least – a mounted army '*cursor*', or official messenger, wore nothing heavy which would slow him down.)

Conscious of the little stir he'd made, Virilis raised a hand and made a little speech on Marcus's behalf, before – with conscious graciousness – he made way for other guests to bring their gifts.

As tradition demanded, these were metal charms shaped like miniature tools and ornaments, some of gold and silver, but most of bronze and tin, and intended to bring good fortune in all areas of life. I counted swords and buckets, an axe, a flower and several lucky little moons, which were all strung on to a silver chain and placed round Amato's neck, over the swaddling, so that they rattled as he moved. Gwellia and I had bought a pretty silver horse, and even Kurso and Maximus, bringing up the rear, offered a tiny trinket each – but, of course, pride of place went to my patron's lovely bell.

Marcus was not the only one to send a gift by proxy. There were several notes and letters from my customers in the town – including an unexpected tribute from Pedronius – and Quintus, to my immense surprise, had deigned to send his slave Hyperius with a little bronze trinket to add to all the rest. Hyperius was immensely condescending, as if he were doing us a favour by attending this affair, though, being just a servant on an errand to the house, he could hardly linger to join us in the feast.

And what a feast it was! The food was served by Maximus, Cilla and Gwellia in the main, though the villa had thoughtfully sent some extra slaves to help, apparently at the suggestion of Virilis himself in his role as my patron's representative. It was a role that he was taking very literally indeed. He even came to help officiate in my place – as His Excellence would have done if he'd been here himself – in offering the traditional taste of every dish to the Roman household deities.

I hope the gods enjoyed it. The mortals clearly did. The bread and cakes were perfect and the lamb was beautiful – so soft and tender that it had fallen off the bones. People were eating it largely in their hands (we did not have enough knives and platters for them all) and had to be careful not to spot their festive clothes, especially once the mead and watered wine was served.

But I confess my own enjoyment was a little marred. I

was watching Maximus moving through the throng, offering a plate of sweet cakes from the town, when it struck me with some force that he was on his own and Minimus was not there to help him serve. I had to turn aside and walk outside the door so that my distress was not too evident to the guests.

Hyperius, I saw, was still standing at the gate, exchanging farewells with another visitor, and when he caught sight of me, he gestured with his hand as if to acknowledge that I was there and to invite me to come and speak to them. But I was still thinking of little Minimus. Aware that unmanly tears were welling in my eyes, and disinclined besides to be summonsed by a slave – even a slave of Quintus Severus – I waved the briefest of salutes, then turned my back on them and pretended some interest in the cooking-pit.

A few moments later I felt a hand upon my arm. Gwellia had seen me leave the roundhouse and had come to look for me. 'What is it, husband? You look quite distressed.' She looked into my eyes. 'But of course. You are still worried about Minimus. Perhaps I should have known. But really, husband, you should come back to the feast. There is nothing you can do in any case until the guests have gone.'

I nodded. 'Once this feast is over, I shall go straight to town and start enquiring – I'll try at every gate. And Junio says that he will come and help.'

She squeezed my arm. 'It's only a pity that you have to walk. That servant of Quintus's was offering a ride. He'd heard from Junio that you were going to Glevum later on, and he came to find me in particular to ask if you wanted to travel into town with him – but I said you couldn't leave the bulla feast before the end.'

So that was why Hyperius was waiting by the lane and why he'd attempted to summon me across. 'I saw him at the gate. I got the impression that he hoped to speak to me, but I was preoccupied with other things.' I glanced at her wryly. 'He has taken a hiring-carriage, I expect, and wanted someone to share the cost of it.'

She shook her head. 'He'd come in his master's carriage, so he said. It's coming back to collect him in a little while. The driver has gone up to your patron's house meanwhile, to deliver a message from Quintus Severus – something about a banquet on His Excellence's return. It's a pity you have to stay here for the guests; it would have saved you quite a walk.'

'If he's using his master's carriage, there'll be no hire to pay,' I said, brightening, 'so it's possible he could wait for me a little while. We could even ask him to join us at the feast. Perhaps that is what he hoped. No doubt he would be flattered to join this company . . .' I turned round, but the carriage and its occupant had already gone. 'Too late! If that was what he wanted, I've disappointed him.'

'You've disappointed him in any case, I fear,' she smiled. 'He was inordinately proud of travelling in such style and was obviously anxious to show off the fact by sharing it with you.'

I nodded. 'I saw him talking to someone at the gate; perhaps he was still trying to find a passenger.'

'Well, he'll be doubly disappointed, in that case,' Gwellia said. 'I'm almost sure that it was Virilis that he was talking to, and being a military messenger, that young man will no doubt have a horse, back at the villa I shouldn't be surpri—'

'Indeed he has,' a cultured voice behind me interrupted us. 'The finest one the army could provide.'

I turned round to find the messenger himself, now wearing a handsome full-length woollen cloak over his uniform, which was why I hadn't recognized him at the gate – though Virilis was a striking enough figure, by the gods. He was an unusually tall and athletic-looking youth, whose easy stride was almost swaggering, and he boasted an impressively square chin and chiselled cheeks. His wavy hair was swept back from his face, and his dark eyes were appraising me with shrewd intensity.

However, his manner was deferential when he spoke. 'Excuse me, citizen, for interrupting your private conversation with your wife. But I did hope to speak to you before I leave, which, unfortunately, I'm obliged to do, as there are other duties to which I must attend. When I saw you standing here, I thought I'd take my chance to come and meet you properly. And your lovely wife, of course.' He flashed a set of perfect teeth at Gwellia, who smiled.

'But we spoke in the roundhouse,' I said ungraciously.

He countered that with a dismissive wave. 'Of course, we did exchange a few words during the naming ceremony, but that hardly counts. It was purely official, wasn't it?' He spoke with the patrician accent of the imperial court, his perfect Latin putting my own to shame, and his long strong fingers, as finely manicured as if they were a girl's, artlessly adjusted his ruby shoulder-clasp. I moved my own stubbled hands so they were out of sight.

'I had heard so much about you,' he went on presently.

That surprised me, but it was Gwellia who said, 'From His Excellence?'

He did the smile again. 'From His Excellence, of course. He is fond of boasting of your husband's intellect and skill, and of how he relies upon him for advice – though he could not insult your family by offering a fee.'

I nodded curtly. That was more than possible. Praise costs nothing and Marcus is often very lavish with it. 'It is an insult I would sometimes be prepared to bear,' I muttered – which was foolish, since it was indiscreet and Virilis very clearly was in my patron's confidence. 'But it is true that I have helped him in solving several crimes.'

Gwellia was frowning warningly at me, but the young courier looked at me with sudden interest. 'Which reminds me, citizen, there is something significant I could impart to you.' He gave me a knowing little smile. 'Apart from that note of introduction which you already have.'

'You have news of my patron? Messages for me?'

He glanced at Gwellia and, almost imperceptibly, shook his head as if to signal that this conversation should not be held in front of her. 'Nothing so formal, citizen, and nothing that cannot wait until a more appropriate time. I am staying in the villa until your patron comes, so we shall be near neighbours for a day or so – I am sure we can find an opportunity. In fact, I understand that you are going to Glevum later on – perhaps we can meet there. And now, I have taken too much of your time. Forgive me, both of you. I will take my leave and allow you to get back to your guests.' And, with a little bow, he turned away and strode back to the gate.

His easy charm and his flashy dark good looks had clearly made a deep impression on my wife. She was staring after him with an admiring smile. She turned to me. 'Did you know he was not just a freeman but a citizen? He was telling me his father was an officer with the legions years ago. Got his citizenship when he retired, and then married – as he was entitled to by then – so his children were naturally entitled to the rank.'

There was something strangely irritating in her open admiration for the youth, so I just said, 'Really?' But she was not deterred.

'No doubt that's why he's risen in the army quite so fast. He's very young to be trusted with dispatches, you'd think. But he isn't just an average courier; he's attached to the provincial governor's household in Londinium and rides all over the country with the imperial mail. That's how Marcus came to notice him and ask permission to obtain his services. Imagine if little Amato could grow up to have a wonderful career like that.'

'Virilis probably has a powerful patron somewhere,' I said sourly. 'Or his father has opened a few doors for him.'

'But he must be a splendid horseman all the same,' she enthused. 'And Marcus seems to think a lot of him. Did you see the note he sent?'

Of course I had. Virilis had given it to me as soon as he arrived. It had been more than fulsome. I was suddenly tired of the wretched messenger and his obvious ability to charm. 'I would not put too much reliance on that note,' I said. 'Marcus has a fondness for handsome youths like that and is always complimentary about their aptitudes – usually rather more so than they deserve. This Virilis may prove to be another. But now, as you were saying before he interrupted us, it is more than time we got back to entertain Amato's guests.'

And, without pausing for an answer, I went back into the house.

Fourteen

It seemed to take an unconscionably long time for the last guest to leave – and that was actually the priest of Mars himself, who seemed peculiarly reluctant to depart as long as a morsel of roast lamb or wine remained. No wonder he was such a portly man. But at last we got him bundled to the gate and into the hiring-litter which he had arranged – and which, it transpired, had been waiting quite a time – and with cries of 'Don't forget to tell your patron, citizens', he lurched off down the lane.

I turned to Junio, who was standing at my side. 'Now, perhaps, we can set off into town ourselves. If you are still willing to accompany me, that is.'

He gave me the old familiar grin. 'Of course. I am as anxious as you are to find news of Minimus. And even if we do not succeed in doing that, I can at least help you finish the Apollo piece today. I know that you are anxious to be paid for that.'

'Especially after that expensive feast,' I teased. But it was not entirely a joke. Even with this payment from Pedronius, money – or rather the lack of it – would be a problem soon. I had been relying on the Quintus contract for a handsome fee and had actually turned down several small commissions on the strength of it. The earnings from the Apollo piece would help to see me through, but I was glad to know my patron was returning very soon. Marcus might be very careful with his own expenditure, but he had enough influence with other purchasers to ensure that my household did not starve, however much ill omen was attaching to my shop.

Junio was laughing at my sally, though. 'At least we shall not require to be fed before we leave! Let us go and tell the women what we plan.' He led the way into his house again.

Cilla was sitting on a stool beside the central hearth, looking exhausted after the excitements of the day, but flushed with a triumphant pleasure too. Gwellia, assisted by the villa slaves, was busy collecting bowls and spoons to wash in the water that Kurso was no doubt collecting from the spring. Amato – the centre of all this activity – was back in his sleeping hammock, dreaming peacefully.

I looked at Junio.

'That was a successful ritual, I think,' he said. 'But now . . .'

'You are going to go and look for Minimus, I hope,' my wife replied. 'Take Maximus to help you. We can manage here. With the slaves from the villa, we have a lot more hands to help than we would have done if Minimus was here. So you go and find him, and good luck to you. Kurso, where's that water?' And she plunged her hands into a metal bowl and set to work to scrub it with a handful of rough sand.

We took this as a signal to depart. We did not change out of our togas – we would get more respect from sentries and people as we were, and we could soak down to our tunics if we went to the villa to strip the linen off the plaque. However, we did pause to seize a cloak and staff apiece, and I took a few *sesterces* from the household store so that I could settle with Radixrapum when he came. Then Junio and I set out to walk to town, with Maximus trotting after us with my box of tools and the spare birrus which Kurso had worn home.

It is a long walk, even in daylight, and – though of course I do not often travel at this time of day – the old track through the woods seemed unnaturally empty. Yet the forest was full of disturbing rustling sounds and a distant howling which might have been a dog or wolf, but – to my over-anxious ears – could have been a rebel signal from somewhere in the trees. Moreover, for a long time we scarcely saw a soul: only a farmer with a panniered donkey lumbering along, who moved grumblingly aside to let us pass. Of course, there were three of us and we were armed with staves, but I could not keep the thought of brigands from my mind.

So when I heard the sound of hoof-beats following, my heart began to pound. I glanced at Junio and saw that his face was set and tense, and – though neither of us voiced our fears in front of Maximus – I knew he shared my thoughts. This section of the lane route is muddy and particularly steep, and it is rare to find a horseman who will choose to come this way at all. But the hoof-beats were coming closer and ever closer still, until they slowed and seemed to follow us.

I stole a furtive glance and saw a hooded figure on a horse.

He came up beside us, reined his mount and stopped.

'On your way to Glevum, citizen?' the rider said, and I recognized the cultured tones of Virilis. He was smiling down at me with that over-charming smile that my wife had found so irresistible. 'I would have offered to take you if you had been alone – I'm sure that my horse could have accommodated us both.'

I thanked him as politely as I could, in a voice still weak with shock. 'But I have not been on a horse at all for many years and certainly never riding pillion.' It was true. I would never have considered such an offer anyway – particularly from an over-pampered pet like him.

He laughed. 'Then perhaps it's just as well. It would not in any case have been a comfortable ride – this route is much more steep and winding than I had supposed. No wonder so few horsemen seem to come this way.' He paused. 'Well, if you're sure there's nothing I can do? Your patron would expect me to help you if I could. Perhaps I could take that box for you, at least,' he went on with a smile. 'It is heavy for your slave. I could easily leave it at your workshop later on – I have to pass that way in any case.'

I was obscurely irritated by this suggestion too. 'Thank you, but I shall require it later on. Maximus can manage very easily,' I said ungraciously, trying to ignore the disappointed look that crossed the page's face.

'Then I will not delay you. I have many calls to make. Arrangements for your patron when he gets back,' he said. 'Quintus Severus is planning an enormous feast, and half the population of Glevum will be there. And there is a special meeting of the curia today. There has been a change of plan. I am to ride and tell His Excellence the result. I will give him your greetings and your latest news. Give my respects to both your charming wives.' He doffed his feathered hat and cantered off again.

'The latest news,' I muttered, as Virilis disappeared from sight. 'Including the fact that I've lost Minimus, no doubt.' The encounter had not pleased me very much and I trudged on with a frown. Maximus, I noticed, was doing much the same.

Junio, perhaps in an attempt to lift the mood, said very earnestly, 'Then we must find Minimus as quickly as we can. Or news of him at least.'

'That may not be possible,' I muttered gloomily.

'Then it is doubly important that you find out what you can. If you can prove the rebels have him, Marcus himself will see that they are caught and punished as severely as the law allows. So let's go over everything you know – up to the moment when he disappeared.'

'Again? I told you yesterday.'

'There may be some detail which you did not realize was important at the time, but which you remember when you tell the tale again. Isn't that what you always say when you are asking questions of witnesses yourself, Father?'

He was right, of course. There was not much to tell him, but I did my best. 'He simply wasn't there when I returned,' I finished.

Junio frowned. 'But he was clearly still there after you had gone. He was seen by the turnip-man sitting on his stool by the workshop counter, awaiting customers?'

'Exactly,' I replied. 'And I haven't found anyone who saw him leave his post. Though he went in a hurry: he'd left his knuckle-bones.'

'Excuse me, masters, but he wouldn't have done that if he could have helped it,' Maximus's voice piped up from the rear. I had forgotten that he was listening to all this. 'It took him months of haggling with the kitchen slaves to get a perfect set – he could not go out to the butcher's stall, of course, to find them for himself. He was very proud of them. They were almost the only objects that he really owned.'

Junio, who had been a child-slave himself, looked rather grim at this. 'So he would not have left them willingly?'

'Not unless there was some crisis and he was called away. He would have put his duty even before his knuckle-bones,' Maximus replied, then added wistfully, 'At least I think he would.'

'Which brings us back to the attack on Lucius, and the message yesterday,' I said. The lane was considerably steeper here and I was rather out of breath. I took the opportunity to take a little rest, by pausing to add thoughtfully, 'And the idea that Minimus witnessed the assault and sent the messenger, thinking that it was me that was attacked? But why on earth should he have thought that it was me?'

'We've been through this before. Lucius was wearing your old tunic at the time, and from the back he might have looked like you.'

'Only at a considerable distance,' I replied. 'And why would Minimus have left the shop in any case, unless somebody forced him?'

'Which is exactly where we started,' Junio said, walking briskly on again. 'Perhaps we should try to find the urchin who brought the message to the house. At the very least he could tell us who sent him. I suppose it is possible that we could find him in the streets.'

'But we don't know what he looks like,' I objected, toiling uphill after him. 'None of us was actually at the round-house when he came.'

'So we'll have to ask around. There are always gaggles of pauper children who hang around the town, hoping to make an as or two by carrying people's purchases or taking messages. More than likely he was one of them. We could make enquiries,' Junio went on. 'Even if he wasn't, they might know who he was and be glad to earn a quadrans by finding him for us. It was a longish errand. No doubt it was the subject of gossip yesterday.'

I nodded. 'Someone must have paid the urchin fairly

handsomely or promised him more coin when he returned. Otherwise he would not have come so far or run so fast,' I muttered breathlessly, thinking of my own attempt to send a messenger to Gwellia the day before, when a quadrans apparently had not been enough. 'And that would hardly have been Minimus, whatever Cilla thinks. He would not have had the wherewithal.'

'But the boy was promised payment on delivery,' Junio pointed out. 'That would make a kind of sense.'

'But if Minimus had sent him,' I said, gloomily determined to support the other view, 'why didn't the messenger say so at the time?'

'The women thought he did,' my son reminded me. 'I only wish our wives had thought to ask a little more. I suppose that they were so concerned about your safety that they thought of nothing else but getting to Glevum as quickly as they could. Speaking of which, here we are ourselves.'

We had turned the final corner as he spoke, and the southern gatehouse was indeed in view. As if by common instinct, we all increased our pace.

'You talk to the sentry, father, and I'll go over there and see if those loitering urchins have anything to tell,' Junio said briskly. 'We'll meet inside the gate – or I'll see you at the workshop if anything turns up and I have to go and find the messenger.'

I nodded. 'Send Maximus if there's anything to report.' I strode off in the direction of the guard.

He was standing stock-still at his post, idly watching people entering the town – looking out for beggars and known fugitives, I suppose – and he scarcely glanced at me as I approached the gate. He was a surly-looking fellow, with a barrel-chest and a general appearance of being bored and hot in his heavy helmet and metal uniform. So it was with some trepidation and a feeble smile that – instead of passing meekly through the arch and scuttling away, like the woman ahead of me with the basket of gathered water-cress – I went up to him.

'Excuse me, sentry-man.'

He turned and looked me slowly up and down. I was still

wearing my toga from the morning's feast, which marked
me as a Roman citizen, but his inspection clearly left him
unimpressed. 'Well?' he demanded.

The brusqueness took my surprise. 'Well, it's like this,'
I said, so non-plussed that I was almost gabbling. 'I have
lost a slave – a small red-headed lad. I think he has been
stolen and I want to know if anyone was seen yesterday
dragging him away, or if there's been a slave-trader through
here who might have had a boy of that description chained
among his wares.'

I waited for an answer but all he said was 'Hmmmph!'
He was still looking at me with something like contempt,
and I added swiftly, 'The slave concerned did not belong
to me but to my patron, Marcus Septimus.'

The mention of my patron had one effect at least. The
square face creased in an unpleasant smile. 'Then I'm glad
that I'm not standing in your sandals, citizen. But I cannot
help you. I have seen nothing since I came on watch.' He
said this with a certain gleefulness, but at any rate I had
prompted him to speech. Indeed, he added a moment afterwards, 'But if you are looking for a small red-haired page,
I suppose the one behind you is not the one you mean?'

I whirled round with sudden foolish hope, but, of course,
it was only little Maximus waiting patiently at a distance
for me to notice him.

I indicated that he had permission to approach. 'The young
master says to tell you that it was not one of them,' the
slave-boy said, giving me a conspiratorial smile to show he
was being deliberately oblique. 'But there is a girl who
thinks she might know who it was – she heard him talking
earlier about the long walk he'd had. She's going to take
us to him. The young master says he'll meet you at the
workshop later on.'

I nodded, and he trotted off again, obviously enjoying
the sentry's bafflement.

I turned back to the guard and was about to say, with
what dignity I could, that the missing slave had been
acquired to be a matching pair with this when a voice from
the gatehouse hailed me heartily.

'Pavement-maker, I want a word with you!'

I looked up in alarm and recognized the soldier with the swagger stick that I'd seen the day before, when he had been commanding the party with the cart – the one I'd nick-named 'Scowler'. He was scowling now and hastening towards us with a determined air. The guard took a step backwards and pulled himself upright, standing to attention as if he feared rebuke.

But Scowler showed no interest in the guard at all. As he approached, he seized me by the arm. I thought that he was arresting me on some trumped-up charge and was about to make a protest, but he hustled me away to one side of the arch. I saw that he was no longer wearing his habitual frown. Indeed, he was giving me a most peculiar smile.

'If you've come here enquiring about that page again – the one that you were mentioning to me yesterday,' he said, murmuring as if he didn't wish the other man to overhear, 'I might have information that would be of use to you. Did I understand that there might be a reward?'

Fifteen

'You know where he is?' Hope was bubbling like a fountain in my veins. 'Wait till I tell my son. If you can take us to him, I'll reward you willingly.' I glanced around to speak to Junio, but there was no sign of him. He and his urchin guide had already disappeared.

Scowler was tapping his swagger stick against his side. 'Now, wait a minute, citizen. I didn't say that I could take you to him, or even that I know exactly where he is, but I do know what happened to him yesterday. That is what I'm offering – if you feel that is something which it is worth your while to know.' He ran a thick tongue around his lips. 'Though it's an official matter – privileged intelligence – and perhaps I shouldn't be telling you at all.'

He was clearly hoping for a substantial bribe, and my store of money was depleting by the day. However, I did want information about Minimus and would gladly pay for news, though the chances were that it was anything but good. The circumstances in which the death-cart officer was likely to have seen the boy did not bear thinking of, but I decided that, even so, I would be glad to know the truth.

I swallowed. 'I'll give you a *denarius*,' I said. 'Half now and another half if what you say leads to my finding him.' *Or at least his body*, I added grimly to myself.

Scowler gave me a wily glance and shook his head. 'I thought that you were anxious to have news of him? This information is worth more than that. Ten denarii at the very least.'

The demand was audacious and deliberately so. It was also more money than I could possibly afford and far more than I was carrying. Perhaps that was what made me stand my ground. 'Then I'll try elsewhere. If you're in possession of this news, then others in the garrison will have heard of it. I'll call on the commander – he knows who

I am, and since this is my patron's slave, I'm sure he'll try to help.'

In fact, I was by no means confident of that: on our previous encounters, there had always been the safety of a Roman citizen at stake, and a citizen of some authority at that. The fate of a humble slave-boy was of no account and therefore most unlikely even to have reached his ears. However, I moved away towards the gate again as if I intended to go to him at once.

Scowler's capitulation was so abrupt that it took me by surprise. He skirted round in front of me so as to block my path. 'Now just a minute, pavement-maker. Let's not be hasty here. I'm sure some accommodation can be reached.'

I raised my hand in a dismissive gesture of farewell, but he was too quick for me. He leaned forward and slapped my palm with his, the age-old signal of a bargain struck. 'A denarius, I believe you offered earlier. On consideration, I formally accept. *Spondeo*. There! We have a binding contract citizen, I think.'

Of course, it was really nothing of the kind. True, a *stipulatio* made in front of witnesses is generally taken to be binding by the market police, but only when the whole traditional formula is used, and Scowler had merely uttered the last response of it. Moreover, I now suspected that I'd promised far too much and he would have settled for a good deal less.

However, several people had seen him strike my hand (including the sentry at the gate, who was very unlikely to contradict a higher-ranking man) and I should have found it difficult to prove my case. Besides, my real concern was to gain news of Minimus, so I let it pass – as, no doubt, he had anticipated that I would. First skirmish to Scowler, I thought sourly.

I rallied by saying as loudly as I could, 'The first half when you tell me what you know; the second if it leads to my locating him.' As I had intended, people turned to look, so the terms of the so-called contract were at least made known.

Scowler, however, seemed alarmed by this and pulled me

back into the shadow of an arch. 'Very well, but don't let people know that you heard this from me.' He had dropped his voice to a conspiratorial whisper. 'He's in custody. I told you there was a warrant out for his arrest. When I got back here to the garrison last night, I heard that someone had already pulled him in, so the rest of us didn't have to keep a lookout any more.'

'In custody!' It was ridiculous, but my first emotion was relief. Minimus might be chained up in a military cell – cold, terrified and hungry, and doubtless beaten too – but at least he wasn't dead or being held to ransom by some vindictive rebel band. If he was in the clutches of the law, there were at any rate established procedures I could try.

'So they are holding him in the garrison?' I glanced across at the grim grey building as I spoke. This altered everything. It would not be easy to get him out of there – especially since Quintus had ordered his arrest – but the garrison commander was a friend of Marcus, and (as I'd told the sentry) I had dealt with him before and knew him to be a stern but not unkindly man. If Minimus was a prisoner under his command, then I could work, if not to obtain an actual release, then at least to improve the lad's conditions till my patron came.

But Scowler shook his head. 'He wasn't brought here to the garrison. The word is he was captured by someone's private guard. And when I say a guard, I mean a gang of them – half a dozen heavyweights, from what I understand. Must be someone wealthy to have a guard like that.'

I closed my eyes. I knew who it would be. Quintus had put the warrant out himself, though I was surprised to learn that Minimus had been caught without Hyperius mentioning it at the naming day. All the same, it was important news. I would have to go and visit Quintus now and try to persuade him that he should drop the charge. In the meantime . . .

'Do you know where they have taken him? The town jail, perhaps?' If so, he would be having an unpleasant time. Without the money to send out for food and drink, the best he could hope for was foul water and stale bread. I could imagine it with dreadful clarity – I had once been held in such a place myself: chained up hand and foot in a subterranean dungeon, dank and airless and wholly in the dark, and forced to lap food and water like a dog, from a communal bowl. There was a good chance that, with a little judicial bribery, I could at least arrange for him to have a better cell.

'I don't know where they would have taken him,' Scowler said. He seemed to be making a habit of repressing any ray of hope. 'But it wasn't to the jail, or I would have heard. We had a dead body to pick up from there today.'

I waved aside this incidental human tragedy. 'But I understand that there's a serious accusation on his head, so he'll be brought to trial. Where else would they hold him?'

He frowned with concentration, anxious to earn that second half-denarius. 'I suppose it's possible they've locked him up themselves. If they produce him for the hearing, that is all that is required.' He brightened. 'That would make a lot of sense, supposing there is somewhere they can keep him safe till then. And I expect there is – a man who keeps a private guard like that won't be short of a denarius or two.'

I nodded grimly. 'What decurion is? It is a requirement that a man has a certain value of estate before he is available to be elected to the post.'

'You know whose guard it was, then?' Scowler looked surprised. 'No one seemed to know.'

'The decurion who put the warrant out, I'm sure.'

'The one who arranged for us to come and get the corpse from you?' He sounded diffident. 'Well, I know where you can find him, if that's so. He'll be at the curia, or on his way to it. The ordo has a special session there this afternoon, and I think I heard the bugle just before you came.'

I nodded. 'Then he will be on his way to the basilica by now. If I miss him there, I'll try his town apartment later on. I know where that is too.'

Though it would not be easy to persuade him to set Minimus free, I thought. Quintus had a stubborn streak and hated to be wrong, and he'd decided yesterday that the slave-boy was guilty – if not actually of killing Lucius, then

at least of stealing his purse and running off with it. No
doubt his accusation would carry weight in court. The only
way to change his mind would be to find the murderer. And
very soon at that.

A chief decurion would have no trouble arranging for a
trial, especially when it did not require a proper magistrate.
In fact, it might not even require a proper court. For the
likes of Minimus, a hearing was often conducted out of
doors, in an open courtyard with someone unimportant
presiding over it – and where an acclamation by the lookers-
on would be enough to seal the poor lad's fate. Unless, of
course, the official torturers had already been to work and
extorted a confession, as they sometimes did. That picture
was so dreadful that I dragged my mind away.

'You say he was arrested some time yesterday?' I said,
already making calculations in my mind. 'When did you
hear of it?'

Scowler pushed his helmet up and scratched his grizzled
head. 'When I came off duty, about mid-afternoon I suppose
it must have been. I tried to tell you then – you seemed to
be so anxious to find out where he was that I knew you'd
make it worth my while. So I went back to your shop, but
I couldn't find you there, so then I tried to keep a lookout
at the gate – I heard you generally pass this way – but there
was still no sign of you, until just now, that is.'

I shook my head. 'Last night I didn't come this way
at all.' Which was a pity – I could have saved myself a
lot of worry if I had. I turned to Scowler and fished
beneath my toga folds into the draw-purse which I carried
at my belt. 'Here's the half-denarius I promised you.' I
scarcely had a chance to hold it out to him before he'd
seized it from me and put it in the arm pouch under his
tunic sleeve. He clearly didn't want the sentry – or anyone
else – to see.

'And the other half?' he muttered. 'When do I get that?'

'When I have located him. And if I find that there is
something more that you could have told me now, I shall
withhold the money. Do you understand?'

Scowler's frown came down upon him like a cloud, but

his tone was wheedling. 'Would I cheat you, citizen?' he said.

I rather thought he might do, if he had the chance, but I didn't say as much. Instead, I attempted to look businesslike. 'Then I shall see you here this evening about the time the sun goes down. If I have found out where he is, you'll have your coin.'

He was still staring after me as I walked through the gate and made my way towards the centre of the town. thinking of what I would say to Quintus when we met.

On reflection, I did not believe that he would let the slave be harmed – not at least while in his custody: he was too aware of who the legal owner was. That was some comfort to me. But equally I did not think that he would let him go. It seemed he genuinely believed in Minimus's guilt – otherwise, why bring the charge at all? But perhaps he would not hasten to a trial. Why take the boy into private custody unless he intended to delay? Or did he, on the contrary, intend to rush it through: to demonstrate to Marcus that I'd been negligent, firstly by not keeping an adequate watch upon the boy and then by encouraging him to independent thought?

Indeed, I realized suddenly, I might find *myself* arraigned – diminishing the quality of someone else's slave, physically or morally, was a criminal offence, tantamount to damaging his goods. That was not a comfortable possibility, and it made it still more urgent that I found the truth.

I was hurrying towards the *forum* all this time, down the wide thoroughfare that led into the centre of the town, still debating whether I should call at the curia at once, or if it was too late and I would have to intercept Quintus later on at home, at the apartment which he kept up in the town. (Like every other office-holder in the curia, he was obliged to maintain a property of a certain size within the walls, although, in common with Marcus and most other wealthy men, he owned a villa in the country too.) Surely he would already be at the basilica by now.

I hurried in that direction all the same, past the serried ranks of statues on their plinths and avoiding the traders who stepped out in my path and tried to interest me in what they had for sale – everything from woven carpets and expensive samian bowls to buckets of live eels – piled up on the makeshift stalls that crammed the pavement and spilled out on the street. I was side-stepping a particularly persistent shoe-seller, who would not believe that I did not want a pair of sandals made for me today, when a quartet of litter-bearers jogged past at that semi-run they often use in town. They were carrying a particularly fancy equipage with embroidered curtains that I recognized at once. This was the litter of Quintus Severus and, as I could make out through the half-drawn draperies, he was himself the only passenger, and he did not seem to be accompanied by Hyperius this time.

That sharpened my endeavours. I disengaged myself abruptly from the sandal-man, stepped over a neighbouring display of leather belts, narrowly avoided upsetting the ink of an *amanuensis* writing letters for a client, and pushed into the road. But I was impeded by my Roman dress (a toga is not an easy thing to hurry in), while the bearers wore short tunics to leave their long legs free. Besides they were strong and youthful men, accustomed to their trade, so by the time I had struggled to the carriageway the litter was already a long way down the street.

I don't know if you have ever tried to break into a run wearing a toga, but if you have, you'll know that it is near impossible. The garment instantly unfolds itself and loops around your knees. There was nothing for it. I could not remove my toga in a public place, so I did the next best thing: stripped off my cloak, wound it into a sort of tourni-quet around my hips, then pulled up my errant toga loops and stuffed them into it. At least, that way, my hairy legs were free. Thus, cutting a most undignified figure, and to the accompaniment of hoots and catcalls from the onlookers, I roused myself into a lumbering trot and set off in pursuit.

Sixteen

They were entering the forum when I caught up with them, and by the time that I had stopped and caught my breath enough to speak – bending over and resting my hands upon my knees, while my chest heaved with the effort of unaccustomed exercise – the bearers had drawn the litter to a halt and Quintus himself was getting out of it.

'Quintus, Decurion . . .' I managed between gasps, positioning myself where he'd catch sight of me. 'A thousand pardons for pursuing you . . .'

He gave me a look I shall remember all my life: such a mixture of outrage, contempt and disbelief that I stopped in confusion. The tanner would have no need of Glypto's caustic brews if he could have borrowed such a look to treat his hides – so scathing that it could have stripped mere hairs off in a trice.

Quintus's tone, when he addressed me, was just as withering. 'Citizen Libertus? Do I believe my eyes?' He sounded quite aghast, and, looking around, I saw that I'd attracted a little crowd of spectators. 'What are you doing here, and in that state of dress? Must you continually make an exhibition of yourself?'

I glanced down at my unconventional attire, undid my makeshift belt and pulled my toga down around me more decently again, painfully aware of its descending loops. 'I'm sorry, councillor,' I panted. It was wise to sound contrite. What I had done was a technical offence – a citizen is supposed to wear a toga in public at all times, especially in the forum, and I had just dishonoured that official badge of Roman pride. I could only hope that stickler Quintus would not choose to make an issue of my lapse. He was very clearly the sort of man who might, so I went on hastily, between painful gasps of breath, 'But it was essential . . .

mightiness . . . that I should speak to you at once . . . on a matter of considerable . . . urgency.'

He looked at me coldly. 'Concerning what?'

I was still panting heavily, but I managed to get out, 'It concerns the slave that my patron lent to me – the one that went missing from my workshop yesterday. I understand you put an order out for his arrest?'

If Quintus's manner had been frosty up till now, it was positively dripping icicles at this. 'I warned you at the time that I intended to do that. Your weakness for the boy has clearly blinded you. The evidence was clear for anyone to see – the empty purse was found upon his person, did you know? Quite enough to have him tried for robbery and possibly for homicide as well. To say nothing of the way that he had run off from his post – against your explicit orders as I understand.'

Of course, I hadn't known that they had found the purse. As Quintus had expressed it, even I had to concede that things did not sound good, and the group of spectators (who had been following all this with fascinated ears) began to hoot and jeer. I said, with what tatters of dignity were left, 'I'm convinced the lad is not a criminal. Just let me talk to him. I'm sure he can explain.'

One lone voice in the crowd called out in my support. 'That's right, councillor. Give the lad a chance before they nail him up. That's only justice!'

My unexpected ally was shouted down, of course, and snatched at and severely jostled by the mob, but he gave me the confidence to press the point. 'Just tell me where you're holding my little slave-boy, Decurion Quintus, and I'll go there at once.' I paused, debating whether to offer payment for the privilege, or whether Quintus would choose to be offended by the thought and accuse me of attempting to bribe a councillor.

The patrician forehead had furrowed in a frown. One hand clutched his toga front and he lifted the other in a commanding stance, as if he were posing for a statue of himself. Then, raising his voice and addressing the onlookers rather than myself, he said, in the formal Latin of the court,

'Citizens! Libertus! You misunderstand. I did put out an order to apprehend this slave and was intending to take him to the jail, but by the time I reached the garrison it seems I was too late. I learned that the boy had already been detained. And with incriminating evidence, as I said before.'

It took me a moment to take in the enormity of this 'You mean . . .'

He looked at me with condescension. 'Exactly, citizen. I do not have your slave. And, before you ask, I do not know who has. Now, if you will excuse me, I have a meeting to attend. Important business concerning candidates for the vacant ordo seat, and we want to get arrangements finished before your patron comes.' And with that he turned away and hurried up the steps.

There was sporadic clapping at this little speech – and a good deal of jeering and merriment at my expense – but after the decurion had left there was nothing else to see, and one by one the onlookers began to drift away.

Clearly there was nothing further here for me either. I was shocked and sickened by the news I had received – the so-called evidence would be almost certain to ensure that anyone accused, in particular a slave, was likely to be tortured until he had confessed – but there was no help for it. I was no closer to knowing where Minimus was held. No doubt Junio would be waiting for me at the workshop now and might have useful information about the messenger, and together we could make renewed enquiries. I ignored the few remaining gawpers, readjusted my dishevelled tunic folds as best I could, put on my cloak again and set off for my workshop as quickly as I could.

I was half-expecting to find Radixrapum waiting at my door, demanding the money that I owed him, but although the street was crammed as usual with passers-by – pedestrians and street-vendors and various scurrying slaves – the shop was closed and shuttered, as I'd left it yesterday, and there was no sign of the turnip-seller anywhere nearby. Neither did it seem that Junio and Maximus were here. Never mind, I would find a stool and sit and wait for them.

I went over to unshutter the door and go inside – I had

never invested in an elaborate lock – but the heavy board was not securely in place. I would have to speak to Gwellia and Junio about that; obviously they had not pulled it properly across the night before, though it seemed they'd shuttered the window space all right. The room was darkened as I pushed the door ajar.

I was about to enter, but suddenly I paused. I knew it was ridiculous, but now that I was here I was all at once reluctant to go into the room – the lingering memory of Lucius's corpse was too much in my thoughts. I even imagined that I could still detect a faint unpleasant smell. Besides, I told myself, the workroom had yet to be ritually cleansed (though I had spoken to the priest about it at the naming day), and if I were to enter it again, this morning's careful purification of myself would be undone. There was no need to go in there till the priest had been – I had my tools and everything I needed for the job I had to do, and Junio could meet me just as well outside.

So I reached around and found Minimus's stool, then took up my position in the outer shop, where I could keep a lookout for Junio when he came. However, I was not destined to be long alone. The tanner had come out into the street and was heatedly talking to a customer at his gate, clearly haggling about the price of skins. He looked over and saw me, and raised one hand in a surprised salute. He went back to his wrangling for a little while, but – though with his crossed eyes it was hard to tell – he seemed to be glancing in my direction all the time.

So I was not entirely astonished, when the deal was struck and his visitor had gone off with his piece of hide, to see my neighbour hasten over, wiping his hands on his sacking apron as he came and baring his one tooth in his gummy smile.

'My greetings, citizen,' he said in his cracked voice, raising his usual mumble to a louder tone. 'How nice to see you here.' His uneven eyes were nearly popping from his head and he was clearly bursting with surprise at seeing me at all.

I could not altogether fathom why. Of course, he knew

about the army cart – he'd mentioned it to Gwellia and my family yesterday – but nothing could be more common-place than my coming to the shop, if only to arrange to have it cleansed. Most likely he was simply curious as to who had died, and I was not anxious to encourage him, so I stripped off my cloak as though I meant to work and said blandly, 'Where else should I be? The naming day is over and I have contracts to complete.' To give emphasis to this, I reached across to my precious stockpile of imported stone and began to sort the contents according to the quality of colour and evenness of grain.

'Of course.' He looked embarrassed. 'Only I heard that you'd had some kind of accident. I was afraid . . .' he tailed off, spreading his stained hands apologetically. 'But I see that it was just another of Glypto's foolish tales.'

'Glypto told you I'd had an accident?' I looked up at him, surprised. I had half my mind upon the stones by now and, before I really thought it out, I blurted, 'Did you send a messenger to my house saying so?'

He looked at me as if I'd taken leave of all my wits. 'That I didn't, citizen. Though I knew that one had been. Your wife and slave both came here yesterday, and I called to assure them that I'd seen you safe and well . . .'

'Of course!' I murmured apologetically, selecting a particularly pretty piece of bluestone from the pile.

He ignored that observation, and went on, 'But when Glypto came to me this morning with this tale, naturally I assumed that they were right and I was wrong, and you'd come to some harm after you left here. And when he spoke of hearing someone on your premises, obviously I supposed that it was one of them come back. So what would be the point of sending to your house?'

It was my turn to boggle. 'Wait a moment. Let me under-stand. Glypto heard this *after* my wife and son were here?'

He gave the ugly grin that showed his solitary tooth. 'Haven't I just said so, citizen?'

I put the bluestone down and shook my head in disbe-lief. 'But this morning I was at the bulla ceremony of my grandchild at my house, and anyone who knows me knew that I was there. Even my customers attended or sent gifts. Who could possibly have come here to the shop?'

The tanner made that spreading gesture with his hands again. 'Probably there wasn't anyone at all. I told you it was only one of Glypto's tales – and he's half-crazy with the tanning fumes. He gets these things confused. He half-heard something from the courtyard in the dusk, I expect, and invented all these tales of people prowling in the dark. Convinced himself, I shouldn't be surprised.' He shook his head. 'Perhaps my wife is right, and I should sell him on.'

But I was hardly listening. 'In the dark?' I echoed. This wasn't making sense. 'I thought you said "this morning"?'

'That's when I heard of it.'

'But Glypto heard something from the courtyard "in the dusk". What was he doing there?' I had visions of him sending the old slave out at night on purpose to spy on my workshop through the gate.

However, I was disabused of that. The tanner looked abashed. 'My wife had left him out there as a punishment. She was so angry with him for staying out so long when he was supposed to be with you yesterday that she put him on short rations and shut him out all night. Gave him a pallet in the courtyard and told him to keep watch – that's how he came to hear the noise, or he says he did. He only half-hears things at the best of times.'

'What noise was this?' I was more and more intrigued. Was this the famous green man come again?

My neighbour shook his head. 'Pay no attention, pavement-maker. I should have known that it was just his foolishness. You are clearly fit and well, so what does it matter what he thinks he heard? Very likely it was fancy, and there was no one here at all.'

'All the same, I'd like to talk to him,' I said. 'I believe he sometimes sees more things than you suppose.'

A strange expression crossed the tanner's face. 'For instance, he insists that he saw the army calling here and taking a body from your workshop, just after he came back from giving you the coals.' He looked at me slyly. 'In fact, I thought I saw the cart myself and the soldiers putting something into it, though I could not be certain that it was a corpse. After all, as I said to my wife, surely you would have mentioned it to us if you had a dead man on the premises – especially since you came to borrow light and coals from us.'

I wondered how best to answer that without insulting him. 'But if there was a body, you knew it wasn't me,' I said, evading his unspoken question by asking one myself. 'Because you saw me leaving later on? So when my family arrived, convinced that I was hurt, naturally you were very curious?'

He seemed oblivious of any suggestion that he might have been deliberately spying on my shop. 'Exactly,' he went on in his curious cracked tone, 'and when I visited the shop – only to reassure your wife, of course – there was no sign that there had been any death at all, and your family clearly had no idea of one.' He sighed and made a small dismissive gesture with his hands. 'So I decided that Glypto was at his tricks again – which only goes to prove it's no good asking him. So I shouldn't bother, citizen.' He paused. 'Unless, of course, there's something which I don't know about?'

So that was it. He knew about the cart and he was offering to trade: information about the identity of the corpse in exchange for a chance to ask Glypto what he'd heard.

I abandoned all pretence at sorting stones and sighed. This tale would be all over Glevum before dusk. 'Well, it is a little difficult . . .' I began, thinking uncomfortably of Pedronius. 'It's a delicate matter and not wholly mine to share.'

He interrupted me. 'It concerns that decurion who came here yesterday, I suppose. People in high places – is that it, citizen?' He tapped his nose as if to indicate that he could keep a secret if he chose.

I clutched at the straw that he was offering. 'Well, in a fashion, I suppose it is.' It was not entirely a lie. Quintus could certainly be said to be involved. If the tanner chose to think there was something more to this and that I was somehow acting on the decurion's behalf, that was hardly my responsibility – or so I told myself.

My neighbour was looking expectantly at me. 'The body of one of the rebels from the wood, perhaps? I wondered if it was, and that's what Glypto saw. I heard a rumour that the ordo was resolved to sort them out before His Excellence returned, even if it led to executions without trial.'

'The dead man was not a rebel,' I said heatedly.

'So there was a dead man?' His tone was so knowing that I realized – too late – that I had made things worse and he was now convinced that I was conspiring with Quintus to conceal a death which might cause the councillor some embarrassment. There were obvious dangers in having that story circulate.

I made a swift decision. 'I'm afraid there was, though it wasn't a criminal, or any of my household or family. It was not even a customer, in fact. It was Lucius the pie-seller, who happened by chance to be calling at the shop because I'd given him a few things recently.'

'Great Mars! What happened?'

'He was overcome quite unexpectedly, it seems, and died. And when you saw me with the turnips, I was on my way to tell his mother. She was happy that the army was going to bury him because she didn't have the means of doing so herself.' I was folding my cloak into a parcel as I spoke and putting it into a space below the counter-top (no doubt where Minimus had kept his knuckle-bones), so that I did not have to look the tanner in the face – although there was nothing actually false in this account. I simply hadn't mentioned the most essential bits – murder, robbery and the disappearance of my slave.

He looked rather disappointed. 'Just a pie-seller? A man who might as easily have dropped dead in the street? And what has your wealthy customer to do with that?'

He was too insistent – and too intelligent. I decided that the truth was now my best defence. I leaned a little closer, as though the paving-stones had ears, and murmured, 'I wasn't anxious for the news to get about, because I was working on a commission at the time and I was afraid the customer would cancel. It is Pedronius, and you know what he's like. He might imagine that the work was cursed, because I'd come across the corpse right in the middle of constructing it. I was halfway through preparing the site to put it in when I came back and found the body in my shop.'

He evidently revelled in the confidence. He nodded sagely. 'I can see how Pedronius might worry about that. Just as well the mosaic wasn't in your workshop at the time – but I can vouch that it wasn't, if you ever should need me to. Might be worth a few sesterces to you some time, citizen.'

I was on my guard. Was he attempting a spot of black-mail? 'What do you mean by that?'

'I would have seen it when I called in to see your wife last night, of course.' He gave me a peculiarly furtive cross-eyed grin. 'Funny a pie-seller should choose your workshop as a place to die. And to think that I was in there shortly afterwards and never knew.' He tapped his nose again. 'Well, I can see that you don't want the story spread around, but – considering that I lent you light and embers yesterday – you might satisfy my curiosity at least. Where exactly did you find the corpse?'

It was a kind of blackmail – of a moral sort. I tried to deflect it. 'You could come in and I'd show you if I'd had the workshop cleansed, but, of course, I haven't, and we don't want to court ill luck.'

It would take more than bad omens to put the tanner off. 'I was in there with your family, so it makes no difference. I'll make sure I ritually wash my hands and face and make an extra sacrifice to the household gods tonight.' He gave me that one-toothed grin of his again. 'Some of us are very careful about that sort of thing.'

I knew when I was beaten. I could see what he would do if I refused to let him in – spread the story that my shop was cursed because I didn't pay proper homage to the gods. 'There is nothing particular to mark the spot,' I said forlornly, but it didn't help. He was already waiting at the door. I led the way into the inner room, crossed to the window space and took the shutter down.

'Over there—' I was about to gesture vaguely at the place when I stopped abruptly short.

The tanner beside me caught his breath. 'Great Mars and all the gods!'

For there was something on the floor, almost exactly where Lucius had been. Something in a tunic and horribly inert. I had been right in my suspicion of a smell. There was a body lying sprawled out on its front and it was very clearly dead.

The tanner turned to me. His eyes were strangely bright. 'Is that the pie-seller? The army brought him back?'

I shook my head, too full of shock and grief to speak, for I recognized the lifeless object on the floor. The last time I had seen it, it was a living man and he was shouting 'Turnips!' in the street.

Seventeen

I turned Radixrapum gently over, but I knew what I would find. The same cruel biting mark of rope around the neck, the bruise where the ligature had been savagely pulled tight, the same protruding tongue and purpled face. But where Lucius had still been pliant and, if not actually warm, at least no more than cool, my poor turnip-selling friend was as cold and rigid as a stone image of himself. Already, over the scent of sweat and turnips, the distinctive sick-sweet smell of death was beginning to appear. He had been dead for hours – if I had not seen him myself the previous afternoon, I might have wondered if he'd been killed with Lucius.

There were other signs as well that this was not a recent death. Blood was already pooling in his arms and thighs, as I could see where his tunic had ridden up them to reveal the flesh. I am no medicus, but I know that this occurs when the body has been lying in one place for several hours. But not this place, necessarily, I thought.

I looked again. There was evidence of abrasion all across the skin, from his ankles to his armpits, as I soon ascertained, and on both front and back, though worse across his chest and around the tattered modesty binding that he wore round his loins. There was no doubt that the scuffing had happened after death. And the toes of the sandals had scraped fresh tracks on the floor, right across the area where the Apollo piece had been. Like the pie-seller, this man had been killed elsewhere and dragged in here afterwards.

I let him roll back on to his front again, so that I was not obliged to look at his distended face, and stepped back abruptly. I was upset and furious. The death of Lucius had been a shock, but somehow this one upset me even more. I had not known the turnip-man very long or very well, but he had proved himself to be intelligent, and when I was in trouble, he'd set out to help: that was almost a definition of a friend.

'Citizen!' The agitated exclamation brought me to myself. The tanner was tugging at my toga in dismay. 'This man did not just die. Somebody killed him! Strangled, I would say. Look at that red mark around his neck.'

I had forgotten that he did not know the details of the earlier death. I nodded wearily.

'Robbed him of his purse too, by the look of it,' the tanner pointed out. 'It has been chopped through at the cord where it was hanging at his belt.'

I hadn't noticed that, but it was significant. If Radixrapum had been killed and robbed last night, then Minimus was already locked up in a cell and could not have taken any part in it. I looked at the severed loop that the tanner was pointing at. 'You are right, of course.'

The tanner was delighted by his own cleverness. 'So, pavement-maker, you are not the only one to notice things, you see,' he said with glee. 'Though you have a reputation for solving mysteries.' Then he saw my face and asked more soberly, 'But I see this person was a friend. Do you know who did this?'

I shook my head. 'I only wish I—' I was interrupted by a noise outside. Almost without thinking, I picked up a heavy hammer from the table-top, ready, if necessary, to defend myself. 'Who is it?' I said loudly. 'Come in and show yourself.'

There was a moment's silence and then the door was pushed ajar – and there was Junio, my adopted son. I dropped my makeshift club.

'What is the matter, Father?' Junio began. 'You sounded quite alarmed. Were you expecting trouble? It is only me. Maximus is following. We have found the boy who . . .' He caught sight of the body. 'Dear Jove! Another one?' He came over and peered more closely at the corpse. 'And the same killer, by the look of it. The method seems to be exactly what you had described from yesterday.'

The tanner looked from my adopted son to me with an

expression of astonishment. 'You mean the pie-seller was murdered too?'

It was no good blaming Junio – he didn't know my neighbour as I did – but I felt my heart sink to my sandal-straps. It would be extremely difficult to hush the tanner now – this story would be all over Glevum by tonight. Any chance of quietly locating Minimus and solving this before my patron came would almost certainly have disappeared – along with most of my likely customers.

Junio looked apologetic, but it was too late. The tanner was already saying in his cracked and mumbling voice, 'And you kept the knowledge from me?' He was obviously aggrieved.

This was going from bad to worse. He would spread rumours that I knew more about these murders than I wanted to reveal. I could imagine what my fellow citizens would make of that.

There was no help for it. I seized him by the arm. 'Of course I kept it from you.' I almost hissed the words. 'Be thankful that I did. It was obviously safer for you if you didn't know. Look at the turnip-vendor. He knew that Lucius was murdered yesterday, and now see what's become of him. Would you want to end like that? Can't you see that we are dealing with a ruthless killer here?'

The tanner had turned pale, even under the dark colour of his trade. 'You mean he only died because he saw the other corpse? I knew that he was round here yesterday, but I didn't realize . . .' He tailed off. The morbid, gleeful interest was gone, and he was staring at Radixrapum now, his boss-eyes glazed with fear. 'You think that he was killed so that he couldn't talk?'

I shrugged. 'What other explanation can there be? He knew about the other body and what was done to it. That's the only connection I can see between the two.' In fact, I realized, this was no more than the truth, and it was disturbing. It did seem that Radixrapum's death had been to silence him. And warn me to silence too. Why else choose my workshop as the place to leave the corpse? Or was there some other connection that I couldn't see?

'I suppose it's possible the two of them were friends,'

Junio ventured in a doubtful voice. As usual, he had been following my thoughts.

I shook my head. 'I don't believe so, from what Radixrapum said to me. He only knew Lucius distantly by sight – and that would accord with his reaction when he saw the corpse: shocked and appalled, but not personally upset. In fact, his chief response was curiosity, I think.'

'And now he's died for it,' the tanner said, obviously beginning to apply this to himself.

I nodded grimly. 'It rather looks that way. Which means that all of us may be in danger too.' I was increasingly aware that this was very likely true. 'You, for instance, tanner. The fewer people who know that you've been here, the better for us all.'

The tanner stared at Radixrapum. It was not a happy sight. 'You'll have to tell somebody about the corpse,' he said. 'You can't just leave it here. Has he got family who'd come and bury him?'

I realized that I did not have the least idea, or any real notion where Radixrapum lived beyond the fact that it was out of town. But it was likely that he had a wife and family, and possibly a plot of land where they could bury him – in that respect at least, he was distinct from Lucius.

'I'll report this to the garrison,' I said. 'They'll have to sort it out. Radixrapum was a farmer so he probably paid tax. If so, the authorities will have a note of it. If not, no doubt they'll send the army cart to move the corpse again.' Thank heaven I had spent today in front of witnesses, I thought, and had a driver who could swear he drove me home the night before. I might have found it difficult to explain the presence of a second dead body in my work-shop otherwise.

The tanner had another unhappy problem on his mind. 'Burial or carnal pit, it makes no difference. In either case, the killer will know that you were here.'

I looked at him, surprised. 'He'd know that anyway.'

'Not necessarily,' Junio put in. 'If he was a comparative stranger to the town, he might have thought that no one was using the workshop currently – when Lucius was killed, it was mid-afternoon and there was nobody in sight. Though he knows by now the shop is occupied, since the first body has been moved away.'

I was about to point out that he knew that anyway, because there had been work in progress on the floor, but I remembered the tanner's wagging tongue and held my peace.

'That's right,' the tanner said, referring to what Junio had said. 'You go to the army and you make it clear you've seen the corpse. If you are right about his motive for strangling this man, then you . . .'

'Must be in danger too.' I was ahead of him. 'Exactly so. He must expect that I would come back to this room again – if only to arrange a ritual cleansing of the place – but he need not know that I had company. So, tanner, be careful that you don't reveal the fact. If you value your own safety, and your family's, it is essential that the killer doesn't know that you were here.'

My warning was hardly needed, it appeared. The tanner gulped. 'You can rely on me. I shan't say a word to anyone at all. Not even to my wife. In fact, if you'll excuse me, I must get back to her.' He made as if to move towards the outer shop and street, but as he reached the entrance he stopped and turned to me. 'Though I shall have to think of something to tell Glypto, I suppose. Do you think that this strangling' – he gestured to the corpse – 'was what he heard last night? There was likely to have been a struggle, don't you think?'

I shot a warning glance at Junio, who seemed about to speak. 'I'd like to talk to Glypto, as I said before,' I answered. 'He may yet know something that may be of help. If you could send him to me, I will deal with him – or, better still, allow him to go out to the midden-pile a little later on and I'll keep a watch for him and try to meet him there.' I didn't mention that Glypto was expecting that.

The tanner sighed. 'Safer than having him come into your shop and see the corpse and put himself in danger as a consequence? That is sensible. I suppose the killer must be watching quite nearby, or he would not know that the turnip-man was here. Oh, great Jupiter!' His cracked voice was getting higher and higher in distress. 'In that case, he'll see me leaving, as sure as Greeks are Greek. There's no back entrance to your workshop as there is in mine. Oh dear Mars, I wish I'd never come.'

I glanced at Junio. This was an outcome I had not foreseen. I had hoped that the tanner would make haste to leave, but, instead, it seemed I'd frightened him too much to go at all. 'I'm sure the killer isn't watching now,' I said. 'I was sitting for a long time on my own outside the shop, and there was absolutely nobody suspicious in the street. I would have noticed it.'

The tanner looked a little mutinous. 'He must have watched the place. How else did he know about your turnip-selling friend?'

'Supposing you are right, and he's a stranger to the town. He kills and robs poor Lucius and leaves him in my shop. He may have come back later on – perhaps to move the corpse – and seen the turnip-man outside the door (which is where I left him when I came to you).'

Junio nodded. 'He may even have supposed that this was the shopkeeper and decided that for safety he must be murdered too. Presumably he followed Radixrapum when he left and chose a quiet moment where he could strangle him.'

'It is even possible the turnip-man led him straight back here. I owed him money so he may have returned, and that would have strengthened the impression even more that this was the owner of the premises,' I went on. 'So, we assume, the killer strangles him and leaves him in the shop, presumably believing that he is safe by now. He surely wouldn't want to linger near the scene in case he drew unwelcome attention to himself.'

The tanner was not comforted at all. 'I suppose all this is plausible. But it is only supposition. If you're wrong, I'm trapped.'

'You could get out through the window space,' Junio observed. 'I think it's wide enough, though you're not very tall. Father and I would have to hoist you up and let you drop the other side. That would bring you into the alleyway that leads down to the pile. It is a little smelly, but it should be safe enough.'

To my astonishment, the tanner looked relieved and, far from rejecting the suggestion as absurd, began at once to think of ways in which it could be done. 'If we brought the table over, I could stand on that . . .'

It was a tight fit through the window space. The man was rather stout, but he was so determined that he managed in the end – at the cost of bloodying his elbows on the shutter-slots. It was not a very dignified descent – he landed in a tangle in a smelly pool – but he picked himself up quickly and, without a backward look, hurried down the alley that ran out to the lane.

Junio and I watched him scuttling away. It would have been comic in any other circumstances, but I was hardly in a smiling mood.

Junio was the first to leave the window space. He gestured to the corpse. 'The tanner was correct about one thing anyway. You knew the murdered man and liked him very much. I see that in your face.'

I nodded. 'This is the man I told you of, who helped me yesterday – which meant he saw too much. If he hadn't done so, I'm sure he'd be alive.'

'So you meant what you said earlier? You really believe this murder was just to silence him?' Junio looked and sounded unconvinced.

'What other explanation is there?' I demanded. 'He saw the other corpse. It is the only link.'

'Apart from the fact that they both sold things in the street,' Junio pointed out.

'But it is hardly likely that there's someone stalking round the town, strangling innocent street-vendors and dumping them on me. I rather think that whatever happened here, it must be something close to what I outlined to the tanner – although, as he rightly said, it is only speculation. I have no proof of it.'

Junio was looking at me with an odd expression on his face: a mixture of pity, concern and disbelief. 'But of course there's a connection. A much more likely link.

Are you really going to tell me that you don't see what it is?'

I turned away. 'Well, there is the manner of their deaths, of course, but I can't see what else. We don't even know where Radixrapum was when he was killed, though I'm fairly sure that Lucius was on his way to see me yest—' I broke off. 'You mean that that's the link? Coming to this workshop?'

He shook his head at me. 'I think it's more than that. Other people came here – Quintus did for one – and he seems to be all right. And so did Gwellia and the rest of us last night. And the tanner, come to that. What did the dead men see that we did not?' He looked triumphant. 'The Apollo piece!'

I had to acknowledge that he had a point, though it was hard to imagine what there was about the pavement that could pose a threat. I said so to Junio. 'Besides,' I added, 'I've seen the pavement too, and so have several of Pedronius's slaves, and up to now, at least, no harm has come to us.'

'I suppose you're right,' he acknowledged ruefully. 'A lot of people saw the pattern too – including me – before the thing was laid. The finished product can't be different and dangerous, unless you take Pedronius's superstitious view and think it's genuinely cursed.'

I laughed, but there was something niggling in the corner of my brain, some other connection that I could not place. It was disquieting. A little shudder ran down between my shoulder blades.

I was about to say as much to Junio when there was a sudden noise outside the shop, followed by a rapping on the outer door.

Eighteen

I was startled for a moment, but Junio grinned at me. 'That will be Maximus and the messenger,' he said. 'They were on their way. I was about to tell you when I first came in, but then I was distracted by discovering the corpse.'

'So you found the boy who brought the message to the roundhouse yesterday?'

He nodded. 'We asked around and it was easier to find him than we thought. That urchin-girl we spoke to knew who it was at once and was eager to help us, for a tip. She even took us to the building where he lived – a flood-damaged ruin in the swampy part of town, where lots of the egentes find shelter overnight. He wasn't there himself – he'd found another errand, taking a urine-pot to one of the fullers in the town – but we tracked him down, and he promised that when he'd finished he'd come and tell you everything he knew. Maximus was going to wait for him and show him where to come—'

Another knock, more tentative this time.

Junio strode to the doorway. 'Shall I let them in? Or . . .?' He nodded towards Radixrapum's body on the floor. 'Under the circumstances . . .'

'Perhaps you'd better not,' I agreed. 'I'll go and talk to them outside.' I was already crossing to the entrance as I spoke.

'I'll come with you,' my adopted son replied. 'In fact, if the lad wants to earn an *as* or two, we might even send him out when we have finished with him here, to make enquiries as to where the turnip-seller lived. There must be someone in the marketplace who'd know.'

He pushed open the door and we went outside, blinking a little in the stronger light. I was already fishing in my purse for a small coin to reward the little messenger for his

willingness to come. But it was no street urchin who was
awaiting us. It was Virilis, my patron's messenger, complete
with military hooded cloak and now with a letter-wallet at
his belt. Clearly it contained some kind of document – from
the shape, most likely a sealed official scroll. For a moment
I wondered if he had been sent with some authority for my
arrest. He seemed equipped for it: as we emerged he was
swishing with his whip at one of the piles of uncut stone
that lay outside my door.

However, he looked as startled to see us as we were to
find him there and, far from being threatening, he came
over with a smile. 'Citizen Libertus, I am glad to find you.
I thought the shop was empty when I first arrived and there
was no immediate answer to my knock. I have just come
from Quintus, who has instructed me to ask if you have a
message that you wish me to convey to His Excellence
Marcus Septimus. I am on my way to meet him, starting
off at once.'

'Really?' I was genuinely surprised, not only by Quintus's
apparent change of heart but also at the idea of setting off
at such an hour to anywhere as distant as Londinium. It
would be dark before he'd covered many miles, though
doubtless as an official messenger he would have access to
the military inns, where he could change horses, rest and
have a meal. 'You mean to leave tonight?'

'Ready and saddled to depart at once, as you can see.'
He gestured to his horse, which he had clearly been leading
through the streets and which was now tied to a tethering
ring outside the tanner's house. 'I am to report the delib-
erations of the curia and the appointment of his nominated
candidate. I should be in Londinium in a day or two at
most. So if you have a message . . .' He smiled at me again.
'About your missing slave perhaps? Quintus Severus seemed
to think you might.'

'Ah!' I murmured. So that was it. The chief decurion had
not regretted his unhelpfulness, as for a moment I had fool-
ishly supposed. On the contrary, he intended to ensure that
Marcus was informed that Minimus was lost. 'No doubt
Quintus told you that I have some news? It seems the boy

has been arrested on a trumped-up charge and is in custody. I'm not entirely sure where he is being held.'

Junio, beside me, made a startled noise. I had forgotten that this all was news to him as well.

'And you wish me to pass this information to your patron?' The cursor cocked a brow at me.

Something in his manner made me think again. 'It might be wiser to wait until he comes,' I conceded. 'Of course, I'll have to tell him all about it in due time, but perhaps it's better if he hears the story from my lips. Besides, I hope that later on today I can discover where the boy is being kept and get him freed, if only on the promise of producing him in court. Or, failing that, at least to speak to him.'

The cursor made a doubtful face at me. 'What makes you think his captor would agree to that?'

He was right, of course, but I said stubbornly, 'The law requires him to. I am not an expert on such things, but I am sure of that.'

I expected Virilis to be anxious to be gone and impatient of these legal niceties, but instead he flashed me an unexpected smile. 'I believe you may be right,' he said in his most charming voice. 'I was witness to a case like this once, in Londinium. The matter came to court and the magistrate decreed that the prisoner had to be produced so they could speak to him. He wasn't freed, of course, but it proved that he was safe.'

I was privately ashamed of my earlier churlishness. 'Go on,' I said.

'The plaintiffs were people of no account in law – just the wife and child and a former slave – so it seems that anyone can make a legal claim, if they can prove they have an interest in the prisoner, that is.'

'Who has a better right to see Minimus than me?' I demanded of no one in particular. 'I am his legal owner while Marcus is away, and I want to hear his version of what happened yesterday. I simply don't believe he took that purse.' I turned to Virilis. 'No doubt you've heard from Quintus about the troubles here?'

Virilis gave me a knowing, unexpected smile. 'Oh, indeed

I have. Quintus talked to me of very little else. He said that when he got here, you'd come across a corpse – some one-eyed pie-seller with a disfigured face – and he'd had to send the army to take it to the pit. He seemed to feel the entire episode was a personal affront.' He gave me a sympathetic grin. 'Do you wish me to tell your patron about it when we meet, or is that another thing you'd rather leave till he arrives?'

He paused, and for a moment I considered this.

'Before you answer, citizen' – he gestured to the document wallet at his waist, and I would have sworn he winked – 'perhaps I should mention that I have a letter to deliver under seal. It's possible that Quintus has mentioned it himself.'

It was a friendly warning and I smiled my thanks. 'Then perhaps you'd better tell my patron everything – including the fact that I've mislaid his slave. But make it clear that nothing's certain yet, and it may be just an accident that I found the corpse at all.' I outlined my theory of the empty shop, and how the killer simply used it as a place to hide the corpse, meaning to come back later and hide the evidence. 'I'm pretty sure the murder didn't take place here at all,' I finished. 'Lucius was dragged there after he was killed.'

Virilis looked suitably impressed. 'What makes you think that?'

'The dragging of the body left scuff tracks on the floor. And I have a witness to prove it . . .' I tailed off in dismay, remembering that Radixrapum was now lying dead himself. 'Or I used to have.'

If Virilis had noticed the last remark, he gave no sign of it. Instead, he nodded briskly. 'Then I'll tell your patron that. And I'll give him an account of your grandson's naming day. I daresay you would like me to convey your thanks for his handsome gift?'

I nodded, embarrassed to have forgotten all about the bell. 'I would be very grateful. I should have thought of it, but with all that has occurred . . .'

He gave me another conspiratorial smile. 'Of course. You

have had a great deal to worry you of late – what with murder and robbery and a missing slave. But never fear, I will express your thanks for you. And now, if you'll excuse me, I must be on my way or I shall never reach Corinium before dark, let alone the staging post I'm aiming for tonight.' He glanced up as he spoke. 'Besides, it may take a little longer than I'd planned. I see it's going to rain.' He gave a little half-ironic bow. 'Your servant, citizens.'

He turned away, picking his way along the muddy street towards his horse.

I paddled after him. 'But you've forgotten something. You have news for me, I think. Something you said you wanted to impart?' He turned towards me, frowning, and I pressed the point. 'Something regarding my patron, I believe.'

The face cleared, but now it was his turn to look a little abashed. 'Ah, of course! But I fear that matters have over-taken me, and it is no longer of very much account, especially now that the ordo has voted as it did. Besides . . .' He caught my glance and gestured towards Junio with his eyes. It was clear that he would tell me nothing more in front of witnesses. 'In any case, Marcus will soon be here himself and no doubt he'll give you his own account of things.'

I was not satisfied with this evasiveness. We had reached the tethered animal by now, and as he reached up to untie the knot which held it to the ring, I insisted in an under-tone, 'This news about my patron, Virilis. Can you not give me some idea of what it was?' I looked around. 'Quickly, while we can't be overheard?'

He laughed a little ruefully and looked up and down the street, but there was nothing of importance that I could see, at least – only the usual customers and tradesmen passing by, and Maximus in the distance hurrying this way, with a small figure tagging at his heels. But Virilis shook his head. 'In this colonia, citizen, the very stones have ears. We cannot be too careful.' He grasped the front pommels on the saddle as he spoke and swung himself effortlessly up and into place.

'You think that there are spies?' I was genuinely shocked. It was possible, of course. Commodus was famous for his network of paid ears and eyes. If Lucius and the turnip-man had fallen foul of one of these, for some reason that I could not see, this put a completely different complexion on the deaths. 'But . . . here? In this humble area of town?'

He stooped down over his horse's neck to answer, in an undertone, 'I am sure of it. Mark what I'm saying, citizen. I speak of what I know. Be careful for yourself. With the present threat from the rebels in the woods, the Emperor has informers everywhere – often the people that you would least expect.' He gestured with his head towards the workshop door, where Junio was still standing, staring after us.

I shook my head, indignant. 'I can't believe my son . . .'

He laughed. 'Of course not, citizen. That was not what I meant. But there are others . . .' He broke off and gestured with the handle of his switch. 'That odd-looking fellow skulking in the alley there. Who is he, for instance? I'm almost certain he's been watching us, though every time I look at him he pretends he's not.'

I followed the direction of the pointing whip and saw ancient Glypto hovering by the pile. I waved at him and he went scuttling off, apparently to put something on the midden-heap, his great boots squelching loudly in the mud.

I grinned. 'That's my neighbour's servant. There's no harm in him. It's simply that he wants to speak to me – he thinks he heard something in my workshop overnight.' I thought about confiding the green man story too, but there was no time for that.

The cursor looked at Glypto with amused contempt. 'Then you should hear him out, perhaps – I'm leaving anyway.' He raised his voice 'Hey, you there!' But Glypto did not even turn his head, just tipped the contents of his bucket on the pile and scurried back into the tannery, leaving the front gate wide open in his wake.

Virilis turned the horse's head towards the road and smiled wryly down at me. 'I wish you good fortune with your witness, citizen – he doesn't seem anxious to run into you.'

To my surprise, I found myself defending the old slave. 'His master thinks that he is addled with the fumes, and certainly he only hears a half of what is said, but I doubt he's as foolish as they all suppose. He might have seen something of what happened yesterday. And I think that he'll be back. I promised him money if he met me at the pile and could me tell anything which proved to be of use.'

Virilis threw back his handsome head and laughed. 'Perhaps he'll buy himself some more conventional attire, instead of that ridiculous loincloth that he wears.' He appeared to compose himself and said more soberly. 'I'm sorry, citizen. I hope that you are right, and he comes back again and you learn something that will lead you to your slave.' He made a little face. 'Though a reeking midden-pile seems an unlikely choice of meeting place.'

I grinned. 'I know. But one where it is easy for a slave to come. He is sent out with rubbish a dozen times a day.'

Virilis nodded. 'I suppose that's true. But in the mean-time, here's another slave who obviously hopes to have a word with you – bringing a companion with him, by the look of it.' This time his switch was pointing down the street, where Maximus was hurrying towards me, accom-panied by a form I thought I recognized.

'Oh, great Mercury!' I muttered. 'He's brought the wrong boy, after all. That's not the messenger that we were looking for! That's one of the egentes that hangs around the town, and if he went to my roundhouse – which I didn't think he had – it's only because I sent him there myself.'

Virilis gave me another conspiratorial smile. 'It seems that you have further troubles, citizen. And I am a messenger myself, as you are well aware, with many miles to ride. It is time I went.' He touched his plumed helmet in a gesture of farewell. 'I'm sorry that I've not known you better, citizen. But, like that slave from the tannery, I too shall be back, if only to bring news of Marcus's reply. I look forward to the next time that we meet.'

And, waving his whip-hand, he trotted gently off, his horse picking its way neatly along the rutted street. The last I saw of him he had turned the corner past the tanner's shop and had raised his pace, riding out towards the military road that would lead him to Londinium and my patron's side.

Nineteen

'**M**aster?' Maximus was waiting politely at the door – a well-trained slave will never interrupt, unless it is a matter of enormous urgency.

I went across to him. The little slave was grinning with obvious delight. 'I have brought the messenger that went out to the house.' He gestured to a child following down the street. 'We managed to locate him. Did the young master tell you that?' He broke off. 'Why what is the matter, master? Is there something wrong?'

I was about to answer when the youngster hurried up, squinting at me as though he could not believe his eyes. It was indeed my little urchin of the day before, and he was even grimier than he'd been yesterday.

'Is this some kind of joke? This is the very man who sent me all that way, and on a wasted errand too! I didn't recognize him until I got up close, because he's in a toga like a proper citizen, but he was only wearing a tunic yesterday.' He turned to Maximus. 'Have you brought me all this way to make a fool of me? Asking me to tell him what my instructions were! Why don't you ask him? He gave them to me, he must know what they are—'

I held up my hand to silence him. 'Wait a minute. Do I understand you right? You did go to my roundhouse with the message after all?'

The urchin looked at me defiantly. 'Of course I did. What else did you suppose? Ran all the way as well, but when I got there, there was no one there. Absolutely no one. Just a waste of time. Or was that another joke at my expense?'

Junio had been behind me listening to all this. 'This is no joke, believe me. You didn't think to leave a message at the house next door? There was someone there. It is my house, and my wife and child were in all afternoon.'

The boy looked baffled. 'Why should I do that? I just

did as I was told. I went to the roundhouse I was directed to and found no one there. Well, what was I to do? There was no written message I could leave behind, and I can't write myself. I waited for a little while but nobody turned up, so there was nothing for it but to come back again.' He looked at me slyly. 'Besides, I reckoned that if everyone was out, it wouldn't matter if you were late or not. So I came back to town. And what thanks did I get? Not even an extra quadrans for running all that way.'

I can take a hint when it is broad enough. I took out the coin that I'd been fumbling with and held it out to him. 'I'm afraid I misjudged you. I thought you hadn't been. And I'm doubly sorry to have dragged you over here to no avail.'

The boy took the money in his blackened hand. 'So that's all you want from me? When I might have been earning something on the street this afternoon?' He sounded disappointed.

'We were really looking for another messenger – one who was sent to the roundhouse later on,' Junio explained apologetically. 'But neither Maximus nor I was there when he arrived – or when you did either – so we didn't know . . .' He stopped. I'd made a startled sound, and he turned and gazed at me. 'What is it, Father? I recognize that look: you've thought of something?'

I realized that I was standing open-mouthed. 'But don't you see? It wasn't later on!'

Junio looked puzzled. 'I don't know what you mean.'

'The other messenger! It wasn't later on! Think it through a moment. When I gave this boy my message to take back to Gwellia, letting her know that I was likely to be late, I was on the way to lay that mosaic at Pedronius's house. Agreed?'

My son nodded doubtfully. 'That is what you told me. So . . .?'

'It might have taken – what? – perhaps an hour at best for this boy to reach the roundhouse, and by that time . . .'

Junio made a whistling sound between his teeth. 'Of course! The other messenger had already been. Gwellia and Kurso were on their way to town.'

I looked at the urchin, who had turned away and was now testing his reward between his teeth. 'Did you pass anyone in the lanes when you were running to the house? Anybody walking? A woman and a slave?'

The ragged child took the coin from his mouth and tucked it somewhere in his tunic folds. 'Now you mention it, I think I might have done, although I can't be sure. I didn't pay much attention at the time – I was too busy running to get my errand done.'

I knew what that meant. 'Would another quadrans improve your memory?'

The urchin grinned at me. It was the first time that I had ever seen him smile and it was not a pleasing sight. Most of his teeth were missing and the remaining few were black and broken. But there was no mistaking his sincerity as he said, 'I did see someone going the other way – an older woman in a cape of Celtic plaid.'

I exchanged a look with Junio. 'That could be my wife. She had a slave with her?'

The urchin nodded solemnly. 'A skinny boy with just a flimsy tunic on. That's why I noticed them. I remember thinking that he was going to be freezing later on because the wind was rising. Even I've got another tunic under this,' he raised his hem, to show the truth of this, though the undergarment was so stained and torn it was scarcely recognizable as cloth. 'Left home in a hurry, without a cloak, I expect. Come to think of it, they had an urgent sort of air as if they needed to be somewhere fast and they'd had distressing news.'

I nodded. 'That was them all right,' I said grimly and ungrammatically, remembering that Kurso had later borrowed my own birrus to come home. I found the promised coin and held it out towards the boy, then drew it back again. 'You didn't see another messenger at all? Another errand-runner from the streets? He would have been ahead of them from what I understand.'

The urchin's eyes did not move from the coin, but he shook his head.

'You seem very certain?' I held the quadrans high.

He did look at me then, as he said earnestly. 'I mean it, citizen. I'm sure I would have noticed if I'd passed a messenger. And if he was a street-boy from anywhere round here, I'd recognize his face. We egentes try to keep out of each other's way by day – so we aren't all working the same area of town – but we often club together to keep a watch at night. Sometimes we even share what we've earned, especially if somebody has been paid with food or has the makings of a fire.'

'So you know all the locals – by sight at least?'

He nodded eagerly. 'Not only their faces, but what jobs they've found each day and, very often, how much they were paid. We generally share that information, so we know what to avoid. So if anybody else had been sent out to your house, I'm sure I would have heard. I was complaining what a long way I had run, and how little I had got for it.'

I did not acknowledge the implied rebuke. 'Which suggests that the messenger was a newcomer – from out of town, perhaps?'

His grimy face wrinkled into a doubtful frown. 'That's the funny thing. I would have heard of that as well. We do get passing beggars hanging around, trying to earn money on our streets, doing the jobs we otherwise would do. So unless there's something special – they're old or very sick – the word gets round and we go and warn them off. There are too many starving egentes in Glevum as it is. But there's been nobody like that, so I can't imagine who it could have been.' He shook his head. 'Unless he was a private messenger, of course. Now, is that everything? The sun has clouded over and it's coming on to rain, and that drives people from the streets so if I don't hurry, I won't find another job today.'

There was already a trace of drizzle in the air, but I persisted. 'This was not a courier, from what I hear of him. He was an urchin, very much like you. And it seems he should have passed you on the road.'

'Well, I didn't see him,' the boy said with some asperity. 'I didn't see anyone of that kind at all. I only saw a horseman, riding southwards with his son, and an ancient woodman with a cart. Oh, and a shepherd with a flock of sheep – I came around the corner and they were taking up the track. I had to dive off into the woods to get around the beasts, but I struck back to the main path as quickly as I could.'

'You didn't try to take a short cut, then?' Junio put in.

The urchin looked impatient. 'I didn't trust the forest tracks – it's easy to get lost unless you know the trails. Besides, I'm sure I heard the howl of wolves, and they say there are rebel bandits in those woods – I didn't want to blunder into them by accident. I suppose this other messenger of yours might have passed in the moments when I was off the path. Now, are you going to pay me or keep me standing here until it rains in earnest?'

I let him have the coin. He didn't test it this time, just hid it where he had put the other one.

Junio laid an urgent hand upon my arm. 'So that may be your answer, father. Either that or the other messenger knew the forest well, in which case he might have taken a short cut through the woods. Perhaps we'll never know. Is it significant?'

'It might help us judge exactly when the false messenger was sent.'

He nodded thoughtfully. 'Whoever sent him must have done so very early on, while you were visiting the pie-seller's mother, perhaps. Certainly not long after—' I gave a warning cough and he broke off in dismay.

I shook my head at him, and he had the grace to blush. He was obviously about to mention Lucius's corpse, and we didn't want the urchin learning about that.

'. . . after you parted company with the turnip-seller,' he finished lamely, signalling with his eyes that I'd stopped him just in time.

I turned to the skinny little messenger, who was smoothing his filthy tunic round his knees again, as though that might offer more protection against the threat of rain. 'Which brings us to another matter. Would you care to earn another coin?'

The boy looked rather doubtful. 'You want me to go running all that way again?'

I laughed. 'No, this time it is something rather different. I spoke just now about a turnip-seller. Do you know the man?'

'The fat one who comes to Glevum once or twice a week, selling his turnips from a handbarrow?' He gave a brief unflattering account. 'We egentes call him "Turnip-head".'

I nodded briefly. 'That seems to be the one.'

'You want me to find out where he is and take a message?' The urchin gave me a calculating sideways look. 'That might take a little time. I haven't seen him on the streets today, and if he's on his turnip farm, I hear that's miles away.'

'But you do know where it is?'

'Not exactly, but I could very soon find out. I know a market stall that he occasionally supplies – I think the man who runs it must be a relative, because sometimes the turnip-seller rides home in their cart. I'm sure the market-trader could direct me to the place.' He flashed his blackened teeth in a triumphant grin. 'Might cost you another as or two for me to go that far, of course.'

I made a swift decision. 'Of course. So I shall not require you to go. But bring me the stallholder within half an hour, before . . .' – I glanced up, but it was already drizzling and there was no way I could estimate the time from the position of the sun. So I improvised – '. . . before the rain fills up that pothole in the road, and you will get your quadrans. Is that understood?'

The boy was a little disappointed, I could see – he had been looking forward to a larger tip – but he nodded glumly. 'You don't want me to look for Turnip-head himself? He may be in the town. I saw him yesterday – just a little while before you came along. Though, come to think of it, until I saw his face I didn't realize who it was – he seemed to have some kind of half-built pavement on his . . .' He brightened. 'Oh, I suppose that it was yours, and that is why you want to send a message to him now? Wouldn't it be easier to have me bring him here? The stallholder might not want to come until the market shuts, and by that time I could have found old Turnip-head himself.'

I shook my head. 'I don't think you could. As it happens, I know where he is and you will not find him on the streets today. Bring me the stallholder and that will suffice. Tell him that it's urgent – there's been an accident. Now,' I added, seeing that he was still havering, 'that's all you need to know. I've offered you an errand. Do you accept or not?'

'Oh, I accept,' the urchin said, 'though it'll take a long time for the rain to fill that hole. You can already see that it drains away as soon as it arrives.' He gave an impudent, triumphant smirk and started off at once, skirting the piles of dampening hides outside the tanner's house.

I turned to Maximus, who had been looking increasingly perplexed.

'I am sorry, master,' he began, 'I brought you the wrong boy. If I'd known, I could have brought you the stallholder instead. Why didn't you send me back there, instead of using him?'

I looked at him wryly. 'Would you know which stall-holder it was?'

He saw the force of this. His freckled cheeks turned pink and he bit his lower lip. Then he said, to cover his discomfiture, 'But what's all this about the turnip-man? Is he the one that had the accident? Is that the explanation for the other messenger?' His voice was so shrill with embarrassment that a passing oatcake-seller turned to look at us, balancing his tray of increasingly soggy goodies on his head. I was suddenly conscious of Virilis's warning about spies.

I took the little slave-boy very gently by the arm. 'You'd better come inside,' I murmured. 'There's something here that you don't know about.'

Twenty

When Maximus saw the body on the floor, he turned so deathly white I thought that he would faint. It was a ghastly spectacle, it's true, but the strength of this reaction shocked and startled me. As I'd said to Radixrapum himself the day before, there are worse sights at the side of every road. And my slave had not even known the turnip-seller.

Perhaps he had never seen a strangled man before and he was less accustomed to the sight of murdered men than I had come to be. But I was startled to see him shaking like a willow leaf. 'Maximus?' I murmured.

He came across and almost huddled close to me, as though tempted to bury his face in my toga hems, like the child he was. He did not speak. I realized that he was close to vomiting with fright.

I put a hand on his shoulder. 'I am not surprised that this distresses you. But try to compose yourself; we may require your help.'

Maximus looked up at me. His face was taut with fear. 'You think that the people who did this have kidnapped Minimus?'

So that was it! Of course, I should have guessed. He did not know what I had discovered about his fellow slave's fate!

I crouched down beside him and looked into his face. 'I promise you, Minimus is safe from this, at least,' I said. 'He is somewhere in the colonia under lock and key, accused of robbery and awaiting trial.'

It was strange information to make him so relieved. 'So he is safe?'

'Comparatively so.' I owed the lad the truth. 'They found him with incriminating evidence, it appears. He may have been ill-treated to force him to confess, but almost certainly he is alive.'

'That will be pretty grim, but I suppose it's better than being questioned by brigands in the woods,' Junio chimed in. 'Can we arrange to see him and help with his defence? Could Quintus be persuaded to admit us, do you think? I assume it was Quintus who arrested him? I heard what you were saying to Virilis at the door.'

I realized that this was true. He'd heard what I had told the cursor, and he'd made what seemed an obvious inference. I struggled to my feet again to ease my aching knees, but my heart was heavy with the news I had to break.

'It wasn't Quintus who arrested him,' I supplied, flapping rather ineffectually at my tunic hems, which now bore the marks of stone and plaster from the floor. 'Or the town watch, either,' I added dismally, as well-trained Maximus hastened to assist, kneeling at my feet to brush my garments properly.

'So it must have been the troops,' Junio said at once. He glanced triumphantly at me, looking for me to commend him on his skill for thinking logically. 'Well, Father, you know the commander of the garrison, and Marcus Septimus has some sway with him, so if they're the ones who've got him locked away, it should be easy for you to . . .' He tailed off, looking at my face. 'Not the garrison . . .?'

I shook my head. 'That's the worst of it. I don't know who it is. Minimus was taken by someone's private guard – I have discovered that much – but I don't know whose they were or where they've taken him. If I did, I would be trying to get him freed by now, though it might require a hearing before a magistrate. Even Quintus has no information, so he says, although the arrest was made on his authority, so he may know rather more than he pretends.'

Maximus looked up, struggling with tears. Years of serving in a Roman house had taught him not to weep. 'But, master, he's accused of robbery, you say? That can't be right. Minimus wouldn't have stolen anything, whatever proof they think they might have found.'

'I am quite sure of that,' I told him. 'But whoever arrested him may have to be convinced.'

Maximus nodded dumbly and went back to his task.

'It must be someone of importance, to have a private bodyguard,' Junio put in. 'Even Marcus doesn't have one as a general rule. A slave or two, perhaps, to clear a way for him.'

'And an armed escort following behind, to protect him if there's any kind of incident,' I pointed out. 'He is a very important person after all.'

'Exactly,' Junio said triumphantly. 'So is this some kind of public official, do you think? It's against the law for private citizens to carry weapons in the streets, and how else could someone have effected an arrest?'

I considered this a moment. 'It is hard to say. There's certainly been fashion this last moon or two for wealthy citizens to keep a bodyguard – supposedly to protect them in case the rebels strike.' It was true. One increasingly saw little groups of burly slaves beside litters and generally accompanying their masters around town, though I had assumed it was generally more for show than anything.

'I think it was a fashion which began in Rome – they say the Emperor is so afraid of plots against his life that he has a hefty escort everywhere he goes.' Junio laughed. 'Marcus will probably effect one when he comes.'

I nodded. 'He is not the only one. I've seen a dozen people accompanying one man, all carrying batons, wooden clubs and staves. It may not create the same effect that swords and daggers would, but it makes for an ugly picture nonetheless. And an effective deterrent, I suppose. That's probably the sort of guard our mystery person has.'

Maximus wasn't listening. He wore a puzzled frown. 'But why should he do it? Arrest Minimus, I mean.' He gave a last flick to my toga hem and, glancing up to be reassured that I was satisfied, climbed to his feet again.

'Presumably he'd heard there was a warrant out,' Junio said at once. 'So it must have been someone who met Quintus after he left here and stopped to talk to him. Someone who hoped to gain favour or reward by fulfilling what he thought was the chief decurion's wish.' He was clearly reasoning aloud and looking to me for agreement as he spoke.

I nodded my approval of his analysis. 'That's certainly a possibility.'

'Though, in that case, wouldn't Quintus have known who took the boy? Or worked out who it was?' Junio mused.

I looked at him wryly. 'And you don't suppose he did?'

He slapped his hands together in irritation with himself. 'I am an idiot! Of course. If the man was a favoured protégé of his, it's likely that Quintus would say exactly what he did – that he had no information – though no doubt he had a very good idea. But couldn't we find out? This person must have been in Glevum yesterday, shortly after the litter had left here, and that should give us a useful place to start.' He brought his hands together with a triumphant clap. 'Find a rich man who met Quintus on the street and you have found the man who captured Minimus. It's the only possibility. Until then, only you and Quintus even knew there'd been a crime.'

'Apart from whoever throttled Lucius, of course,' I said drily, echoing what Radixrapum had once said to me.

My son looked chagrined. 'I had forgotten him. But naturally, you're right. In fact' – his voice was eager now – 'not only was the murderer aware there'd been a robbery, he had a lively reason for arresting Minimus – if only to deflect suspicion from himself. But then there was the purse they found on him . . .' He paused and looked at me. 'Oh, great Jove! I should have thought of that. The murderer could easily have cut that off himself and simply pretended that he'd found it on our slave! What could be more—' He broke off as there was a tapping on the door.

Events had made us nervous. We exchanged a startled glance.

'That can't be the urchin back again so soon,' I said. 'He wouldn't have had time to fetch the stallholder by now. Indeed, he would scarcely have had time to leave the street. More likely the tanner come to have another look!' But I picked up my heavy hammer as a weapon all the same, before I said to Maximus, 'You'd better answer it, as usual, to make it seem that things are normal here.' I gestured to the corpse. 'But don't let anybody come inside. I'll be right behind you. I won't let you get hurt.'

The slave-boy nodded nervously. He half-opened the door, then, to my surprise, disappeared round it and shut it after him. An instant later he was back again, looking much relieved. 'It is the urchin, master, but he hasn't been to town. He has a message for you from the tanner's house, he says, but he won't reveal it except to you alone. I think he has been told that there might be a tip.'

I nodded. 'Very well, I'll go and speak to him. In the meantime, you two, deal with things in here. Junio, set some candles round the head and use my birrus to cover up the corpse.'

'It won't bring curses on us, master?' Maximus blurted out, with a look of superstitious terror on his face. 'Dealing with the body of a murdered man?'

I was about to say that I had done so yesterday, and so had Radixrapum, but I saw the flaw in that – in the light of what had happened since, this remark was hardly likely to allay his fears. Instead, I told him gently, 'It will make no difference now – we will have to purify the workshop and ourselves in any case. Besides, the best way of soothing an unquiet ghost is to afford its mortal body proper rituals.'

'That is why you want to find his family, I suppose, so they can arrange a funeral?'

'Exactly. And to call him by his proper name and put money in his mouth to pay the ferryman. In the meantime, we will treat the body with respect. I will come and help you when I've spoken to our little messenger.'

With that, I slipped round the door myself and went out into the street.

The drizzle had set in, in good earnest by this time, and the urchin was waiting there impatiently, hopping from foot to foot among the stones and trying to find shelter close against the wall, but he stopped at once when I appeared and stood there silently.

'You have a message for me from the tanner, I believe,' I prompted, remaining in the shelter of the doorway as I spoke.

The ragged child looked doubtful. 'I don't think it was
a tanner – not the man I saw. An old man in a loincloth
who said he was a slave. Gypso or Glyppo or something
of the kind. He said that you would recognize the name.'
Rain was dripping from his hair on to his ragged tunic as
he spoke.

I frowned. 'I know the man you mean, and he's indeed
a slave. But what was he doing sending you to me?' It was
a reasonable question in the circumstances. It isn't usual
for servants to send private messengers, especially to somebody who only lives next door.

The boy rubbed his wet nose with a grimy hand. 'I don't
know, citizen. Perhaps the fellow's mad. I rather thought
he was. The message that he gave me was very strange
indeed, but he swore that it was important and you would
want to know.'

I was still frowning. 'Then why did he not deliver it
himself?' I did not add that I had an arrangement to meet
him later on.

'I think he would have done.' The scraggy urchin rubbed
his nose again, then wiped his fingers on his tunic skirt.
'He said to tell you he'd been looking out for you, but
hasn't had a chance to speak to you alone. He doesn't know
how long he can keep coming to the pile, especially now
that the rain is setting in. His mistress is suspicious of him
running in and out and is threatening to punish him if he
does not tend the fire.'

I allowed, rather grudgingly, 'That makes a kind of sense.'
I glanced towards the tannery, fearing that Glypto was being
soundly whipped. But there were no sounds of anguish from
the compound opposite. Indeed, there was no sign or sound
of anyone, although the gate was open and, despite the rain,
a rack of skins remained forlornly on display.

'Well, I'm glad to hear that it makes sense to you, citizen.'
The skinny shoulders shrugged expressively. 'Nothing he
said made any sense to me and I had to shout at him to tell
him anything. I was tempted to ignore him and go straight
on into town to find that stallholder, but the slave was so
insistent that I decided to come back – in case it was as

urgent as he said it was.' He looked at me slyly. 'He even suggested that you'd be prepared to pay.'

'Then you'd better tell me what the message was,' I parried. 'Another half a quadrans for you when you do.'

'Well . . .' He ran a nervous tongue around his grubby lips and burst out in a rush, '. . . he told me to tell you the green man was here again.' He paused and looked defiantly at me. 'There! I told you it was nonsense—'

I interrupted him, trying to work out the implications of the news. 'When was this, did he tell you? Did he see the man? Or did he only hear him in my workshop overnight?'

The urchin shrugged his shoulders. 'I don't know any more. That is all he told me.' Drips of rain were running down his face by now, making little paler channels in the dirt – he had given up attempting to wipe the water off. 'I didn't believe a word of it, in fact – just thought that he was moon-crazed and tried to humour him. Green man, indeed! But I see it does mean something – I can read it in your face.'

I was cursing my carelessness in betraying that – I did not want the urchin telling tales around the town. 'It's just his name for someone,' I said, as airily as if I knew exactly who was meant. 'But thank you for the message, and I am prepared to pay – when you come back with the stallholder. But be very quick, and this time make sure you're not waylaid!'

'I will be faster than the wind,' he promised, and – judging from the pace at which he set off down the street, his worn-out sandals flapping and squishing through the mire – he meant to try to make that promise good.

Twenty-One

I had promised to help my son and slave with the task of affording some dignity to Radixrapum's corpse, so I went back to do it. (I do not altogether believe in tales of vengeful ghosts haunting the place where their mortal bodies had not been shown respect, but I certainly didn't want to take unnecessary risks.) The two of them had been busy in my absence: the floor was swept and cleaned, and they had turned the corpse over and laid it on its back. Junio had spread my birrus over it and, with Maximus's help, he was now setting tapers at the head and feet.

Junio looked up at me as I came in. 'What did the tanner say? You didn't ask him for some embers to light the altar fire again? That would be useful. We could light the candles too. I know we brought some tinder, but that wouldn't be as quick, and if you're talking to the tanner . . .'

I shook my head. 'The message wasn't from the tanner after all. It came from Glypto, that ancient slave of his.'

Junio got to his feet, dusting his toga down, though the floor had been sprinkled with water from the jug and his hems were not as dirty as my own had been. 'Anything of interest? I know that he heard noises in the workshop here last night at dusk. Does he know who it was?'

'He says he saw the green man here again.' I frowned.

'So that is almost certainly our strangler,' Junio said. 'The green man was nearby when both the victims died.'

'Monsters?' Maximus looked up. He was in the act of setting the taper on a spike and he almost impaled his finger in his evident alarm.

Junio laughed. 'It's all right, Maximus. Father doesn't mean some creature from the underworld. It's the just old slave's word for somebody he saw, very close to this work-shop, when Lucius was killed. The trouble is we don't know why Glypto calls him that – it doesn't seem that he was wearing green. We wondered if it might have been because he limed his hair.'

The little slave-boy was looking much relieved. I had forgotten that he hadn't heard all this before – Gwellia had whisked him off to bed while I was telling Junio the tale last night.

'So the message was really that the murderer was here? But we already knew that, because we found the corpse. I wonder why it was so urgent to tell you, in that case.'

'But Glypto couldn't have known that,' I reminded him. 'He hadn't seen the body of the turnip-man.'

'The tanner did, though,' Junio put in. 'Do you think, in spite of everything, he might have told his slave?'

'I doubt it very much, but we can soon find out. We'll act on your suggestion. Get the empty brazier, Maximus, and go next door and ask the tanner for some coals.'

'But don't *you* want to talk to Glypto?' Junio enquired.

'Certainly I do, but since it's obvious I have a slave with me, it would look remarkable for me to go myself. If Glypto is not able to meet me at the pile – as, from his message, I presume he won't – it will give the tanner an excuse to send him over here, without his wife suspecting anything. In the meantime, I will go outside and see if by any chance I'm wrong and Glypto has somehow contrived to get away.'

'Let's hope he has done,' Junio said to me as Maximus scuttled to obey. 'You will learn a lot more from him on his own, though the coals will be useful in any case, of course. In the meantime, I am to stay here and guard the corpse?'

'If the stallholder should come while I'm away, try not to let him in. You know what to tell him. I want to trace where Radixrapum lives, so I can send and tell his family what's befallen him.' I looked at the unhappy bundle on the floor. 'I shall be lucky if they don't suppose I murdered him myself. I'm fortunate that the tanner is so inquisitive – otherwise I would have no witness that the man was dead when I got here today, and that there was no corpse here last evening when I left.' I left him to it, hoping to find Glypto waiting at the pile.

Despite the drenching drizzle, it was a relief to be outside, away from the increasingly sick-sweet smell of death and the silent reproach of Radixrapum's corpse. I paused for a moment to retrieve my cloak, happy to be breathing the fresh air again. I glanced towards the tanner's house, expecting to see the small form of Maximus, but the gate was still ajar and there was no sign of anyone. Indeed, the whole street was deserted now – all the normal passers-by had taken shelter from the rain – so I wrapped my cloak around myself and set off squelching down the little alleyway in the direction of the midden-pile.

But the alleyway was empty; you could see that at a glance. Only the raindrops splashing on the pile and washing little eddies of filth towards my feet, and a pair of drenched and starving dogs, fighting over something on the far side of the heap. There was no Glypto anywhere in sight.

The dogs had stopped at my approach to snarl ferociously at me, baring their yellowing teeth in a distinctly threatening way, and I had no wish to tangle with their jaws. I left them to their unspeakable supper and beat a swift retreat back into the more salubrious surroundings of the street. As I emerged, I saw Maximus come out on to the road – accompanied by the tanner – through the open gate next door. The page was carrying the brazier of embers, I was glad to see.

The tanner saw me and came hurrying across. He too was wrapped in a heavy cloak from head to foot against the rain, and he peered closely at me from underneath the hood, each of his boss-eyes glinting with concern. 'Citizen Libertus, I thought that it was you. What have you done with Glypto? My wife is very cross.'

'But—' I was beginning to protest, but he waved the words aside.

'The daft old fool has let the fire go out, he's been away so long, and the whole of the mixture must be done again, she says. She's blaming me, of course. Says I should never have agreed to let him talk to you at all.'

'But—' I said again.

'Well, I didn't mean to tell her, but you know what she's

like. She wormed it out of me that I'd agreed that he could come – though I didn't tell her about the corpse, of course – and my life won't be worth living if he's not back at once. She's threatening to leave and take her dowry too. I don't care how important his information is, you'll have to send him home.'

'But I haven't seen him,' I said, when he paused and allowed me – at last – to get the sentence out. 'I came out to find him, but he wasn't at the pile. See for yourself.' I gestured down the alley-gap.

He stared in that direction, but there was clearly no one there. Even the dogs were silent, gnawing at whatever stinking thing they had found among the heap. The tanner threw a baleful look at me.

'And he isn't in your workshop?' he said suspiciously.

I shook my head. 'Why, in that case, would I be out here in the rain, looking for him?' I demanded.

The tanner looked non-plussed, biting his lip with his remaining tooth. 'Well, if you haven't got him, where in Dis has the old fool got to? He wouldn't run away.' The eye in my direction glared at me. 'Unless he'd heard about the murders taking place next door. He did see the army take away a corpse. That might have frightened him, I suppose.'

I frowned. 'There may be something in that,' I conceded thoughtfully, to my neighbour's evident surprise. 'He did send a message to me a little while ago – not personally but by a messenger – to say that he had seen the green man here again. That might account for why he isn't here.'

The tanner boggled. 'You don't believe that tale?' He gulped. 'Though they do say that corpses from the under-world turn green-skinned as they rot. You don't think—'

He broke off as Maximus gave a yelp and dropped the brazier on the ground, spilling half the contents in the miry damp.

'Absolutely not,' I said severely. 'If Glypto had seen a walking corpse, or any kind of ghost, he would have told us so – in graphic terms, no doubt. He simply said 'a man' and I'm sure that's what he meant. He even heard him speak

– quite normally, it seems.' I turned to Maximus, who was
still whiter than the toga of a candidate, and said as matter-
of-factly as I could, 'Maximus, pick that brazier up and
take it to the shop, and light the candles while that ember
is alight. Don't stop to pick up the others that you dropped,
just take the one you have. Hurry up or this rain will put
that out as well.'

The little slave looked up at me and nodded thankfully.
He picked up the brazier and trotted off with it.

'And you'd better light the fire on the altar too, while
you are about it,' the tanner called out after him. He turned
to me apologetically. 'You can't be too careful when spirits
are about. And I'm worried about Glypto. Where do you
think he's gone?'

I shook my head. 'I've no idea,' I said. 'Taken shelter
somewhere, if he's got any sense. And we should do the
same – he clearly isn't here.' I turned as if to go.

'Wait just a minute, citizen!' The tanner tugged my cape,
which was distinctly damp by now, and made it impossible
for me to move away. 'Didn't I hear that you had lost a
slave yourself? I'm sure I heard you telling Glypto so the
other day – I was just inside the gate and I couldn't help
but hear. It's true. I see it in your face. Oh, great Dis,' he
added in his strange rasping tone, 'do you think some
madman is creeping round the streets, murdering tradesmen
and kidnapping the slaves?'

'My slave has been arrested,' I said unwillingly. 'By
Quintus's decree. I don't think the green man had any part
in it. Though I do think it's possible that he is the murderer
– though I don't know who he is, and I can't imagine why
he'd want to kill those men. And as for why he wanted to
leave the corpses in my shop . . .'

'Who knows? Perhaps he did it by mistake.' My neighbour clearly had no interest in discussing my affairs. He
was still holding me firmly by my cape and he shook it
with both hands as he said urgently, 'But Glypto heard the
green man talking. You said as much yourself. Suppose that
Glypto heard him speak again – last night, in your workshop – and recognized the voice?'

I could not counter this; I'd thought as much myself.

'Suppose it was the green man, and Glypto knows it was?' the tanner babbled on. 'You think that might frighten him enough to run away?' He paused, the raindrops dripping from his hood.

I shook my head. 'In that case, surely, he'd have done it earlier. I saw him at the midden-pile a little while ago.'

The tanner looked doubtful. 'I suppose he would have had the opportunity. He must have been out there a dozen times today.' His grip was slackening.

'Exactly.' I extricated myself gently from his grasp. 'Whereas, if he was feeling under threat, surely you'd expect him to try and stay inside – not seize every opportunity to go into the street. Yet he sent me that message not half an hour ago, because he hadn't managed to speak to me alone and didn't think he could contrive to get outside again.' I looked at him. 'You're sure he hasn't had an accident indoors? Fallen into one of your tanning vats, for instance?'

'Dear Mercury! I hadn't thought of that,' the tanner said. 'Or he might have hidden in a rack of skins. I'll go and have a look. And if you see him, for the love of Jove, send him home before my wife walks out on me, or there'll be another murder – in the tannery this time.' And he was gone before I even had time to answer him.

I turned back, rather damply, towards the workshop door and was about to push it open and walk into the dry when a brusque voice from the corner of the street prevented me. 'You the pavement-maker, are you?'

I looked up to see the speaker bearing down on me. It was not, as I had first supposed, a man, but a strapping woman in a full-length woven cloak. Her burly form was shapeless as a sack, her hands enormous and her feet – set on solid ankles – looked as large as mine and were encased in a stout pair of boots with wooden soles. Her hood was pulled up firmly around her head and it concealed her hair, but as she strode towards me I could see her face: round, wrinkled and weatherworn, with shrewdly bright grey eyes. I realized that this woman had been lovely once.

'I am Libertus, the mosaicist. You wanted me?' I said.

'On the contrary. I heard you wanted me. Something about my husband, as I understand. I gather you have news of where he is – well, I'm glad to hear it. I've been worried sick. Stayed up waiting for him half the night, with his dinner burning on the fire, and when he hadn't come this morning, I came to town myself. What has he done now? Got himself arrested or something, I suppose? Has he done something to offend the market police?'

I shut my eyes in horror. I had not expected this. It was no surprise that Radixrapum had a wife – it is next to impossible for a man to tend a field and sell his produce in the market without a family – and I knew that his death would be a fearful blow to her. But I had not for a moment envisaged meeting her and having to tell her the dreadful news myself. What made it worse was that, despite their differences in looks, this woman's practical good sense and clear intelligence fiercely reminded me of my own dear Gwellia.

'Come, pavement-maker,' she was saying, 'don't prevaricate. I know that you have news. I was talking to my husband's brother in the marketplace. He has a stall there, near the forum, and he often gave Radix a lift home on his cart when he had sold his turnips. So I was in the act of asking if he had any news when an urchin-child turned up and said you wanted him – my brother-in-law, that is. You had unhappy information about my husband, he explained, and were intending to send word to me, so naturally I got directions and hurried here myself.'

'And what happened to the messenger? I owe him something for his services.' I forced myself to look her in the face.

'I paid the boy what you had promised him,' she said with dignity. 'Two sesterces. I would have paid twice that to learn where Radix is.'

I mentally acknowledged the urchin for his ingenuity. It was a great deal more than I had undertaken for, of course, but I did not tell her that. This poor woman had sufficient woes. 'I fear you will not think so, when you hear the truth.'

The grey eyes clouded. 'Not the prison, then? I feared that the aediles might have marched him off, for giving short-weight coin or something of the kind. It has been known before when someone passed it off on him. But it is more than that – I see it in your face. There's been an accident? Or worse – someone has attacked him and he is lying hurt? I know there are rumours of rebel bandits in the southern woods.' Her eyes still searched my face. 'Dear Jove! Worse still? Don't tell me he is dead!'

I knew that I was witnessing the death of hope. I saw it written in those troubling grey eyes.

I shall not forget, until I die, the dawning pain in them as I said, as gently as I could, 'I wish that I could tell you otherwise.'

Twenty-Two

S he was magnificent in grief; I must acknowledge that. No wealthy Roman matron could have been more dignified. There was no screaming or shrieking or beating of the breast; only a sudden stiffening and stillness of her form, and one long juddering painful sigh to betray how deeply the news affected her. I could see that there were glinting tears behind her eyes, but she did not let them fall, though she pressed her lips together to stop them quivering.

'I'm sorry,' I said, sounding as helpless as I felt.

She didn't answer, just stood there staring at her roughened hands. Then, in a tiny voice that did not seem to come from her at all, she asked, 'What killed him?'

'He was murdered – strangled – set on in the street.' What else could I say? She would see him soon enough, and there was no softening the blow. 'I have no idea who murdered him, or why.' Then, after a moment, 'I only know it wasn't me, or mine.'

She dragged her gaze from somewhere centuries away and focused it on me. 'I didn't think it was.' Suddenly her face was tired and old, and all the beauty had gone out of it. 'Where is he? What have they done with him?' she said.

'He was dragged into my workshop, and I found him there today. We have covered him and lit some candles round his head—'

She cut me off abruptly. 'Take me there and let me see,' she said.

I took her the few steps to my counter and called out for Maximus. The little red-haired slave-boy was there at once, rushing to open the workshop door for me. When he saw the woman at my side, he gaped.

'This is the turnip-seller's wife,' I said, and stood back to let her in. The tapers at the head and foot were both alight, I saw, and the flame on the altar was also burning bright, but there'd been no attempt to light the workshop fire, perhaps for fear of heightening the pervasive smell, of which I was now painfully aware. She must have smelt it too, because she made a little noise and clapped both hands around her nose and mouth. However, she recovered instantly and strode across to where the body was.

Junio had moved over from the window space and would have greeted her, but she scarcely looked at him. She just said bluntly, 'May I look at him?'

I motioned to Maximus to move aside the cloak, expecting that when she saw the purpled and distorted face she would be much distressed, and as soon as she had glimpsed it, I made a sign to Maximus to cover it again. But as he moved to do so, she prevented him. She pushed back her hood, revealing a knotted plait of greying hair, and knelt beside her husband for a moment silently. Then, bending forward, she kissed that tortured brow. Only then did she rise and allow Maximus to put the birrus back.

'I will make arrangements to have the body moved,' she said in a voice that trembled on the brink of tears. 'As soon as possible. Thank you for doing what you could for him.'

Maximus was unable to disguise his sheer relief at this. He actually smiled, though he recalled himself at once.

Junio hastened to ask the widow courteously, 'Will you be able to arrange the rest yourself – find someone to provide a proper bier and herbs and everything? And what about a pyre? Our slave could assist you by running messages.'

She looked at him a moment as if he'd been speaking Greek or some other language which she didn't understand. 'I will arrange to have him taken home and given burial. There will be no pyre. Our family is Celtic and prefers the ancient ways. And as for the offer of your slave, there is no need for that. His brother and my son will help me bury him, and my two daughters will pick the herbs for me and help me put him in a winding sheet. We'll lay him in the ancestral grave-site just outside the farm, where his parents and our dead babies lie – that is what he would have wanted,

I am sure – and where I expect to join him, in my turn, very soon.'

There was an awkward silence. She would not welcome comfort – she was a stranger here – but it was hard to deal with shock and grief so deeply felt. I said at last, 'Then one of us will stay here till your family comes.'

It shook her into action. She said, in the gruff and businesslike tone she had used when we first met, 'I won't be very long – my son came into town today to help me search for him. Well, I have found him now. I'll send him and his uncle with a shutter board to carry him away. I'm sure my brother-in-law will find room on his cart and take it home for me.' She pulled the hood up round her head again and made towards the door. 'Thank you, citizens. I'm sorry for any inconvenience this may have caused to you. I will have your birrus laundered and returned to you, of course.'

She made me feel so helpless that I spread my hands. 'If there is anything whatever that we can do for you . . .'

She looked at me, the grey eyes glinting in the shadows of the hood. 'You can find his killer, citizen. Oh, I have heard of you. You have a reputation for solving mysteries, so that even His Excellence – with all the resources at his personal command – relies on the pavement-maker for advice. Everyone in Glevum is aware of that. Perhaps that's why the killer left the body here – simply to taunt you that you could not solve a crime left on your own doorstep, quite literally so.' She raised her roughened hands. 'By all the ancient gods of stone and tree, prove him wrong, citizen, and tell me who did this.'

I muttered something about trying to do that anyway, because I wanted to find out on my own account.

She shook her head. 'Simply trying isn't good enough. Promise you'll succeed. Tell me who would want to kill an honest, humble man like my poor husband there, who never did a bad deed in life and never had a single enemy.' Her voice was trembling, but with anger now, not grief. 'You tell me who it is and I'll go on from there. I won't just drag him before the justices – being thrown to the beasts is far too good for him – I'll call curses on his head that will make him writhe in this world and the next. So, if you really want to help me, citizen, that's what you can do. Find out who the killer is and let me know his name.'

I could hardly promise that, but I reiterated that I'd do my best.

She nodded abruptly. 'Then I look forward to your answer. Till then, good afternoon. I will send the shutter to you as soon as possible.'

She had reached the door by now. Maximus scuttled to escort her from the room, but at the threshold she turned back to me. 'And when you find out anything, make sure you send me word. Any market stallholder will tell you where I live.' And, this time, she was gone.

There was a startled silence. Junio looked at me. 'Her faith in your abilities is rather touching, Father, don't you think?'

I sat down on the corner of the workshop bench – the only place inside where there was room to perch. 'Embarrassing, I'd call it,' I said bitterly. 'Of course I'd like to find out who killed the men and put their corpses here. Anyone would want to solve the mystery of a body in their shop – let alone two bodies – and no motive one can see.' Maximus had poured a cup of mead for me, from the store that I kept underneath my workbench at the back, and – almost without thinking – I accepted it. 'I am no further forward than I was at the start.'

The mead was cold, of course, not warm and spiced as I prefer, and it was ill luck to drink in the presence of a corpse – unless it was a funeral libation to the gods – but all the same I took a sip of it. Somehow the thick liquid seemed very comforting.

Junio, however, waved his cup away. (If it had been Roman wine, I thought, he might have taken it!) 'You don't suppose that Radixrapum's wife was right, and that these murders were aimed purposely at you, just because you have a reputation in such things? Perhaps there was no real motive for the killings after all – simply that these people were on the doorstep here.'

I didn't answer. The idea seemed preposterous to me.

But Junio was warming to his theme. 'So it might have been significant that they were street-vendors after all, though it didn't matter who they were or what their business was. Perhaps the strangler didn't even know, since he attacked them from the back.' He paused, then shook his head. 'But, of course, it can't be possible. No one would murder random passers-by, simply to prove that he was cleverer than you. Only a madman would do a thing like that – and these murders are too cold to be the product of a raving mind.'

But suddenly I almost choked upon my mead. 'By Jupiter and all the gods, I do believe you're right.'

Junio gaped at me. 'You think that we are looking for a lunatic? Someone so crazed with self-importance that he'd do that to somebody?' He broke off and gestured to the unfortunate body on the floor.

I shook my head, still spluttering with mead. 'That isn't what I meant. Dear gods, why didn't I think of this before? Even the tanner said the murderer might have done it by mistake!'

Junio looked baffled. 'I don't know what you mean.'

'Think, Junio! You suggested that the murders were aimed purposely at me. Suppose that you are right?'

Junio sat down heavily on the trestle by my side. He had turned deathly white. 'Great Mars! You mean, the murderer thought that it was you!' He shook his head. 'Then it must have been someone who knew you not at all. Lucius was so ugly that you could hardly miss the fact—'

'Not from the back, he wasn't. He was much my height and build, and he was wearing an old tunic that I'd given him. And it seems that Radixrapum was murdered in the dark, though I don't know what he was doing at my workshop at that hour.'

'After he had been wheeling your pavement through the streets!' Junio said. Almost without appearing to notice what he did, he seized the second cup of mead that Maximus had poured and drained it at a gulp. He made a face. He didn't care for mead. 'So anyone who glimpsed him might have thought that it was you and followed him back here.

Dear Mercury! Father, it looks as if you're right.' He saw that I was frowning. 'You've thought of something else?'

'Only that Radixrapum left his barrow on the lane outside Pedronius's country house. I thought that he got into a wagon with a friend, but perhaps I was mistaken. My would-be killer could not have followed someone in a cart.'

'Your would-be killer!' Junio echoed disbelievingly. 'But who on earth would want to murder you? And why? I know that Marcus Septimus thinks highly of your mind, but – no disrespect, Father – you don't have influence, or serious wealth and power. I suppose a casual robber might set on you for your purse, as we thought had happened with Lucius at first, but two planned attempts to kill you? Who would benefit?' He shook his head. 'Perhaps the turnip-woman was right after all. It was a madman, pitting his crazed wits against your own. Besides—'

He broke off as there was a commotion at the door.

'The stretcher already?' I said to Maximus. 'You'd better go and let the bearers in.'

But it was not the stretcher. It was the tanner's wife, and her raddled face was a mask of what looked like rage and shock. She shouldered her way past Maximus and burst into the shop.

With one accord, Junio and I moved to stand between the woman and the cloaked shape upon the floor – to mask it if we could – but she did not so much as glance around the room. Even the now-pervasive smell did not seem to register. She sought me with her eyes and glared at me.

'I might have known that you would bring trouble on our house. I told my husband so, but would he listen? Of course not, he knew best – as usual. All this lending burning embers and sending our best slave to talk to you for hours – and not even making any charge for it. Well, you won't be talking to Glypto any more. I hope you're satisfied.'

'He *has* run away, then?' I said stupidly. 'I'm sorry if you think that was on my account. I think it was because of something he had seen which he thought was dangerous. He's doubtless hiding till he thinks the threat has past. I'm sure that you will find him.'

She gave me a look that would have withered stone. 'It was dangerous all right. And we've found him already. You'd better come and see.' And, without waiting for an answer, she turned and strode outside.

Junio and I exchanged a startled glance and, leaving Maximus to keep vigil on the corpse, we meekly followed her.

Twenty-Three

The tanner's woman did not turn her head to glance at us at all, but stumped imperiously on. She did not, as I expected, move towards her gate, but walked straight past it to the corner of the block and down the street that led towards the main road from the town. We were in the northern suburb here, just outside the gates, and I thought she was going to lead us to the high road further out, which was flanked with tombs and led off eastwards towards Corinium and beyond.

But, to my surprise, she doubled back again, down the narrow lane that led behind her premises and so back to the alley where the midden-pile was, so that we were now on the other side of it.

For the moment, however, I could not see the pile. The alleyway was narrow at the best of times, and now there was a crowd of people clustered into it, all of them craning to get a better view. One of them turned to glance as we approached and I recognized him from the tanner's works – he had been one of the people scraping hides the day before.

The tanner's wife had recognized him too. 'Out of my way, you oaf!' she barked. He backed away, and instantly a sort of path appeared, thanks to a general shuffle in the crowd. I realized that this was the workforce from the tannery. The stout little figure of the woman struggled through the gap, and as we tried in vain to follow her, she climbed up on a cracked pot at the bottom of the heap and turned to face the milling bystanders. 'Get back to your work, the lot of you. There's nothing more to see. Servus and Parvus, go and fetch a skinning board, and we'll put this on it and carry it inside, and send for the slaves' guild to take care of it. The rest of you – there's tanning to be done. Stay here another moment and I'll turn you on the streets.'

This outburst had an immediate effect. The two men that she had nominated – obviously slaves – trotted off at once in the direction of the house, and all the other workers seemed to melt away like dew. Junio and I were left alone with the tanner's wife and found ourselves able to approach the midden-pile and take a look at it.

This side of it had clearly been recently disturbed, revealing something that had been roughly hidden beneath the surface rubbish – something that looked at first sight like a pile of bones and rags. It was still partly covered by a piece of filthy sack, but I hardly needed to examine it. I understood, with sinking heart, what those dogs had been so excited by a little while before.

'Glypto?' I murmured, genuinely shocked. 'When did this happen?'

'I don't exactly know.' It was the tanner's rasping voice and I turned to see him standing very close behind. I had not seen him till that moment, though clearly he'd been there. 'One moment he was hobbling to and from the house, and the next he'd simply gone. It must be . . . I don't know how long . . . since I saw him last.'

His wife gave an impatient, disgusted little snort. 'Then you've even fewer brains than I supposed you had. The last time I summoned him, it was to stoke the fire in the tanning house. I watched him do it – he shirks it otherwise – and now it has almost completely burned away. That would take half an hour or so at least, and when I looked and found he wasn't there, the cauldron was not only off the boil, but it was starting to cool down. I was furious, of course. I had to stoke the fire myself to keep the tannage warm. That's why I wanted him so urgently – to bring more fuel to get it brewing up again – but I couldn't find him then, and we have been hunting for him for a long time since. So the answer to your question, citizen, is an hour, more or less.'

I nodded. That accorded with what I knew myself. 'Shortly after I saw him at the pile, when I was talking to the cursor on the street,' I said.

The woman glowered again. 'And whose fault is it that the poor old fool is dead?' she demanded angrily. 'If it hadn't been for you, and my foolish husband there, Glypto would not have been lurking in the gap, getting himself stabbed to death and buried in the pile.'

'Stabbed to death?' That was a real surprise. I hadn't taken a close look at the corpse, which was anyway still part-covered by refuse from the pile: the top half obscured mostly by the piece of sack, but the legs still under what looked like kitchen waste. I noted rancid fat and vegetable skins as well as hooves and bones and fur-scrapings from the nearby factory. I had caught a glimpse of bloodstains on the length of tattered loincloth I could see, but I'd put that down to the gruesome activity of the dogs.

'You are sure of that?' I'd supposed that he'd been strangled like the other two.

She gave a mirthless grin. 'It rather looks that way. Something pointed has made a hole between his ribs.' She wouldn't meet my eyes. 'Take a look yourself. I had them pull that piece of sacking over him. I didn't want the rats and dogs to gnaw him any more.'

I moved the piece of sack and knelt down on it myself – fruitless to try to save my toga now – and took a closer look at Glypto's corpse. He had been thin in life and he was thinner still in death, no more than a skeleton encased in wrinkled skin. The woman was quite right: there was a knife wound in the chest and it had bled a lot, not only on the loincloth but on the pile beneath – presumably fresh blood was what had drawn the dogs. They had gnawed the wound quite badly, and the arm as well, but the rest of the body was more or less intact. When I brushed off the rubbish, I could see the heavy boots – the skinny feet still in them – and the sight of the iron collar round the neck gave me a little jolt.

The knife, which had been carefully removed, had struck with deadly skill. There was no sign of struggle or of other injury, and the old face looked – oddly – more surprised than pained.

It was clear that, once dead, he had been shoved down on the pile, and some of the contents pulled down over him, though even if we had not known it for a fact, we could have deduced that the body had not lain there very long: the stinking wet of rotting waste had not had time to seep deep into the clothes, only to damp the edges, and the hair, though full of leaves and rubbish, was not matted to his head, despite the recent rain.

In fact, I thought, we should be grateful to the starving dogs. If they'd not been driven to scrabble in the heap and dig the body up, it might have lain there quite a long time undisturbed until it had disintegrated into rot itself, the stench lost in the general stink that always permeates the heap.

Junio was tugging at my toga sleeve – more like his slave self than my only son. 'Father,' he whispered, 'this proves that we were wrong. No one could stab Glypto thinking it was you. He doesn't look like you, or dress like you, or wheel your pavements round the street for you – none of the things we spoke of earlier.' He shook his head. 'Or is there a second killer, do you think? I suppose there could be – there's a different method used. Glypto wasn't strangled.'

I didn't answer. I got slowly to my feet. I was feeling very old. I turned to the stout woman still glowering at my side. 'Madam, I am sorry that you have lost your slave. I can see it is a blow. If I can prove who killed him, as I hope I may, there is a possibility that you could claim redress. I will let you know as soon as I have news. In the meantime, I see your slaves have come, bringing the skinning board to take the body on. No doubt the slaves' guild will arrange the funeral. Send me word when it happens, and I'll attend the pyre.'

The woman gave me a baleful glance. 'Claim redress!' she muttered. 'What? And buy myself another servant in his stead? You think that is so easy? You are nothing but a fool. Worse than my husband, if that's possible. Parvus and Servus, pick this body up!' She whirled around, to my astonishment, and almost spat at me. 'And don't go anywhere near his funeral, do you understand? He was my slave, and you killed him, whatever you may say! As surely as if you'd plunged that knife in him yourself. So don't pretend you're sorry and come snivelling around his pyre.' And following the slaves, who had scooped the body up, she seized her silent husband by the arm and marched, as rigid as a centurion, back down the alleyway and round towards her door.

Junio looked helplessly at me. 'Just because you told her that she might claim redress. That's hardly gratitude.' He frowned. 'You don't suppose she did the deed herself? Stabbed him in a fit of rage, because she found him out here at the pile again when he was supposed to tend the fire? She might have done. She's quite strong enough, and there's plenty of sharp knives in the house – after all, they use them for skinning all the time.' He was warming to this theory now. 'Suppose she came out carrying a blade, struck him harder than she meant and killed him, more or less by accident. Wouldn't she have tried to bury him a bit – scrabble a bit of the rubbish over him – and then sent in for help, pretending she'd just found him? By her own admission she put the sacking over him. Perhaps it wasn't even such an accident.'

I put a fatherly hand upon his arm. 'I don't think she killed him. I think he was killed because of what he knew – and most likely by the strangler himself.'

'But we know she hated him. She flogged him dreadfully, locked him out all night, kept him with that chain around his neck—' He broke off. 'Oh I see. Glypto always wore that heavy collar round his neck. Even if the strangler had wanted to slip a cord around his throat – like he did the others – he couldn't have done so, because that was in the way?'

'Exactly so,' I said. 'Using the knife may have been an unexpected last resort.' I went towards the midden as I spoke, half-wondering if there was a way to clamber over it, but it was far too high. High enough, as Glypto had observed, to hide a child – or a corpse – that was on the other side. I cursed myself for my lack of curiosity when I'd come out to search for Glypto in the rain. I turned and began to walk the long way home again.

Junio trotted after me. 'Well, I still think there is something strange about the tanner's wife.' He was reluctant to cede the argument. 'She was behaving very oddly after he was dead. You don't think it was guilt?'

'On the contrary,' I said, pausing at the corner to let him reach my side, and dropping my voice in case the tanner was in earshot just beyond the wall. 'She always acts like that. In fact, if anything, I think she's feeling grief.'

He looked at me, puzzled. 'Grief? For Glypto? But she despised him. She was always saying so. She thought he was a fool. She was always threatening to get rid of him.'

'But she never did. And if her husband had ever tried to sell him on, she would have left the house and taken her dowry with her – he told me that himself.' I saw his look of blank bewilderment. 'Glypto had been her slave since she was just a girl. She treated him appallingly, of course, as you so rightly say, but, in her own peculiar way, he was probably the only thing she ever cared about. And I think the tanner knows it.'

Junio swallowed and said pensively, 'And he put up with it? Simply to keep the dowry, I suppose. I wonder what will happen to that household now?' He stared thoughtfully towards the rear entrance of the tannery, which we were now passing. Clouds of acrid smoke were pouring out of it and swirling round the lane – obviously the tannage process was in full swing again. 'Perhaps it will help if we can solve the crimes and find out who killed Glypto. At least she cannot blame you for it then, as she seems prone to do.'

I said heavily, 'But the tanner's wife is right. I am very much to blame. Glypto was killed because he tried to come to me, to offer information. I did not see the danger and I let him down.'

'It's not your fault that someone planned to murder him.'

I paused at the corner of the street to say, 'I don't believe that Glypto's death was planned – not like the other two. I think it went like this. The murderer found out that Glypto knew too much and that he was planning to meet me at the pile, so then, of course, he knew he had to act. He kept a watch for Glypto somewhere close nearby and found him loitering in the alley-gap. It was raining by then and there was no one else about, so he took the opportunity to slip a knife between his ribs and covered him quickly with rubbish from the heap, thus giving himself the time to make his own escape before the body was discovered. And he might have got away with it, if it wasn't for the dogs.'

Junio looked at me. 'You seem very certain – almost as if you'd worked out who the green man is.'

'I wish I had,' I told him. 'But every time I think I have an answer to all this, something happens which makes me change my mind. But don't let's stand and talk about it here. As Virilis told us, the street has ears and eyes, and there is still the problem of Radixrapum's corpse. But we must talk it over – I am sure there's something very obvious I've missed – and very soon indeed. I need to solve this mystery before my patron comes. There might be dreadful consequences for us otherwise.'

Junio misunderstood my train of thought. 'Because the strangler is still after you?' He sounded quite appalled. 'Of course! He has already made two attempts upon your life – if our deductions so far prove to be correct – and both times he failed. So you are still in danger. Don't stay here in the street. The strangler might be somewhere very close nearby, and, as the tanner said earlier, he may be watching us – as he was obviously watching Glypto too.'

'He can hardly strangle both of us at once, and I'm quite certain that he works alone. As long as there is someone with me, I should be quite safe,' I said, wishing I believed it.

But Junio was already tugging at my arm. 'Come back into the shop. Maximus and I will try to make quite sure that you're not left alone at all – not until the killer has been caught.'

I submitted to his pleading and permitted him to hustle me towards the workshop door – just in time to meet Maximus coming out of it.

Twenty-Four

'Ah, master – and young master – there you are at last.' Maximus was breathless with relief. 'I did not know what had become of you. The turnip-seller's son and brother have arrived to take away the corpse. They brought the tailboard from the cart to put him on and a blanket to put over him, so I have let them in. I'm glad you're here now – you can talk to them.'

I nodded and went in, but there was little to talk about, in fact. The two men had already put the body on the makeshift bier. Shrouded by the blanket, it seemed less grotesque, and the presence of fresh herbs and flowers, which they'd obviously brought, gave at least the impression of a normal funeral. When Radixrapum made his final journey through the streets, he would attract no special stares. I was glad of that for him.

The brother – there was no doubt that they were siblings, he was so like Radixrapum that it was startling – had folded up my birrus and put it carefully aside and was now engaged, in silence, in sweeping down the floor, using a broom-bundle we kept by the wall. His nephew – another, younger version of the same – was walking behind him, sprinkling the brushed area with drops of water from the jug.

The younger man looked up as I came in. 'We have done our best to purify the place,' he said. 'Sprinkled some ashes from the altar over there, just as we would have done if we had been at home.'

It was hard to know how to reply to this, but I thanked him rather awkwardly.

The uncle turned a pair of grey, distrustful eyes on me. 'It wasn't our idea. My sister-in-law told us to. Seemed to think that you'd been kind to her, and to my brother, though I can't see how. If I had my way, I'd have the town watch here and have you marched off to the magistrates, but she swears you didn't do this and will find the man who did.' He shot me a scornful look. 'Well, I hope she's right. Perhaps at the same time you can find out why anyone should want to see my brother dead. He was a kindly man who never did any harm to anyone. On the contrary, he always tried to help.' He vented his feelings by swishing viciously at the corners with the bunch of broom.

'He was trying to help me,' I admitted with a sigh. 'I think that's why he died, though I don't yet know for certain who was responsible.'

The young man stopped his sprinkling and said very quietly, 'Go on.'

'I've tried to piece together what must have happened here. I think your father came back to the shop to see me late last night, because I owed him money for—'

Radixrapum's brother interrupted me. 'Well, you are wrong already. He never came back here, and I can swear to that. He came to see me in the market in the afternoon – quite late, not long before I'm usually packing up the stall – and said he had an errand to run outside the gates. He had something on his barrow, a pavement of some sort ...' He looked around as if the thought had just occurred to him and added bitterly, 'I suppose that it was yours. He was going to deliver it to Pedronius's house, he said.'

I nodded and was about to tell him more, but he went on without a pause.

'At all events, he said he would be late, and asked if I could pick him up outside the villa when I had finished for the day, because the road to my farm and his turnip field runs outside the gates ...'

'You live close together?' My turn to interrupt.

He paused in his energetic efforts with the broom to give me a look of ill-disguised contempt. 'His turnip field abuts my smallholding, of course. It was all one property in my father's time, but it's divided now. Each of the sons was left a part of it, though, as the eldest, I had the largest share. But we still cooperate. He grows the turnips and I sell some on the stall, as well as the ones he hawks around the streets, and in return on feast days he peddles my cheese and

buttermilk for me. Of course, I don't have room to bring
him into town when the cart is full of produce early in the
day, but I often take him home – even with his barrow . . .'
He faltered suddenly. 'Or, at least, I did.'

'And that is what you had arranged to do last night?' I
said. 'I heard that an ox-cart had stopped outside the house.'

'Well, it wasn't mine,' the man said bitterly. 'I don't have
an ox. Only an old mule. I leave it with a hiring stables
just outside the walls – I pay them to look after it and the
cart as well – and I pick it up each evening when the market
shuts. That's what I did last night – as the hiring stables
will no doubt tell you, if you care to ask – and I drove out
to the villa, where he told me he would wait. I waited for
a long time, till it was almost dark, but in the end I had to
leave.'

Any chip of stone tile that wasn't on a stockpile, neatly
sorted out, had been swept into his heap, together with the
dust of ages by the look of it, and he was looking round
for somewhere to dispose of it. I gestured to a corner, where
I'd roughly swept the debris from the shop before, ready
to be gathered up and join the midden-heap.

He pushed his pile in that direction with his broom.
'Naturally I was worried about where my brother was, and
the man on the gate there had no news of him. I wondered
if someone had already taken him – all the big villas have
farm wagons they can use – so I went home to see. But he
wasn't there, of course. How could he be, since he was
lying here?'

'So perhaps the ox-wagon did take him to the town,' I
said.

'He would not have done that, when my uncle was going
to pick him up.' The young man was splashing drops of
water on my workbench as he spoke, and on the coloured
stockpiles of assorted stone.

'Or he'd have come straight to tell me if he had,' the
older man agreed. 'Besides, if he'd come back to Glevum,
I would certainly have heard. From the hiring stables, if
from no one else. You can't walk through the gates without
someone seeing you.'

I had to acknowledge there was truth in this. But I was following a different train of thought. 'Then I wonder if he was brought back to the town against his will?' *Or was already dead*, I added privately, although I did not voice that thought aloud. 'These wagons from the villas – are there many on the roads?' I hoped he would identify the one the gateman saw.

He disappointed me. 'There are always lots of them. I saw half a dozen of them yesterday, queuing at the gate.'

'Why would they go to Glevum at that time of day, if they came from country houses fairly close nearby?'

The nephew dispensed the last few drops of water from the jug. 'I suppose they bring in fresh produce from the villa farms to supply the owners' town houses, but it's easier to bring things in on horseback if you can. Then you don't have to wait till dusk to bring them in.'

His uncle nodded. 'Like those hangings that decurion had brought in yesterday – the one who made the speech at the basilica today, congratulating Gaius Greybeard on capturing the vote. . . .' He turned to his nephew, 'Though, come to think of it, I saw his cart as well . . .'

But I had lost interest in wagons, suddenly.

'Gaius Greybeard! That doddering old fool! Elected to the ordo?' I shook my head in total disbelief. 'I knew that he was standing as a candidate – he has done that for years – but there must be some mistake. Surely they cannot have elected him! I understood that Marcus Septimus had proposed a candidate.'

'Well, so he did,' the older man replied. 'And that's why Gaius won. He was the nominee. Of course, the whole election was a formality once it was known that His Excellence Marcus had endorsed him for the post.'

I could not believe my ears. I knew that Marcus had no patience with the man and his repeated efforts to become a councillor. Too easily influenced, my patron always said, too inclined to do anything for gold, and with no more judgement than the average fish. Marcus would not endorse him for a post as street-sweeper, let alone as town councillor in the curia.

I must have looked as startled as I felt. 'Don't look so disbelieving, citizen,' the stallholder exclaimed. 'I can assure you that it's true – I heard the proclamation of the news myself. We were in the forum market together at my stall when the chief decurion came out on to the steps and made the announcement about the outcome of the vote. He actually mentioned that it was His Excellency's wish.' He gave a rather peculiar sort of grin. 'The bystanders were a bit surprised at first, I must agree, but most of them decided that he'd been well paid for his support.'

I looked across at Junio who had been listening to all this.

'Are you thinking what I am thinking?' I enquired.

Junio nodded slowly. 'Marcus would never have nominated Gaius for that seat. Unless he was coerced. Certainly he'd never stoop to take a bribe. He's always been scrupulous in avoiding any hint of that. There has been some mistake. Or someone tampered with the message on the way . . .'

'There was no mistake.' Radixrapum's brother was peremptory. 'And how could anyone have tampered with the scroll? It had his seal on it. I saw it come myself. It was brought to the forum yesterday by that official messenger in the fancy clothes – Virulus or Virilis, or whatever he is called . . .'

But I was no longer listening. His words had struck a sudden echo in my brain. I felt my jaw drop open and my mind began to whirl. 'Dear gods,' I said. 'Of course! That is the solution! How could I be so blind? The answer has been here in my workshop all along.'

'What is it, Father?' Junio was instantly alert and at my side. 'You have thought of something? Something related to the murderer?'

I was quite excited. 'I believe so, Junio. It all fits into place. I don't know why I didn't think of it before. It was Radixrapum's brother who gave me the idea. You heard what he just said?'

'That he was in the forum when the message came?'

That had not been my meaning, but it sparked another

thought. 'And that was in the morning!' I exclaimed. 'I should have seen that it was odd. I am even more stupid than Gaius Greybeard is, if that is possible.' I turned to the two mourners. 'I am sorry, gentlemen. I shall have to ask you to move the bier as soon as possible. Junio and I must go to the garrison at once. People are in danger and the killer must be stopped. I only hope that we will be in time.'

'But who is it that we're stopping?' Junio enquired in a tone of anguish.

For the first time since the bulla feast, I allowed myself to smile. 'Why, the green man, of course. Glypto is deaf! Have you not understood?'

Radixrapum's son sidled up to Junio. 'Who on earth is Glypto?' he enquired, as though he was talking to the only person still sane. 'And what has a green man got to do with it? Does this mean your father thinks he knows who strangled mine?'

'I think so,' Junio answered in an undertone. 'And Glypto is the latest victim of the same murderer. Though I don't understand what Father thinks he knows.'

'Then let me show you something.' I bent to the stockpile of assorted tesserae and picked up a little sliver of green stone. 'What is this, Junio?'

They were all looking at me now as though I'd lost my wits, but Junio humoured me. 'It looks like a piece of lapis viridis,' he said.

'Exactly,' I couldn't keep the triumph from my voice. 'Lapis is the word for the material, and viridis . . .'

'You mean . . . the colour?' Junio always thought in Latin – he had no other tongue – but the connection had just occurred to him.

'Precisely! We thought when Glypto said the man was green, he was giving a description of him in some way. It never occurred to me that he thought it was his name. He told me that he knew the man was green, because he heard them talk. The other speaker – the urchin – must have used the word. And Glypto misheard it. Virilis and viridis – the sounds are very close. And once you have seen that, a lot of things make sense. Who – except the tanner and ourselves

– knew that Glypto was going to meet me at the pile and tell me what he knew about the murders here? Only Virilis – I told him so myself. It troubles me. I didn't see the danger at the time, and half an hour later Glypto was found dead.' I sighed. 'The tanner's wife is right. I might as well have slipped the dagger in his ribs.'

'But Virilis had set off to meet Marcus by that time!' Junio protested.

'You think so? We saw him leave, of course – he made quite sure that we did – but it would have been quite easy for him to double back and wait in the rear lane for Glypto to appear, then stab him and hide his body in the pile. It was raining by then and few people were about, so even if he had to leave his horse tied up somewhere again, there was nobody lingering around to notice it.'

'But how did he lure Glypto to the far side of the midden-heap? Or did he simply toss the corpse across the pile?'

'I've thought of that,' I said. 'But Glypto would naturally go that side of the heap – it was nearest to the back door of the tannery – but though (as Glypto said) the midden-pile was big enough to hide a child from view, it's not so high that you can't see over it. So when he came out with his bucket, for the umpteenth time today, and saw me talking to someone on the street, he came around this way to try to speak to me. But when he got here, Virilis was there, and Glypto recognized him somehow as the man he'd seen before. It may have been the military cloak or perhaps the voice, but he knew who it was and tried to send me warning as soon as possible. But it was too late by then. Virilis had noticed him, and I had sealed his fate.'

Junio whistled. 'So when he said the green man was here again, he didn't mean he'd heard him here the night before? Or is it possible he heard him then as well? I suppose we'll never know.'

Radixrapum's family had been listening to all this, but, in accordance with my earlier request, they had put on their cloaks and hurried to secure the corpse a little more firmly to the makeshift bier. Now, as they moved into position to lift each end of it, the younger man said thoughtfully,

'So you think the cursor was the strangler, but he stabbed the slave?'

'Indeed I do,' I said. 'Using that dagger he carried at his chest, though normally, I think, he preferred to use his sash – thin plaited silk would make an excellent strangulation cord.'

Junio was reluctant to accept all this. 'But you can't still think his real intention was to strangle you. What motive would he have? He hadn't even met you until the naming day.'

'That's quite true, of course. And that's how he came to murder the wrong man, twice before. Not because he attacked them from behind, as we supposed (although in fact he did), but because he didn't know what I looked like anyway – only what my work was and where I was most likely to be found.' They were looking doubtful and I spelled it out for them. 'Lucius was in my workshop: Virilis thought that it was me. Hardly surprising when you think of it. And the same with our poor turnip-seller here. He was wheeling a mosaic pavement round the streets, to a place where I was known to work. The cursor had no way of knowing who I was – not till he met me at the bulla feast today.'

'But you think he was trying to kill you all the same?' Radixrapum's brother was incredulous. He looked at his nephew. 'I can't believe that's true. What kind of person murders a complete stranger in cold blood, just because some other person asks them to?'

'Apart from an executioner, you mean?' I said.

I heard Junio's sharp intake of breath. 'You think that's how he saw it?'

It was a relief to say it openly. 'I am quite sure he did. He was acting on instructions. Someone told him where I lived and what I did, and where I was likely to be that afternoon. Someone of importance, that he was working for. I don't imagine that his services are free.'

'But Marcus sent him here,' Junio observed. 'You can't think it was your patron who ordered him to strangle you?' He shook his head decisively. 'I don't believe it.'

'Nor do I,' I answered. 'But I think I know who did.'

Radixrapum's son had left the bier by now and had come round to confront me, arms folded on his chest. 'Tell me his name and I will strangle him with these bare hands' – he made them into fists – 'and that Virilis too.' He shook his head. 'What did he hope to gain? How does he profit by my father's death? Or yours?' he added, as an after-thought.

'Preferment in his chosen occupation, I should think,' I said. 'I knew he was ambitious – even my wife Gwellia saw as much and commented that he probably had powerful friends somewhere. Indeed, he was already very highly placed – already an official cursor, at his age, and he told me that he'd worked for the governor before, and even been to Glevum with a message once or twice. What kind of promotion could such a youth expect? Not to be commander of a troop of horse – that would require too much experi-ence. But to join the *speculatores* – that is different.'

The mention of speculatores brought a sudden hush. The very name was feared throughout the Empire. The specu-latores had begun as simply mounted scouts, but under successive emperors their powers had evolved, and now they were known not merely as paid spies, but as ruthless killers of imperial enemies. And, as Virilis himself had warned us earlier, Commodus saw plots and treason every-where.

'Dear Mars!' said Junio, turning almost white. 'You think he might have been? One of the emperor's infamous elite – the mounted spies and assassination squad?'

'Not a *speculator* yet, I think,' I said at last, 'but aiming to prove that he is equal to the task. And doubtless Quintus promised him support.'

'Quintus Severus? The chief decurion?' Radixrapum's brother said in a voice that was suddenly squeaky with anxiety. 'You don't think he's involved?'

'Who else was giving Virilis orders in the town? Of course, it did not seem remarkable – as you say, he is decu-rion. He must have known Quintus from visits earlier – we know he's carried previous messages.'

'But how could Quintus have organized the killings?'

Junio said. 'Besides, he turned up at your workshop the day that Lucius died – he wouldn't have done that if he'd tried to have you murdered not very long before.'

'On the contrary,' I said, 'that is exactly why he came, and how he knew that the first attempt had failed. He had intended to come across my corpse, in front of witnesses – it was designed to look like random violent robbery, of course – and no doubt he would have set up a hue and cry and offered a reward for anyone who could find my murderer. I might even have been given a splendid funeral. No wonder he was startled to find me at my door. I thought he looked astonished at the time.'

'And what about the pavement for the basilica?' Junio said.

'He never intended to commission that at all. It was merely an excuse for him to come to me – I should have been suspicious that he agreed to it. *You* were, I remember.'

Junio looked pleased. 'When he found you were alive, he had to cancel it, I suppose. And hurry back to Virilis to point out the mistake. He must have been beside himself with curiosity when you told him there was a corpse inside the shop – and he knew it wasn't you! And what about the—'

I raised my hand to silence him. 'Not now, Junio. We've talked for long enough. These gentlemen are ready to get the body home, and we must start the chase for Virilis. Of course, he will not know that we are on his tail, but all the same we must catch up with him tonight, or Marcus is in danger.'

'Marcus?' the three men said in unison. Radixrapum's relatives had picked up the bier, but they put it down again, exchanging startled looks.

Junio was horrified, and said, rather tactlessly, 'But I thought you said the danger was to you! Marcus is a wealthy, powerful man, supposed to be related to the Emperor himself. Surely no one is going to try to murder him?'

'But that must be exactly what this is all about,' I said patiently. 'Quintus wouldn't bother to have someone strangle me for my own sake alone – I am not important. It is

Marcus, and my contact with him, that is seen as dangerous. And I'm beginning to see why. As soon as my patron is safely home again, he'll make it clear which candidate it was that he endorsed – and it won't be Gaius Greybeard, I'm quite convinced of that. But I can't stay any longer. We are wasting time, and Virilis is getting further from us every minute that we lose. Come with me to the garrison to find the commandant, and I'll answer any other questions on the way.'

Twenty-Five

J unio and I allowed the turnip-seller's family to remove the bier – it would have been unthinkable to push in front of it – and immediately afterwards we set off ourselves, leaving the workshop in the care of Maximus.

The slave-boy had been waiting outside the workshop door and was desolated now at being left behind, but there was no time to explain. I would simply have to tell him later what this was all about. I said as much to him.

He nodded glumly. 'Master, I am at your command.' And then, as if he could not help the words, 'But if there's any news of Minimus, you will send word to me?'

'I will,' I promised with a heavy heart, though I'd begun to fear that Minimus might, after all, be dead. Virilis was too cool a murderer to hold his hand, if my slave had proved to be a threat to him.

Junio must have read my feelings in my face, because as soon as we rounded the corner and were out of sight, he turned to me. 'What is it, father? Something is amiss. Are you still worried about Minimus? I thought that we were fairly certain he was safe, even if he is a prisoner somewhere. And if you can prove what you've been saying, it should not be hard to get him freed. He was only arrested at Quintus's behest.' He paused, partly to cross the wider road, which after the recent rain was very sticky here, so that we had to pick our way across it on the granite stepping blocks, carefully positioned an axle-width apart.

When we reached the further pavement and were side by side again, he went on. 'But, I suppose, they claim to have that purse and you don't have any actual evidence of who the killer was. And Glypto, who might have been a witness, has been silenced now. And you can't prove who killed him either.'

'If they catch up with Virilis tonight, I think there will be circumstantial evidence at least,' I told him grimly.

'He won't have had the opportunity to change his clothes, and I'm certain that there will be spots of Glypto's blood on him – and on the dagger-hilt, though he will have wiped the blade. No doubt he'll tell some story at the military inn – fighting off a bear or something – to account for it. That's where strangling is so much easier.'

I was hurrying onwards as I said this, and Junio had to scurry to keep up with me. 'But, Father, surely, if you're right, the cursor won't have left the town? He's made two attempts to kill you and not succeeded yet. You would expect him to try again.'

'He has done, Junio. Don't you realize that? Twice today he has come to look for me – once when we were walking into town and later at the workshop. Looking back, we should have seen that it was strange. It is rare to see horsemen on that stretch of lane – I thought so at the time. Even a skilled rider like Virilis would avoid it if he could.' A sudden thought struck me, and I almost laughed. 'I suppose that's why Hyperius was suddenly so keen that I should ride back to Glevum in his company. I imagine that Virilis put him up to it – it would have been much easier to attack me then.'

Junio nodded. 'But he did not attack you when he passed you in the woods.'

'There were three of us,' I reminded him. 'That's what saved my life. And the same thing at the shop, though Virilis probably thought that he would find me on my own. Doubtless he discovered that we'd parted company when we first arrived in Glevum. Quintus saw me in the street with no attendant at my side – I met him when he was on his way to oversee the vote, and we know that he'd been talking to Virilis since then. The cursor had just come from the curia when he called on me, and the decurion had given him a letter under seal. He told me so himself. And that's another thing which I should have questioned at the time! Why should Quintus suddenly send him to enquire whether I had a message for Marcus Septimus? Of course, he did not do anything of the kind – it was just a ruse of Virilis's, made up on the spot.'

Junio nodded his agreement. 'Considering the outcome of the ordo vote, you'd think, if anything, Quintus would try to prevent you from sending word. Though, of course, you hadn't heard the news about Gaius Greybeard then. I do see what you mean. It does seem Virilis expected to find you on your own, but it's hard to believe that he meant to strangle you. He was so charming. He gave no hint of it.'

We had almost reached the centre of the town by now, but I changed my route to avoid the enclosure where the forum was, and where, of course, the basilica and curia building lay. I did not want to meet Quintus anywhere.

'Charm was the weapon he most relied upon,' I said. 'He certainly charmed Gwellia – and my patron too. You heard the glowing testimonial that Marcus gave to him. And as for hinting, I think perhaps he did. He told me that he had something for me when we could be alone. Something that I did not expect and was connected with my patron – all of which was true – except that the 'something' was a piece of twisted silk around my neck. I suppose it amused him to play games with his prey.'

I had to check my stride and step into the road. The pavements here were cluttered with stalls of every kind.

Junio, too, was dodging the displays. 'Then we'll make sure you always have someone at your side. But if you manage to have Virilis caught, there won't be such a threat.'

I frowned at him. 'Be careful what you say.' Since we'd turned into this crowded area, I'd been avoiding names. Virilis was right. The town was full of spies, including, as he'd warned me, the ones I'd least expect. I wondered if he'd really, in the end, had some respect for me. It was a peculiar compliment, if that were true. I turned to Junio. 'The man you speak of was an expert at his trade, if you can call it that. The deaths he meted out were swift and merciless. Let us hope that a different danger doesn't face us now: a meeting with some other person's gang of brutal thugs.'

'You mean Qui—' Junio left the decurion's name unsaid. 'Oh, dear gods, I hadn't thought of that. You still think he's behind this? And that Marcus is in danger too? I hope you can convince the garrison commander of all this.'

'So do I,' I told him. 'We will soon find out. We are very nearly at the garrison.' I brushed aside a trader who was offering me belts – 'Finest leather, citizen. A special price for you!' – and turned down a narrow lane, where we rejoined the main street that led towards the gate. I could already see the tower of the guardhouse block where the commander had his headquarters.

I was just hastening towards it, quickening my step, when I was halted by an imperious voice. 'Citizen Libertus! Imagine seeing you. I had supposed that you would be busy with your pavement work today.'

I whirled round to see a curtained litter which had drawn up close to me, and the face of Quintus Severus peering out of it. 'I am on my way to Pedronius's house right now to admire your handiwork,' he went on, with a smile that did not reach his eyes. 'I hear it's very fine. Perhaps if you are going there, I could save you the walk, though there is only room for one of you in the litter, I'm afraid. Or, if you are returning home, my slaves could take you there? They have nothing particular to do when they've delivered me.'

Junio, beside me, had stiffened visibly, but I tried to match the decurion's mirthless smile with my own. 'Thank you, councillor, but there is no need of that. I am only walking to the garrison. I have a message for the commander there.'

I saw momentary anxious puzzlement in his eyes, and an idea came to me.

'Thank you, by the way, for sending Virilis to me. I have sent a message by him to my patron, as you suggested I might do, though doubtless it largely duplicates your own,' I said, pausing to let my next words take effect. 'But I'm sure that he'll be anxious to learn the latest news – the result of the election was such an unexpected one.'

There was no mistaking now the look of doubt that crossed his face. I could see my ruse had worked. He must be wondering if his plans had gone awry, and Virilis was in the pay of Marcus rather than his own. After all, it rather looked like it. I was still alive and Virilis was gone, and Quintus could not know how I had learned about the vote.

'Slaves, put the litter down!' The smile had vanished now, along with all pretence that this meeting was polite. 'And you, Hyperius, get that man into it.'

The stolid slave, who had been lingering on the other side, came round the litter and seized me by the arm. It happened so quickly that I did not resist and he might have managed to force me to get in, but Junio was a younger man and far too strong for him. He grasped the startled servant by the throat and pushed him violently. Hyperius fell backwards, spluttering on to the paving-stones.

'Here! You two! What's the meaning of this?' There was a sound of ringing hobnails, and there was Scowler running up. His swagger stick was stuck into his belt, and he had drawn his sword instead. One of his companions was panting after him, carrying Scowler's helmet and a dagger of his own.

By the time that Hyperius was on his feet again, Scowler had reached me. 'Oh, it's you again!' he said.

Quintus leaned back in his litter, his face a mask of cool disdain. 'I see that you're acquainted with this citizen.'

Scowler gave a self-important nod. 'I met him yesterday. You had us go and move a murdered pauper from his workshop floor.'

'Exactly!' Quintus gave me a triumphant, poisonous smile. 'And there has been another murder at his shop today. So it will not surprise you that I am arresting him.'

Scowler looked doubtfully at me. 'Is this true, citizen?'

'That there was a body at my workshop, certainly. But I had no part in either of the deaths. On the contrary, I believe that the decurion ordered them. I had some information from the slave next door.'

The decurion turned purple. 'But you can't have had. This is preposterous. Why should I want to murder a pie-seller and a turnip-man? And who would trust the testimony of a simple slave?'

I gave him the best smile that I could conjure up. 'Very likely nobody, decurion, it's true. But how did you know it was a turnip-man? Or did you work that out from the description that your hired assassin gave? And, come to that, how did Virilis know that the first corpse had one eye?'

Scowler, who had placed himself between the two of us, bent towards the litter as if to wait for a reply.

'I don't know how he knew that,' Quintus snapped impatiently. 'He didn't hear from me. I wasn't at the workshop, as you may recall, until the pie-seller was dead, and even then I didn't go inside. And he didn't describe the turnip-man to me. You can't implicate me in what Virilis may have said.'

'But you do agree that it was Virilis who strangled them?' I said. 'Especially since he doesn't deny that fact himself?'

It was a gamble. Of course Virilis had not denied that he was the murderer – nobody had taxed him with it up to now. But Quintus didn't know that and I hoped that I could lead him to conclude something which I had already hinted at: that Virilis was secretly acting for Marcus all the time, and that he – the decurion – had been betrayed and duped.

But Quintus shook his head. 'If he maintains I paid him to try to strangle you, he's lying!' he declared. 'Trying to protect the man he's really working for, I expect, and earn a lenient sentence by accusing me. He'll be claiming I have dealings with the rebel bandits next, and that I am plotting to deliver certain people to their hands. Well, I deny it, do you hear! If Virilis planned that, he did it on his own. And as for this presumptuous mosaic-maker here . . .' – he was addressing Scowler, but he waved a hand at me – 'he may not have been responsible for the murders at his house, but he attacked me earlier. Hyperius here was witness to the fact. Is that not so, Hyperius?'

The audacity of it took my breath away, but Quintus had already turned towards his slave. Hyperius was looking flabbergasted too, but after a long moment he inclined his head. 'Certainly, master. Exactly as you say.'

I was about to protest my innocence, but Scowler already had his sword-point at my throat. 'And when exactly did this incident occur?' He did not look at Quintus, but kept on watching me as though I might somehow be tempted to make a dash for it.

Quintus leaned back in his litter, clearly satisfied, and made a vague gesture with his seal-ring hand. 'Oh, just a little while before the ordo vote was held. I had just heard the bugle-call to tell us to convene. This fellow approached me at the door of my own home and threatened me with violence. Pushed me against a doorpost and banged my head on it. Hyperius saw it all. And even then he followed me to the basilica, shouting that I had his slave in custody, which I certainly did not! Crowds of people were witnesses to that.' He favoured Scowler's colleague with a winning smile. 'And, of course, at that time I thought he'd committed the murders at his house. I didn't know that Virilis had confessed to them. I simply knew that this man was violent, and guilty, at the very least, of *iniuria atrox* against a magistrate. I was planning to drag him before the justices. I was trying to arrest him when you came along.'

I had to acknowledge his ingenuity. The way he told the story, it did sound plausible, and no one was going to take my word against that of the chief official in the town curia. I would find it difficult to prove my innocence, especially if Hyperius was prepared to testify. Moreover, given that he'd made a proper charge, I was likely to be taken into custody for this, probably by the decurion himself – in which case some unpleasant accident was almost certain to befall me before I came to trial. And Virilis was getting ever closer to Marcus all this time. I could feel the cold sweat running down my back.

But Scowler had lowered his sword-point and stepped back suddenly. 'I think you've misremembered, decurion,' he said, putting his weapon carefully in its sheath again. 'This couldn't have happened at the time you claim. A moment after the ordo bugle blew, I was talking to this citizen myself. He was here at the gatehouse and there are witnesses. Your apartment, as I understand, is on the further side of town. He could never have got there in the interval.'

Quintus was glowering, but still irascible. 'Then it was earlier in the day. Hyperius would know. I was so shaken that I can't recall.'

'But,' Scowler said slowly, 'he'd just come into town. I watched him through the gate. And – before you say anything else you might regret – I happen to know there was a bulla ceremony at his home today that didn't end till almost noon. I heard that from the high priest who conducted it. It would not be difficult to prove it, I presume.'

There was a silence. Quintus had turned pink. 'I still say he assaulted me. It doesn't matter when. Perhaps I got the day wrong. I want him brought to trial . . . if only for appearing in the forum in improper dress. There are certainly dozens of witnesses to that.'

I saw an opportunity and seized it instantly. 'Then, soldier, you had better take me under escort to the garrison yourself. Put me under charge. I'll appeal to the commander. I believe I have that right, and I would like to speak to him as soon as possible. I have some information he'll be interested to hear.'

Quintus seemed ready to leap out of the litter and lay hands on me, but the presence of Scowler and his fellow soldier prevented this, of course.

'I'll make you pay for this,' he muttered, as he pulled the curtains to. 'I'll find a way to prove you guilty, don't imagine otherwise. And don't suppose you'll ever see your little slave again – I'll make quite sure you don't. Slaves, pick up the litter and take me quickly home. At the double or I will have you flogged.'

The litter jolted off. Scowler stood beside me as it vanished out of sight, with stout Hyperius panting after it. 'I'll have to arrest you, citizen,' he said when it had gone. 'I could have argued otherwise, but you agreed to it.'

I nodded. 'Don't worry about that,' I said. 'You may have saved my life. If I'd been forced into that litter, I doubt I would ever have got out of it alive. And I wanted to go to the garrison anyway. I meant what I said. I must talk to the commander as soon as possible. It's vital that I do. We've lost too much time already, and there are lives at stake.'

Scowler pulled out his swagger-stick and scratched his head with it. 'What's all this about? Did that Virilis fellow really kill those men?'

'I'm afraid so. He thought that they were me. That's why he put them in my workshop afterwards. He took a lot of pains to put them there, too. That poor old turnip-seller you heard me talk about just now must have been carried halfway through the town, draped across his saddle in the growing dusk, wrapped in those hangings from the curia. The gate-keeper on duty when Radixrapum disappeared told me that there was nobody in sight, except an ox-cart – and a young man carrying a roll of something on his horse! That was Virilis, of course – that tallies with something that the market-trader said. I even saw the marks of the pommels on the corpse, though at the time I didn't realize what they were.'

Scowler took his helmet and plonked it on his head. 'I still don't understand. Why has that decurion got it in for you?'

I shook my head. 'There's no time to explain. Take me to the garrison – and, Junio, you take a carrying litter and go, as fast as possible, to Pedronius's country house. Get the youngest, strongest bearers you can find, and never mind the cost. I'll see that they are paid.'

My son was boggling at me. 'But I promised not to leave you!'

'I'll have an armed and armoured escort,' I reminded him. 'Being under guard has some advantages.'

Junio nodded. 'So when I reach the villa, what am I to do? You don't just want me to finish off the pavement, I presume.'

I shook my head and smiled. 'You can tell the gatekeeper that it's what you came for, if you like. That should ensure that he will let you in. Then find the steward and ask for Minimus. I think you'll find he's got him locked up some-where in the place.'

'What makes you think so? Something Quintus said?' Junio was still havering. 'And isn't he intending to go out there himself? He said he was going to.'

'Exactly so,' I said. 'Which is what makes me suppose that Minimus is there. That, and thinking through what happened yesterday. Though I can't explain it now.'

'Just a minute, citizen!' That was Scowler now. 'I have a vested interest in all this – you owe me a half-denarius if you find that slave today. So answer his question. Why do you think he's there?'

I was impatient to be taken to the garrison, but one cannot argue with a sword. 'Well,' I said reluctantly, 'I was called out to the villa on a false pretence: one of the garden slaves appeared and asked for someone to come out to the site. At the time I didn't question it – I'd seen the boy before – so I hurried over, but Pedronius wasn't there. I thought nothing of it – it happens all the time – but, on reflection, I don't think it was chance. Normally, Junio, you would have been with me in the workshop too. So if there was a summons to do something to the site, and I was expecting an important customer, what would anyone suppose that I would do?'

'Send me to do it,' Junio replied. 'But I was buying provisions for the bulla feast that day.'

'Which Quintus – who would not dream of buying things himself – had not allowed for in his plans.'

'That would have left you with Minimus all the same.' Scowler observed, earning his name again.

I nodded. 'They obviously had plans for diverting him as well, probably to carry something to the site, where he could be imprisoned and later charged with theft – I think they always meant to plant that purse on him. I believe that the garden-boy met up with Virilis, no doubt by appointment – he told me he had another errand to perform and he would have to let the cursor know the coast was clear. When Virilis heard I'd gone in person in answer to the call, and realized that only Minimus was left behind, he came up with a plan. It was so simple that it was spectacular. After a little while, he sent the garden-boy again, saying that there'd been an accident to me at Pedronius's house and telling Minimus he was to come at once. But Minimus complicated things by trying to send a message home.'

'So he did send the messenger after all?' my son exclaimed.

'A red-haired slave, exactly as described. And he gave the message to the garden slave, who seems, in fact, to have delivered it after he had spoken to Virilis again, though this time Glypto found them at the pile and heard him saying that "everyone was out" and, by implication, that the coast was clear.'

'Dear Mars!' said Junio, 'So Minimus hurried to the villa, supposing you were hurt, but when he got there . . . what?'

'I imagine that the steward took him in and sent to Quintus for orders what to do. I'm sure that Minimus was there. The gatekeeper told me that he'd seen no visitors, except a slave in a blue tunic. I thought he was talking about a different one –a boy that I myself saw scurrying out – but I realize now he must have meant Minimus all the time. The steward was no doubt perplexed in any case – first I turned up and then my slave-boy did, when he'd been told each time he was expecting you. He had orders to detain you in the garden, I expect.'

'So he knew all about it? The attempt to murder you?'

'I doubt that very much. It would be too dangerous. He was just obeying orders, as he always did – he used to work for Quintus after all, and no doubt his former master retains him as a spy. The man was saving for his slave price, and I'm sure he'd just received a small donation to the fund. When I went back later on, I saw him counting it.'

'So he was the one who locked up your little slave?' Scowler was incredulous. 'I heard he'd been arrested by a private guard.'

'Well, in a sense he was, though doubtless it was Quintus who began that rumour too – just as he lied to me when he denied that he knew who'd taken Minimus.'

'But wouldn't the whole villa staff have known of this? Someone would have told you when you visited the house,' Junio objected.

I shook my head. 'Not necessarily. Pedronius wasn't there, and the steward, in his absence, has full authority and controls the keys. In fact, when I went there the first time in answer to the summons that never was, I did not even see a door-keeper. The steward came out to me himself to tell me that my errand was in vain – quick thinking, since he was expecting you! With no one at the gate, it would have been easy for him to let Minimus come in and march him to some storeroom and turn the key on him. Quintus had really put a warrant out, of course, and the steward probably believed what he had been told – that the slave-boy was a thief – especially when Quintus later sent the purse, claiming it was evidence against the boy.'

Scowler was still scowling. 'This is all speculation. You have no proof of it.'

'I think you'll find that it is what happened all the same. As I am hoping that Junio will find out – if he gets there before Quintus Severus, that is.' I turned to the soldier. 'Then you can have your half-denarius.'

A crafty smile spread over Scowler's face. 'I think we can arrange that, citizen, don't you? We heard the decurion tell his litter-men to take him home. If we can delay him for a little while . . .' He turned to his companion. 'Get over there at once. Say that the garrison needs a written charge from him regarding this assault. Make sure you slow him down. And don't say who sent you or anything you've heard, or I'll have you down the lead-mines as fast as you can blink.'

The soldier nodded and set off at a run.

But Junio was still trying to follow what I'd said. 'So when Virilis knew the coast was clear he came back to the shop and lay in wait for you? He must have spent a long time hiding close nearby. He might have been discovered – that was dangerous.'

'Not for Virilis. He hid himself by visiting the tannery next door, pretending to be interested in buying hides. The tanner told me he'd had a customer with a jewelled cloak-clasp, and, of course, the cursor had one with a ruby set in it. I only saw the implication when it was far too late.'

'Speaking of lateness,' Scowler's voice broke in. 'I'm due off duty soon. Besides, you are supposed to be under my arrest. Come along, citizen, or I'll have to draw my sword.'

'I'm coming,' I told him and made to follow him.

'But, Father,' Junio bleated, 'suppose that you are wrong? Or the steward just denies that Minimus is there? Or locks me up as well!'

'The steward thinks our slave-boy is a criminal and that

he is holding him until he can be tried. Tell him that armed soldiers are already on their way, to take Minimus into official custody,' I answered. 'I'll talk to the commander and try to make it true.'

Scowler pushed his helmet back and scratched his head again. 'If it's worth another half-denarius, I will make it true myself. As I say, I am off duty soon. Give me a few minutes and I'll follow this young citizen. I'll bring the slaveboy back to the guardhouse, if we find him there. If we have a bargain, that is, citizen?'

'We have a bargain, soldier,' I told him thankfully. 'You bring the lad back safe and I'll pay twice as much.'

So I let him march me towards the garrison while Junio scuttled off to find the bearers and the chair.

Twenty-Six

Even then it was not as easy as I'd hoped that it would be. There was no problem with my being charged, but my request to see the garrison commander was refused. He was very busy, the *optio* on duty told me with a sneer, trying to trace the owner of a murdered slave whose body had been discovered in the woods.

'Hardly a matter for the senior officer,' I said.

'Depends what you believe. The commander seems to think the rebels are involved and that the boy was being used to carry messages. Nasty business: the brutes had strangled him.'

A strangled slave-boy! I felt my blood run cold. I took a swift decision. 'It may be that I can help. Did this slave-boy have red hair by any chance? And a light-blue tunic?'

The soldier shook his head. 'Not as far as I know. Scruffy little thing. We thought he was a street urchin, but he'd got a brand on him. Possibly a land slave, it says in the report. Dark-brown tunic and big boots. Nobody mentioned the colour of his hair.'

I got up from the wooden form where they had made me sit. (If I hadn't been a citizen, it would have been the floor.) 'Then I believe I do know who it is. And I know who owns him – or I think I do.'

He looked up from the written orders he was looking at. 'And who would that be?'

'Pedronius the tax-collector, if I am correct. I think this used to be a garden slave of his, though I believe that the boy's been out on loan. To Quintus Severus, I think that you will find.'

The optio shuffled his bark sheets aside. 'Then I'd wish you'd been here earlier. It would have saved a lot of time. It's taken the commander half the afternoon to find out that it was the tax-collector's slave brand. It seems you do know something. You'd better come with me.'

He led the way into the inner court and up the staircase to where the commander's private office was. When we were summoned in answer to our knock, the optio pushed me in ahead of him, then stood stiffly to attention in the middle of the room. There was a smell of armour polish, lamp fat, sweat and grease.

'In the name of his Imperial Divinity . . .' the optio began.

The commander waved these formalities aside. 'Oh, very well! Forget the formula.' He pushed away the pile of documents before him on the desk and leaned back on his stool. These – apart from a handsome oil lamp on a stand and the shadowy statue of a deity in a niche – were the only furnishings in this spare and spartan room. 'What is it that you want?'

'A prisoner requesting an audience with you, sir. Brought here on a charge, but has information on that dead slave in the woods.'

The grizzled eyebrows rose an inch or two, and the commander turned a pair of weary eyes on me, but when he saw me his manner changed at once. 'Citizen Libertus, you are here again?' He sounded at once exasperated and amused. 'Why is it that every time I find a corpse you are not far behind? Never mind. If you have information, I'll be glad to hear. Optio, you may leave us.'

The soldier snapped his sandal-heels together in salute and clattered off downstairs.

'Now, what is it?' The commander turned to me. He was a lively, weather-beaten man, with a stern though kindly face, who took his position of command more seriously than most – he had declined a position in the senate house at Rome in favour of continuing his military career. 'I understand that you're a prisoner in my custody? Do you deserve it?'

'Only for tying my toga-ends around my waist,' I said. 'And for discovering the truth about the chief decurion, which, incidentally, is related to that slave-boy's corpse you found. I think you'd better hear it. If I'm correct, my patron is in danger of his life – and so am I, of course. And there may even be danger to the state.'

He leaned forward, making a spear-point of his hands. 'Then tell me all about it – from the beginning, please.'

I told him the whole story: the fruitless visit to Pedronius's house, the discovery of the pie-seller's body, and how Virilis had mysteriously known the details of the face, when no one but myself and Radixrapum were supposed to have seen the corpse.

'What about the soldiers who brought the army cart? Could one of them have told him?' the commander asked. He was scribbling down details on a piece of wax, though he'd nearly filled the writing-block by now.

I shook my head. 'We'd bandaged up the face. It was not visible,' I said.

He nodded and poised his pointed stylus once again. 'Go on.'

I went on: all about Glypto, and the message that brought my wife to town, and the appearance of Virilis at the naming day. 'He must have been astonished to find me there,' I said. 'When he killed Radixrapum just the night before, he thought that he had strangled *me*.'

'So both of the murders took place yesterday, and you think he moved the turnip-seller to your workshop after dark? Which means that he rode to Marcus's villa very late indeed – though he was an expert rider, I suppose. Yet he had already been there earlier in the day, I think you said.'

'In the morning, after he had visited the curia,' I said. 'And that's another intriguing thing. Of course, the forenoon is when the council generally meets – unless it is some special session like today – but how could a messenger, riding from the west, have contrived to arrive there yesterday so early in the day, deliver a message, wait for a reply and still have time to get to the villa before noon? Even Corinium is at least two hours away, even on horseback, at this time of year.'

The commander gazed at me. 'Meaning that he had probably spent the night nearby?'

'I'm almost sure of it. It may have been an inn – I don't suppose that Quintus would ask him to the house, but I expect the two made contact that evening all the same.'

'We'll make enquiries of all the establishments nearby.' He scratched another sentence on his writing-block. 'If they were seen together, that will prove you're right. And you don't believe the message that the cursor brought – naming Gaius Greybeard as his nominee?'

I looked at him a moment. 'You know Marcus. What do you suppose?'

He made a wry face. 'I was doubtful too, but eventually I concluded – as I'm sure many people did – that Gaius had offered money and Marcus had succumbed, perhaps when the candidate he really favoured refused to stand. I have seen it happen many times before.'

'But not involving Marcus,' I said indignantly. 'He is sometimes foolish, but he never takes a bribe. Not over anything important anyhow.'

The sharp eyes twinkled. 'I won't tell him you said that. Now, about this murdered turnip-man . . .'

I went on with the story, and he made notes of it, occasionally pausing to ask me to expand. When I had finished, he leaned back on his stool and folded his arms across his armoured chest.

'So, in summary, you think that Quintus tried to have you killed because he'd falsified your patron's message to the curia – presumably in return for a considerable bribe – and he thought you'd find him out? You have a high opinion of your talents, it appears.'

'It isn't my opinion that is relevant,' I said, feeling a little snubbed by this remark. 'If Gaius feared me, that might be enough. Perhaps he thought that I would write and tell my patron too, since it is no secret that I send to him each moon with news of what is happening in the town.'

'Such as the unexpected death of that town councillor?' The commander grinned at me. 'I know that your patron found that very interesting. He wrote to me about it under seal. It was inconvenient, he said, having a sudden vacancy when he wasn't here himself, and he intended to propose a trustworthy candidate.'

'Inconvenient is not a word I'd choose. I wondered if it was a little *too* convenient.'

'So did he, Libertus. That's why he decided to come home so suddenly. But, returning to your patron's nominee, it had to be someone with sufficient property, of course, and he told me he would need me to look into that before the voting day.'

'So he didn't nominate a candidate at all? Because he didn't know if the man he had in mind owned enough to qualify?'

The old soldier got slowly to his feet. 'Oh, he had decided on a nominee all right. He told me who it was. Can you really not guess whom he intended to propose?'

I shook my head. 'It would have to be someone who'd agreed to it. I suppose that one could make enquiries and find out who it was he had approached. There are not so many people who would qualify.' I broke off suddenly. 'It wasn't Pedronius by any chance?'

'It was not Pedronius.' He was smiling now. 'The man that your patron had in mind is a troublesome old fellow, though he's bright enough and honest in a dogged kind of way. A pavement-maker who has a workshop on the northern edge of town . . .'

I was gaping at him. 'Me! But he never mentioned it! And I don't have a property within the walls at all.'

'That was the reason he consulted me. However, the councillor who died possessed a large estate, including several properties in town. He had no family, so everything went automatically to the residual heirs – Quintus, as you know, received the country house. Your patron got a town apartment as his share. He wanted me to go and look at it, to see if it was big enough to meet the regulations. If so, he was intending to make a gift of it, on condition that you kept it up and left it to his son.'

I was still reeling. Of course, this was the kind of gift in which Marcus specialized: I would have had to keep the place in good repair, at my own expense, and in the end his family would reap the benefit. And public life required the lavish financing of public works and games, which would be crippling, though it was possible to recover something of the cost through patronage. But if Marcus had instructed me to stand, I could scarcely have refused. Thwarting the wishes of a man like that is apt to be severely detrimental to the health. Fortunately, I had not been called upon to choose.

I said, 'But Marcus never wrote to me of this!' And then I realized. 'Or at least I never received it if he did.'

'I am sure he meant to. I know he was planning to send a present for your child.'

I nodded. So that was the explanation for the expensive gift! It was a kind of bribe, by proxy as it were. 'And that was the reason Quintus wanted me removed?' I made the link at last. 'Not simply because he was afraid I'd find him out, but because I might have been a rival to his chosen candidate.'

'I am sorry if that is an insult to your pride.'

'So I was wrong in my assumption. Marcus is not in danger after all.'

He whirled around on me. 'But of course he is. More than ever, after what you've told me here. I thought that he'd asked you and you had refused, and he had succumbed to Gaius's pleadings in disgust. But if that is not the case, and Greybeard was elected on the basis of a lie, then Quintus cannot expect to get away with it for long. Obviously, Marcus will reveal the truth as soon as he returns.'

'So Quintus will want him silenced? By Virilis, no doubt, since he is on his way to see my patron now.'

'I doubt that the attempt will take place straight away – that would be too suspicious. It will happen nearer home. But after what you tell me, we cannot take the risk. I shall send a rider after Virilis at once and have him stopped. Wait here a moment.' He took a piece of vellum from the drawer beneath his desk, dipped a sharpened quill into a bowl of soot-black ink, scribbled a sentence and then folded the paper and attached a seal, pressing his seal-ring on to wax that he had melted at the lamp. He went outside and shouted down the stairs, 'Optio!'

The man was there so quickly that it seemed he must have been fired from a bow. 'You called me, sir?' he panted.

'Have this sent at once. The fastest messenger. It is to

be relayed to every military inn between here and Londinium. It is only to be given to the commanding officer, who is to send it on at once. The man named is to be put under immediate arrest and brought back here as soon as possible. He is not to be permitted his weapon or his horse, or to change his clothing. Oh, and send a detail to the house of Quintus Severus as well. I know that he's the chief decurion, but have him brought in here for questioning. Is that quite clear?'

The optio was looking startled, but he rapped out a reply. 'Clearly understood, sir.' He clattered off downstairs.

The commander sat down at his desk again. 'We'll catch him, Libertus; have no fear of that. We'll have fresh horses and fresh riders at our disposal at the inns, and Virilis won't know that we are after him, so he will be making no especial speed.' He sighed. 'We'll pick up Quintus too, though your accusations of conspiracy might be hard to prove, since he never actually murdered anyone himself. Besides, as decurion, he would not be put to death, even if we did find proper evidence – the most he could expect is lifetime exile or confiscation of his property. Though I am very interested in what he said to you: that Virilis might accuse him of assisting the rebels in the wood. Why would he say that if there's no truth in it? And, of course, Quintus is an *Ordovicius* by birth. But, as he says himself, it will be hard to prove.'

I nodded. 'Virilis might agree to testify, of course. That would be sufficient confirmation to convict.'

'Then let us hope he will – either under torture or in return for a promise to spare his life. Meantime, we have adequate evidence for a corruption charge, so we can bring Quintus in for questioning on that. If we can find him. He might have fled by now, and, unlike the case of Virilis, we won't know where to look. And to think I had him in this very room this afternoon and let him go.'

'You did?'

He nodded. 'We were discussing the transport of some valuable items to the town – which seems ironic in the light of this.'

'I see,' I said. 'So what will happen now?'

'You are going to tell me about that body in the woods. Pedronius's land slave, I believe you said. You have some idea what he was doing there? I suppose you're going to tell me that Virilis murdered him?'

'Well, that's what happened, if I am any judge. I hear he was strangled, like the other two. I presume that the cord had been removed? And perhaps there were marks on his armpits and his thighs, where he'd been carried on the saddle of a horse?'

The commander nodded. 'Very well. Suppose that you are right. Why did he do it?'

'Because the boy knew too much. It would not have mattered if the plan had gone aright, but it all went badly wrong. *I* went to the mosaic site instead of Junio, so the slave had to go and report to Virilis, who was forced to send him back to tell a blatant lie – that there had been an accident to me – which the boy knew was not true. That made him dangerous, though when Minimus sent him over to my house, taking the same message, Virilis let him go, knowing he could catch up with him on horseback later on and dispose of him. I think you will find that they were actually seen, and I can find you an urchin who could swear to it and no doubt identify the corpse and rider, if he got the chance.' I frowned at him. 'What made you think the rebels were involved?'

'The fact that they had very clearly searched the corpse. Every seam and hem had been undone, his boots had been removed and even the soles had been slit open with a knife. They were looking for something – a message, we supposed. And someone is giving them information, I am sure. Before your patron left for Rome, we had defeated them – driven them back into the forests in the west – but recently they have been having more and more success. They evade our ambushes and there are constant raids – every time a convoy of military equipment passes through.' He sighed. 'Ever since Quintus became decurion, in fact. You don't suppose . . . He couldn't have used the same boy as a messenger to them as well?'

'Why not? It wasn't his slave, if he did get caught. He used to borrow him from Pedronius, ostensibly to move kindling about – and where would that take him other than the wood? And why move kindling, come to think of it? Unless there was a message of some kind in its midst, which the slave-boy might not know about, especially if the wood was bundled as it often is—'

He interrupted me. 'Well, Quintus won't tell us, you can be sure of that. And the slave-boy's dead, so we have no proof at all. If only we could lure the rebels to a trap. They must have a signal, but we don't know what it is.' He got to his feet and stretched out a hand to me. 'Well, goodbye, Libertus, thank you for your help. I'm sure we'll catch Virilis before he does his worst, but that's the best that I can offer, I'm afraid. I wish I could prove your case against the chief decurion, but I can only hold him on suspicion of corruption as it is. So there you are. By the power vested in me, I fine you one sestertius for indignity of dress, and declare that you are innocent of any other charge. So you are free to go. You can pay the optio if he is back by now. And I believe that I can see that red-haired slave that you were looking for, walking across the courtyard with a soldier by his side. And your son is with them, by the look of it.'

But I wasn't moving. Not yet anyway. 'Just a moment,' I said slowly. 'What you said just now. Something about a signal. I've just had an idea.'

Epilogue

I was not invited to Pedronius's feast to welcome Marcus home, and I didn't join the crowds who lined the streets to see him pass, scattering fresh rose-petals and herbs beneath his carriage wheels. But I did go to wait on him the next day – not too early, by his own request.

He kept me waiting, as he always did, but finally a pretty fair-haired page appeared and asked me to follow him to the *triclinium*. He didn't know the way and I was forced to point it out – obviously the child had been purchased overseas – but dates and wine appeared, and shortly afterwards His Excellence himself.

'Libertus, my old friend, I'm glad to see you!' he exclaimed, extending his ringed hand for me to kiss, while I made a low obeisance at his feet. 'Get up and let me see you. You're in good health, I see. I'm glad of that. I gather we have much to thank you for.'

He meant, of course, that he owed me his life, but I didn't mention that. Instead, I murmured, 'No more than my duty, Excellence, and a pleasure too, of course.' I risked a compliment. 'You're looking well yourself. And what a splendid toga.'

He looked down at the pale-blue garment that he wore. 'Ah, the *toga picta*. It's all the rage in Rome. Used to be a fashion for it long ago, they say. Not sure that I like it. It doesn't bleach, like white. I've got a red one too. But that one's at the fullers – it suffered a mishap.' He shot a look at me. 'Your idea, I gather – and a complete success.' He reached out jewelled fingers to select a juicy date. 'What was it gave you the idea about the wolf-howl anyway?'

I could have spelled it out to him, of course, but I did not. If truth were told, I was a little bit ashamed to think I'd been so slow. Glypto had told me that wolves were getting scarce, and that it was hard to keep the army well

supplied with skins, and yet I'd heard that eerie howling in
the woods – not only at night, but at all times of day, especially when Virilis was in the woods – and still I had not
realized what it was. It had even crossed my mind that it
sounded like a signal and I'd dismissed the thought again.
But, of course, that was exactly what it had proved to be.
And once we had searched a pile of bundled kindling (which
mysteriously appeared one day beside the path) and found
a note, it had been fairly easy to set up a trap.

Quintus had obligingly walked head first into it, by
arriving unsuspecting at the meeting point and helpfully
agreeing to provide the optio – in his temporary role as
rebel chief, of course – with further funds and useful information about likely troop movements. The decurion's
distress, when he discovered his mistake, was apparently
quite comical to see, and his willingness to confess to almost
anything, provided that he was not sentenced to the beasts,
provided all the evidence required to see that the real rebel
chief was caught and crucified. The plan for killing Marcus,
which he suddenly seemed very anxious to divulge, was
not to have him strangled by Virilis at all, but set upon, at
a predetermined signal, by rebels on the lane outside his
home, and put instantly to death, together with his unsuspecting wife and child.

Virilis's only role in this was to delay the entourage,
which, at another signal, would be permitted to arrive and
discover the carnage. The blame would have fallen on the
rebels, naturally, but after all – as their leader commented
– one can only suffer crucifixion once, and one might as
well face it for substantial reward and the lavish pickings
of a wealthy man as for the paltry purse of some hapless
traveller.

Of course, the carriage that they set on was not Marcus's
at all – the wolf-howl signal had made sure of that – and,
with the help of a half-century of men disguised behind a
wall, the soldiers in it had rounded up the rebels in no time,
with the loss of only a dozen men themselves. It had all
been very satisfactory, especially to me, since Quintus had
confirmed that I'd been right in everything. He had been

stripped of his office and everything he owned, and sent into lifelong exile, but he'd escaped the sword by confessing everything and conniving at the capture of the rebel force. Virilis, whose sentence had been death, had appealed to the Emperor and was going to Rome, where – so the commander told me – he was likely to be instantly reprieved and recruited to the ranks of the speculatores.

I did not say all this to Marcus. I just said, 'The wolf-howl, patron? It simply came to me. An inspiration from the gods, perhaps.'

He nodded, as though he had expected this. 'Of course.' He took another date. 'And speaking of white togas – as we were, I think – it occurs to me that we'll need another councillor on the ordo now.'

I knew what he was referring to, of course. Candidates for office always dress in spotless white, the so-called '*toga candida*' in fact. I said evasively, 'A chief decurion, you mean?'

'They will appoint a chief decurion from the serving ranks, of course, but had you thought of standing for the other vacancy? I gather the commander had a word with you.' He bit the last remaining date neatly into two and swallowed it. 'We could arrange for you to meet the property qualification, I think. Perhaps he told you that?'

I had my answer ready. 'I'm flattered, Excellence. And naturally, if you wished it, I would be glad to serve – with your kind endorsement, I would be elected I am sure.' (In fact, I was anything but sure of that. The choice of Gaius Greybeard had caused quite a stir, and not everyone was ready to believe that Marcus had not sanctioned it. 'Everybody has his price,' the common gossip said.) 'But,' I continued, mentally blessing the commander as I spoke, 'I fear that, after all, it will not be possible. The town apartment which I think you have in mind has been measured most carefully and is a foot too small.'

Marcus was looking positively vexed. 'I am sure some small adjustment could be made . . .'

'But if a property is bequeathed to you, and then you alter it before you pass it on, you will have acted as owner and be liable for tax.' I had no idea if this was true or not. It was only based on something that I'd heard Pedronius say, but it seemed to work. I saw the look of mild alarm that crossed my patron's face. Marcus was a rich man, but famously careful with his wealth.

I took advantage of the moment. 'Have you thought of inviting Pedronius to stand? He would be a worthy candidate and very grateful for your support, I'm sure. Look at the splendid banquet that he arranged for you last night . . .'

Marcus waved a lofty hand at me, but his expression cleared. 'I expect you're right. Perhaps an ordo member should have experience of managing finance. And of public life, as well. I'll speak to Pedronius on the matter when I can – in fact, he is coming here to feast with me tonight. And perhaps you will bring Gwellia to see us very soon. I know my wife would like to speak to her – in fact, I think she's brought her home a gift.' He looked round vaguely at the table-top. 'I was going to suggest that you took her home some dates, but I fear we've finished them.' He smiled. 'I'm glad you liked the bell.'

'And the town apartment, Excellence?' I put in wickedly, noting that our invitation had not been to dine. 'What will you do with that?'

'Oh I shall sell it, since you won't be needing it. I'll use the money to buy some vineyards, I expect – something to occupy my son when he's a man. But, in the circumstances, you should have some reward. Can you think of anything?'

He knew as well as I did how I would reply. The answer was waiting just outside the door. 'Well, Excellence,' I murmured, 'since I have a choice . . . what about a pair of non-matching red-haired slaves?'

And I knew, from everybody's smiles, that I had chosen right.